THE SAFE BET

BRITTNEY SAHIN

EMKO MEDIA

The Safe Bet

By: Brittney Sahin

Published by: EmKo Media, LLC

Copyright © 2015 EmKo Media, LLC

Third Edition © 2018 EmKo Media, LLC

Original title: *Silenced Memories*

This book is an original publication of Brittney Sahin.

Editor: Sarah Norton, Chief Editor, WordsRU.com

Third Edition Proofreading: Judy Zweifel, Judy's Proofreading

Cover Designer: Mayhem Cover Designs

Paperback ISBN: 9781720002352

❀ Created with Vellum

PROLOGUE

LANDSTUHL REGIONAL MEDICAL CENTER, GERMANY - SEPTEMBER 2010

"ARE YOU OKAY?" MICHAEL'S MOM GENTLY SMOOTHED THE BACK of her hand over his bandaged scalp. Her eyes no longer brimmed with tears, because she'd been releasing them steadily since she showed up at the hospital yesterday.

"You've been asking me that every hour." He squeezed the emotion down his throat, his stomach tightening at the memory of what happened in Afghanistan.

"And she'll keep asking you until you're out of this place—and out of the service," his dad said glibly from the chair where he sat. "Your sister's flight just left New York, by the way."

"She didn't need to come." But he'd be happy to see her.

He closed his eyes, falling back into the combat zone—back to where he'd lost so many of his men.

His hands fisted at his sides, and he fought like hell to crawl out of his mind and to the present, to his family.

He'd lived.

1

So many had died.

How the hell could he keep going?

"Michael."

It was Jake's voice, his teammate who'd made certain he survived to see another day.

He bore down on his teeth and forced his eyes open. "Hey, man." The pain in his chest and ribs was nearly unbearable, even with the heavy meds he was on. "You look good."

Jake tipped his head to Michael's parents in greeting and approached the bed wearing civilian clothes. "Can we have a minute?"

Michael nodded to his parents and held his breath as they left, feeling guilty at the buzz of relief he felt to have them gone. He needed time to make his own decision without choosing to leave the Marines because of pressure from them.

"How's the rest of the team?" *The ones who made it out . . .* Michael tried to sit up, but he groaned and found the pillow again.

"They're hanging in there." He gripped his temples and sighed.

"You talk to Eddie's wife?" Michael thought back to the wedding—Jake, their buddy Aiden, and Michael, had been groomsmen not too long ago. And now he was gone in the blink of an eye. "How is she?" God, he was going to be sick.

"Not well, but I promised her we'd always have her back."

Without a doubt.

"There's, uh, something I wanted to let you know." Jake paused to take a heavy breath. "I've decided to get out. I'm going to Quantico in three months."

"You're gonna be a Fed?" He allowed the news to settle for a moment. "Wow. Congratulations."

Jake looked heavenward. "I don't want to push, but maybe it's time for you, too?"

Michael tucked his tongue in his cheek in thought. "My mom put you up to this?"

He didn't respond, which meant Michael was right, at least, in part.

"There are plenty of ways you can continue serving." Jake's arms hung heavy at his sides. "Just something to think about."

"Right." Michael closed his eyes, the drugs making his body nearly heavier than his thoughts.

"Glad you're okay. The world can't afford to lose you." A pinch of emotion caught in his tone.

"We lost a lot of good men." His heart stammered as a blanket of memories blew through his mind, yet again.

Would he ever be the same? He could almost feel his heart hardening.

"The price of war," Jake said in a low voice as if he were trying to believe his own line.

Michael looked back at Jake and his stomach tucked in. "Okay," he bit out. "If I get out . . . I have to keep helping, somehow."

Jake flashed him a smile, and his Southern accent deepened when he said, "I wouldn't expect anything less of you, man."

CHAPTER ONE

PRESENT DAY

"YOU HERE ALONE?"

Kate lowered the martini glass from her lips as she looked over at the guy next to her. "Yeah."

He smoothed a hand over his red beard. "You like this place?"

"My first time. Seems okay." She averted her attention back to the blush liquid in her glass.

The rosy color reminded her of the failed wedding she'd planned the weekend before. The bride's cheeks had turned beet red at the altar as she crushed the poor groom. "I can't do this," she'd admitted, then she'd raced down the aisle like Julia Roberts in *Runaway Bride*.

That had been a first for Kate. But weddings weren't her usual gig, anyway. They took entirely too long to prepare. That was yet another reason why she hoped her meeting with Julia Maddox tomorrow went well.

"You want to dance?"

"No, but thanks."

It'd been months since she'd gone out, and she missed the feeling dancing used to give her. Loud, thumping club music had a way of syncing with the rhythm of her heartbeat, which always caused a tingling sensation throughout her body, mimicking chills —the good kind.

Music and dancing helped shed her anxiousness. It was a way for her to let go.

And in this city, particularly, she really needed to unwind. After the long, nightmare of a day she'd had traveling from New York City to Charlotte, she at least deserved a drink.

Kate squeezed her eyes shut, wondering what she'd done to warrant a year's dose of bad luck all rolled into one hellish day. She'd not only missed her flight but spilled coffee on herself at the airport. On the later flight, she had to sit next to someone who reeked of stale cigarettes, and—oh yeah—her hotel had been overbooked.

Maybe she should never have agreed to tomorrow's meeting— was her dad right when he'd asked her not to go?

"I really think we should dance."

A hand on her leg had her flinching and opening her eyes. *Mr. Red Beard. Just great.* She shoved the guy's hand from her thigh and slipped off her seat in a hurry, nearly stumbling in her heels.

His gray eyes combed over her chest as his tongue peeked out of his mouth and slid across his bottom lip. "If you change your mind, I'll be here."

She couldn't stomach a response. She left her drink and turned away, tugging at the hem of her dress as she edged closer to the dance floor, feeling the need to hide the area where his hand had been.

She watched the attractive men and women shuffle around, dancing to the beat of a new Calvin Harris remix.

Her head tilted back, and the music washed over her like waves licking the silky sands of the beach, and she allowed her body to drift with the beat.

Her eyes shut, and the music pulsed through her, electrifying her senses. She danced like she was alone in the room, the music reverberating through her soul.

After twenty minutes of dancing, she startled when someone pressed up against her from behind. She turned to face the man who was intruding on her personal space. Although he was attractive in a dark-haired, haunted, wiry sort of way, she had no interest in rubbing against some Adam Levine lookalike.

"I'm good," she mouthed while shaking her head.

He held his hands up and moved away from her.

As she continued dancing, she caught sight of someone at the bar.

Not the creepy, red-bearded man, but someone else. He was muscular, blond, and sitting with his hands on his lap at the edge of the bar. His eyes were focused on her, and something about him created an eerie sensation in her gut.

He stood, his eyes still on her, and her palm landed on her chest as worry climbed into her throat.

She squeezed her eyes tight for a moment, willing him away. When she looked again, she caught sight of his back as he headed toward the exit.

Thank God. She checked her watch, wondering if it was too late for another drink with a morning meeting.

With the blond man gone and Mr. Red Beard out of sight, she approached the bar. "French martini, please." She shifted in her four-inch, nude heels, which she was beginning to regret, and checked her phone. Two missed calls from her father. He was damn persistent, but that was the story of her life.

"Kathryn?" the spiky-haired bartender said, eying the credit card she placed before him. He shook his head and slid the card back to her. "No need."

She followed his pointed finger to find her fifty-something-year-old martini buyer, who gave her a slight nod.

Kate pressed her lips together in a polite smile but prayed he wouldn't attempt to join her. Maybe if she just shifted away . . .

She slammed into what felt like a concrete post. *What the!* The contents of her glass sloshed and cascaded over her wrist and onto a dark-gray, luxuriously soft fabric.

"Shit. I'm so sorry." She set her glass back down on the bar and reached for a napkin.

She began to dab at the stain, taking note of the sculpted abs beneath the shirt. But when she dragged her gaze back up to the hard jaw of the man in front of her, she inhaled a sharp breath, and her hand froze.

The man stared down at her with the most intense blue eyes she had ever seen.

Cerulean blue. Cobalt. Sapphire. She couldn't decide as she rummaged through the crayon color list in her head to find a match for those unbelievably blue eyes.

I seriously had to spill my drink on Michael freaking Maddox?

He was a man who could have been carved out of granite. That's what she had thought about him when she looked at his photo the other day as part of the research she'd done in preparation for her appointment. Before her now, he was hard as steel.

And yet, his firm lips were curving at the edges with the hint of a smile.

"Let me pay for your shirt," Kate offered in a small voice, once she was able to look away. Michael's hand gently wrapped around her wrist, and she realized she was still touching his chest with the napkin.

"That won't be necessary. Let me replace your drink." His voice was deep, but also like silk, blowing across her skin in a hot caress.

She kept her eyes on his, feeling lost for words. Then she cleared her throat and retracted her hand from his grasp.

She was free, but he'd left a mark. His touch had lit a sudden fire inside of her.

The feeling of desire was . . . unplanned. And she didn't handle the unplanned very well. No, she needed lists and predictability, which was one reason she wanted to swear off weddings. Coming to the club tonight had already been a rather wild step for her.

"Please, I insist on paying for your shirt." Even though he was worth millions, she had to do the right thing. "I think my martini ruined it." As she reached for her purse, he placed his large hand over hers, his touch warming her body.

"Just tell me what you were drinking, and that'll be payment enough." He pushed back a brownish-black lock that had escaped the gel of his purposefully unruly hair. His gaze penetrated deep into her eyes, and his lips parted. He edged closer to her, and she breathed in his cologne. He smelled exotic, like rosewood and amber.

Her mind raced, trying to come up with something to say—hell, anything, at this point. All that dared escape were the words, "French martini."

"Michael, sweetie, I thought that was you." A woman with long, brown hair and perfectly honeyed skin, placed a hand on Michael's shoulder before briefly glancing at Kate.

Michael ignored her, his gaze never swerving from Kate's.

"I—um . . ." *What is wrong with me?*

"Michael?" The woman's clipped voice rang in Kate's ears as she touched the side of Michael's face, attempting to guide it toward her.

"I have to go," Kate said once she realized Michael had no desire to look anywhere but at her. Before she could give him a chance to respond, she pivoted in her heels and started for the exit.

What the hell just happened?

She'd worked with plenty of powerful and good-looking men before, but God, Michael Maddox was in a league of his own.

She'd had an instant crush on him when she saw his photo online, but his picture was a pale substitute for meeting him in person.

She hoped to hell he wouldn't be at the meeting tomorrow. Of course, if she landed the job, she'd have to work with him eventually, wouldn't she?

Damn my bad luck.

CHAPTER TWO

KATE SIPPED A SKINNY VANILLA LATTE AS SHE WALKED TO JULIA Maddox's office at the center of town. It was about ten minutes before 8 a.m., and she soaked in the sun as it slipped between the two towering structures to her left, splashing onto her arm.

She stopped a few minutes later once outside the tall glass building that housed Maddox's office.

The doorman tipped his head in greeting to Kate before opening the door. "How you doing, miss?"

His Southern accent washed over her, warming her like the sun. People were so much nicer here than in New York. "I'm wonderful. And you?"

"Better now." The older man winked and shut the door behind her as she entered the lobby.

Kate stopped in front of the mirrored elevator doors and waited among the gathered men in suits. Looking at her reflection, she found herself wondering whether she should have opted for her classic black heels instead of bold red pumps. But so far, nothing about this trip had been exactly standard for her.

She took in a deep breath and pressed her nervous palms over her black and white, sleeveless dress.

As the elevator doors dinged and opened, her phone buzzed in her purse.

Not now. She couldn't handle talking to her dad before the meeting. She knew what he would say, so she ignored the call and turned off her phone as she stepped with weak knees into the elevator.

Knowing there was a chance she may see Michael Maddox again today had her tossing and turning in bed all night. She played out various scenarios of what she would say to him if they were to meet again.

Planning. Always.

Well, almost always. If she'd gone to bed early like she should have, she would never have spilled her drink on Maddox.

Focus. She ran a successful event planning business and had a fantastic track record with clients, although Maddox would be the biggest client she had landed to date. And the sexiest.

When the elevator doors opened, Kate entered a bright white lobby, which boasted beautiful splashes of color in the modern art that hung on the walls.

"Hi, I have an appointment with Julia Maddox."

The secretary picked up the phone. "Julia, your appointment is here." The woman waved her hand in silence, gesturing for her to have a seat in the lounge area.

"Thank you." Kate placed her bag by the chair and attempted to get comfortable. She looked out the large wall of windows to her left to see the corporate Bank of America building beside her.

"Kate," Julia's voice sang through the lobby.

Kate's attention shifted as she rose to her feet. Julia Maddox was an impressive woman, just like her brother. Tall and lean, but with curves where they should be. Her long, black hair settled in soft waves to mid-back, and her bold, blue eyes lit up the room.

"Hi." Kate reached for Julia's outstretched hand.

"I'm so glad you could make the trip here on such short notice. Thank you so much." She smiled. "Cindy, hold my calls for the morning," she instructed. "Please, come with me. Can I get you some coffee or tea?"

"I'm fine, but thank you," Kate replied as they went into Julia's office. The wall was made of glass, and the room was swank, mirroring the contemporary furnishing and colorful abstracts from the hall.

"Have a seat." Julia motioned for her to sit at a large, wrought-iron-framed table near the floor-to-ceiling windows. "I know you mentioned on the phone your schedule is pretty jammed, so I really appreciate you taking the time to come here."

"Hosting an event for the Maddox Group would be an honor." Kate opened her bag and retrieved her tablet.

"I know I didn't give you too many details on the phone, but I'm in a bit of a bind. My brother fired the last three event planners —the best in the area. Our company has locations in Manhattan and Charlotte, however, and we really need someone who can spearhead events in both locations." She paused and set her hands on the table. "Kate, when I read that article about your business in *The New York Times* last week, I just knew you were the one." She shot Kate a contagious smile. "I love what you've done with the company since you took over for your mom."

"Stepmom," Kate said softly.

Julia nodded. "You expanded to Boston, and I understand you are even contemplating opening a third spot here in Charlotte." Julia clasped her hands on the table and leaned forward, somehow maintaining her poise.

"I'm thinking about it." Would three locations be too many? She wanted to give Charlotte a chance. "May I ask . . . why now? Mr. Maddox is not exactly known for throwing lavish social events."

"You're right. He deplores the idea of even attending fundraisers or balls, let alone hosting one." She inhaled before releasing what appeared to be an exhausted breath. "Michael hasn't actually agreed to have the event. Not yet, at least."

Kate's shoulders arched forward in surprise. *This is a plot twist.*

"Michael believes in paying it forward, but he doesn't like to get the media involved—to take advantage of the spotlight. I assume you know, but Michael was in the Marines, part of a special operations team. He's been a civilian for five years now. And in his time home, he's witnessed a lot of veterans struggling."

Kate had read the Maddox company profile after she'd taken the call from Julia, but somehow hearing it firsthand made it more real.

Michael was a military hero. A patriot. And now a millionaire.

Julia stood and faced the window. "Three years ago, he launched a small business initiative for veterans. He's very passionate about his projects, but it would be nice to garner support for our vets from others as well." She turned back around and eyed Kate. "I've already sent the invitations and secured a location for the gala. It's scheduled to occur one week from tomorrow."

Kate tried to hide her shock. She couldn't expose any chink in her armor. But was Julia really expecting her to pull an event together with such lightning speed? And for a man who didn't even want to host it? "Are you serious?"

"You've worked miracles before. I did my research on you after I read that article. You can pull it together, and I'll help. Between the two of us, I believe we can convince Michael to agree to the fundraiser, and then I'd like to see a replica of the event in New York, soon, as well." Julia crossed her arms. "Michael's shouldering a burden that neither of us could understand, and he's wearing himself out," she said with a sigh. "He's always working. Always stressed. He needs help, but he's stuck on this idea that people should help because it's the right thing to do, not because it's a PR opportunity. He doesn't even want the public to know about his good work."

"Wow." She'd heard of rich people being private about charity before, but the notorious playboy image of Michael she had in her head was quite a disconnect from the philanthropic picture Julia described.

"He needs to come to terms with reality. People rarely do anything unless they're going to get something out of it. We need help from others, and so we need to play the game, give them a tax write-off or public recognition—whatever it takes to get more support." Julia's hand slipped to her chest as she reached for the chain she was wearing beneath her silk blouse.

Kate caught sight of what appeared to be a military ID tag as Julia rubbed her hand over the small, silver object. She took a moment to think and smiled. "When do we start?"

"Now."

Kate rubbed her hand over her cheek as her thoughts drifted to Julia's brother. Would she really be able to do this?

"Come on. Let's get some coffee. We can brainstorm some ideas and make a plan that'll win Michael over."

Kate nodded but was unsure whether another dose of caffeine would be good for her nerves. Somehow she'd have to perform two miracles. Make Michael attend his own event . . . and not turn into a complete idiot when she was in his presence.

* * *

MICHAEL SLOWED THE TREADMILL DOWN TO A STEADY PACE, staring out the gym window that overlooked the hotspot Whiskey River. People rushed to work, attired in fashionable business wear. He'd been donning a suit for almost five years, and he hated the damned thing. Wearing heavy combat gear in an Iraqi summer was more comfortable than a tie around his neck.

"Maddox, at the gym so late?"

Michael averted his attention to James as he stepped onto the neighboring treadmill.

"I thought you got your workouts done at, like, six in the morning." James looked down at his Rolex and back at Michael.

"It's near nine." He smirked and powered on the machine, increasing the speed.

"Late night," Michael responded before stopping the treadmill and stepping off. Although not as late as he would have liked—the blonde at the bar had gotten away without even giving her name.

"What's your excuse, man?" Michael reached for his phone and glanced at the screen. Fifteen missed calls.

"You know I play hard every night. Can't make it to the office before ten. But hey, it's one of the perks of being your own boss." He flashed Michael a smile and began running.

Michael hated the guy. He was an arrogant prick, much like many of the guys he had to deal with on a regular basis.

"Later," Michael said after wiping down the treadmill, and then he went to the locker room to wash off.

He showered in a hurry and dressed. He tamed his semi-wavy hair with a little gel and parted it to the side. He pulled his laptop case and black blazer from his locker before exiting the room.

"Michael."

He glanced over at the brunette who was approaching him. "Hi, Lana. How are you?" he asked, annoyance tingeing his voice.

She tapped his muscular arm with her fist. "I've missed you, stranger. Haven't seen you at the club."

"I was there last night, but I didn't stay long." He gave her a polite smile.

She pulled on her long braid and stepped closer to him. "Maybe we can get together again? I had fun last time." She looked up at him from beneath long, black eyelashes.

He studied her for a moment, wondering why some girls wore makeup to the gym and little else. "I have to get to a meeting," he lied. "See ya around," he said, his back already turned to her.

Outside the door, he shook his head, relieved to be free.

Once at the office, he greeted the doorman and headed up the elevator.

"Good morning, Michael," his receptionist welcomed him

when he arrived. "I was worried about you when you weren't here at your normal time."

It wasn't like him to be late, but September was a rough month . . .

"I'm fine," he grumbled.

"Well, uh, have a good day."

"Yeah, thanks. You too." As he walked back to his office, he noticed his sister's room was empty.

Unlike her office, he didn't have glass walls. He preferred his privacy. He sat behind his large walnut desk and loosened his tie. The tie didn't usually make it past noon.

Before he had a chance to get situated, his office phone began ringing. It was Cindy.

"I forgot to tell you when you came in, but you asked me to give you a heads-up the next time Julia invited another event planner here."

"And one's here?"

"Yup."

"Where is she?" Michael's quads tightened as tension darted through him. He wasn't in the mood to fire someone again. When would his sister finally get the message?

"I, uh—I don't know. Sorry. She and Julia left ten minutes ago."

"Okay. Thanks. Could you let me know as soon as they return?"

"Of course."

Michael ended the call and leaned back in his chair, pinching the bridge of his nose. "Julia," he muttered under his breath. "What have you cooked up for me this time?"

CHAPTER THREE

"LET'S CUT TO THE CHASE. THERE'S NOT GOING TO BE AN EVENT. So, no event planner needed."

Kate folded her arms and eyed Julia's phone, which had rung the second they entered the office. Julia had put her brother on speakerphone so Kate could hear. "How did he even know I was here?" she mouthed to Julia.

"Would you just come down to my office so we can talk in person?" Julia pleaded.

Kate grimaced as her stomach muscles clenched. *Don't do that.*

"I'm not wasting time on this," Michael bit out. "No fundraisers."

"Kate's different. You'll like her. Please, hear us out."

"She's an event planner, so no—I won't like her."

Kate stared at the phone, annoyance ripping through her, peeling back the nerves until only her confidence was left. "Actually, I'm a business owner, much like yourself, Mr. Maddox, and I do a lot more than plan events."

Julia smirked. "Michael?"

"Dammit, Julia. Take me off speakerphone. The poor girl doesn't need to hear this."

Poor girl? "Mr. Maddox, I run a very lucrative company in both New York and Boston," she explained, trying to keep her voice calm and polite. "I have an MBA from Harvard. I am by no means a 'poor girl,' and I'm certain that I can handle whatever you dish out."

The line went dead.

"Well, he'll never be able to fire you now."

Kate smiled, although now that her anger had receded a fearful nausea was taking its place. "I think he already did fire me. He hung up."

Julia moved her hand in front of her face as if she were swiping a fly. "Sure, but that's only because he's on his way here right now."

Kate's stomach lurched. Battling on the phone was one thing, but did she have the backbone to face him in person? After all, in his presence last night she'd become a puddle. Any longer and the bartenders would have had to mop her off the floor.

Michael pushed open the glass door of his sister's office and stopped in his tracks when Kate turned toward him. He shut his eyes for a second, but even when he opened them, they betrayed the slightest hint of astonishment.

Kate smoothed a hand over her dress as she approached him, and his eyes captured hers, making her a little dizzy. Insecurity crept inside of her again. "Hi, I'm Kate Adams of Marissa Adams Events," she said, her voice trembling as she extended her hand. "My stepmother's Marissa Adams."

He remained in front of the door. With his sleeves rolled to the elbows, exposing his strong forearms, it took her a moment to pull her gaze away from the ripple of flesh.

Michael finally reached for her hand. "Hi." He cleared his throat. "I'm sorry, I didn't mean to insult you on the phone."

She released his hand and took a step back. He somehow made her feel like she might lose her balance. Her pulse ticked at a high speed as she watched his eyes drift down her body. There was no way she could go head-to-head with this man. His chiseled features, well-sculpted nose—hell, his perfect face, who could deny it?—were like kryptonite to her. How could she stand up to him when she was short of breath?

"Maybe we could sit down and talk?" Kate suggested—because there was no way she could remain upright much longer. No man had ever impacted her like this, so why the hell did it have to happen now?

He glanced at his sister and tipped his head in the direction of the nearby table, a silent way of agreeing to talk.

Kate waited for Julia to sit before taking her previous chair. She crossed her legs but took in a short breath when she realized his eyes were lingering a bit longer than necessary on her calf muscles.

"Listen, I'm sure my sister has explained to you my hesitations about having a fundraiser, and my opinion on the matter has not and will not change." He walked closer to the table where his sister and Kate sat, but he remained standing and crossed his arms. He arched his shoulders back and stared down at them.

A power play. Her mind was spinning. The sexy tone of his voice rendered her speechless—again. She shifted in her seat and tried not to look at his strong, clenched jaw, which read "uncompromising." After a calming breath, she folded her hands in her lap and studied him for a moment. His blue eyes pierced through her.

"Mr. Maddox, I . . . I think that . . ." *Get the words out.* "I think that you will totally hate my idea."

Julia looked over at Kate with a what-are-you-doing? expression. At no time during their morning chat had Kate mentioned she'd be throwing those words at Michael.

"But it'll work well to raise awareness for your veteran business initiative. You'll probably detest my idea . . . but it's not about what you want, is it?" She forced herself to remain calm as she stood, wanting to be on a more even playing field with him. Of course, he still towered over her, but she felt a little better, anyway.

"Go on." The soft tone of his voice surprised her, but also filled her with hope.

Kate peeked at Julia. Relief filled her as Julia's look of concern disappeared from the smooth lines of her face. Julia nodded and returned her attention back to Michael.

"When you got out of the Marines you became an overnight success story. You created and engineered ideas to better improve the intelligence systems that our military use, and you built a company around those ideas." She bit her lip before continuing, trying to maintain power over her nerves. "You sold your company and are reaping the benefits." *For three hundred million dollars.*

"Your point?"

She swallowed. "A lot of those who exit the military aren't you. They're not as lucky. But instead of hoarding your money away like many rich men in this country, you're focused on using it to help fellow veterans." She paused to catch her breath. "The thing is, despite everything you do, it's still not enough. You're only one man. Imagine what ten men like you could do. Or a hundred. Why go it alone?"

Michael remained staring at her now, hands in pockets, lips sealed.

"My kid brother joined the military as soon as he turned eighteen. I worry about him every day. This is personal for me. In fact, caring for our military men and women should be personal for everyone." Worrying about her brother had become about as normal as brushing her teeth. It was never ending. And she knew she'd always stress as long as he was putting his life on the line.

His brows stitched together. "What do you want to do?"

Julia rose to her feet. "I'm going to leave you two alone to work out the details. I have a call to make, but I trust Kate can take the lead on this. I'll just go and use your office, Michael." Before Michael or Kate could refuse, she hurried out of the room.

Michael looked away from the door as it swung shut, and turned back to Kate, who was reaching for her tablet.

She pushed her long hair off her shoulders and onto her back, wishing she could concentrate. She opened an app that housed her notes, trying to ignore the way her hairs stood on end knowing he was behind her.

"Did you tell Julia that we've already met?"

Startled, Kate slowly turned toward him. "I'm so sorry about your shirt. You should let me pay for it."

"Did you know who I was last night?" he asked with a deep voice.

She swept a hand to the nape of her neck. "Yes."

"Why didn't you say something?" His eyes narrowed on her, and he took a step closer.

"I . . ." Could she tell him she had been completely tongue-tied by meeting him in person? "Honestly, I didn't think you would remember me, and then I was in a hurry, so I kind of rushed out when your friend showed up." Her poker face was failing her.

"You thought I would forget you?"

She allowed his words to hang in the air for a moment, free of gravity, as she contemplated the appropriate response.

"Mr. Maddox, how would you feel about an auction?"

"Call me Michael." He walked over to the coffee machine behind Julia's desk. "Want one?"

"No, but thank you."

He turned toward her after a moment, holding his coffee in one hand and placing his other in his pants pocket. He looked out the wall of windows. "An auction might be a good idea, but how will we get enough items for the auction in a week?"

She bent over and reached into her bag. "I'm sure you have a few things you could auction, and I have some connections. I'll make some calls." Her cheeks reddened when she caught his eyes focused in the direction of her ass. She exhaled and attempted to concentrate. "Open to page forty-nine," she instructed, tossing a magazine in his direction.

He cocked his head and raised his brows.

She mentally berated herself as she watched Michael open the magazine after setting his—thank God—full cup of coffee down on Julia's desk.

"Why do you have this?" His tan face darkened a touch as he looked down at the article, which proclaimed him sexiest businessman in Manhattan. He shook his head and chucked the magazine on the desk.

"I do my research on clients. I need to know their likes and dislikes."

"You clearly know my dislikes well enough to throw them in my face. Literally."

He was growing edgy. Shit, she was going to lose him. "Here's the part of my plan that you'll hate." She closed the distance between them until she stood a few feet away. "I think you could earn top dollar . . . and ensure a hundred percent attendance, maybe even increase the number of invites."

"And how would we go about that?"

"I'm talking about auctioning a date with you. People would come to see the elusive Michael Maddox put himself up for auction, and women would pay." *Stay confident.* "I know this sounds crazy, but you have to think about the purpose—the long-term goal. Think of the money this could bring to your cause," she implored, looking up at him as he stared back at her, his face unreadable.

He reached for his coffee, his white shirt straining over the pull of his taut muscles. "You're right, it does sound crazy. Next idea." His jaw was firm, his face resolute. He took a seat behind his sister's desk, set the coffee in front of him, and rubbed his temples.

She stepped in front of the desk and crossed her arms. "Remember, this is for the veterans. Can you please swallow your pride for one night?" At that moment, gone was the timid woman she had been last night. Gone were her checklists and schedules. She was standing her ground and, even if he was about to toss her out, it felt good.

He ran his tongue over his bottom lip and clasped his hands on the desk. "If you did your research, you would know that I'm a private guy."

Without thinking, she replied, "If you're so private, why do you date supermodels?" Of course, maybe the magazines had him wrong.

He stood back up and walked with slow movements before stopping a foot shy of her. "I wouldn't call it dating exactly."

God, how can you make casual sex sound so . . . sexy? She could feel the heat crawl up her neck and into her cheeks.

Since the tabloids were right, maybe she needed to rethink her doubts about Roswell and Area 51?

"I'm not asking you to marry someone. Just go on one date. One dinner." She found herself walking back toward the table where she had stacked her belongings.

Maybe she should go. Maybe she wouldn't be able to work with him, after all. But what about Julia? What about her own business that could flourish tenfold with the Maddoxes as clients?

No, she had to convince him.

"Mr. Maddox—Michael—I'm sorry. I don't mean to be pushy. I know this is a strange request for a man of your, um, stature, but I'm certain it will be the best way to maximize attendance while simultaneously increasing the money raised for your business venture." She bit her lip and waited for a response.

His eyes softened a bit as his gaze drifted to her mouth. "Hm. Maybe."

"Really?" She pressed a hand to his firm chest, and her eyes widened when she realized what she'd done.

His jaw tightened as he placed his hand over hers. "In what world does maybe mean yes?"

She exhaled, pulled her hand free from his, and took a large step back. "I'm so sorry. I don't know what came over me. I was excited."

She cleared her throat, waiting for him to speak, but he remained silent. "Michael, I promise everything will be perfect. Tasteful and sophisticated."

He blew out a breath. "I've lost my damn mind." He shook his head. "Fine."

"Great." She clapped her hands and tried to will away the embarrassment from her unprofessional touching moments ago. "I was also wondering if you could ask one of the models or celebrities you know to be auctioned off as well. We need to cater to the men attending the event, too."

"I can make a few calls. It's short notice, but I'm sure I can find someone." He began tugging at his tie, as though it were strangling him.

"Thank you."

He nodded, but it was clear the whole idea of the auction pained him. "I have a meeting." He retrieved the coffee he'd set on Julia's desk. "I should get going."

"Thank you again for this opportunity." She turned toward him in haste, almost knocking the coffee onto his shirt. "Oh, God. I am dangerous, huh?"

"Yes." He cleared his throat, his eyes darkening. "Yes, you are."

* * *

"THE LOCATION'S PERFECT," KATE SAID TO JULIA AS THEY EXITED the hotel. "Now we just need everything else."

Julia handed her car ticket to the valet and turned toward Kate. "I still can't get over how you handled my brother this morning. I wish I had it on camera to watch over and over again. How you got him to not only agree to the event but become a part of the auction is beyond me," she said, pulling her thick, black hair up into a loose bun.

"I guess he realized that he needed to put the needs of his foundation ahead of his own desires."

"Any ideas on what we can auction? Aside from my brother?" Her lips quirked at the corners into a grin.

"I'm sure Michael has some artwork he could donate. Does he have season passes to any sporting events?"

"I can definitely access art, but I think I can even do you one better on the sports tickets. Michael and I are friends with a few of the Giants. Perhaps we can offer tickets and dinner with the players."

"Wow. That might fetch an even higher price than Michael." Kate laughed and followed Julia toward the red Ferrari that pulled up to the curb.

Julia tipped the valet before getting behind the wheel. "Looks like we'll need to work all weekend." She shifted gears and joined the traffic. "But there's no reason why we shouldn't go out and celebrate. How about drinks tomorrow night? You like to dance? There's a place I go to all the time."

"That sounds good. I have somewhere I need to go tomorrow after work, but I'd love to go out and dance later." At least this time she wouldn't be alone.

"Great."

"Thank you for this opportunity. I believe in what you guys are doing with this foundation." Kate took in a deep breath and glanced out the window. "I'm always so nervous about my brother's safety. Every time he reports for another tour of duty, I feel sick."

"I can totally relate."

"My stepmom stopped functioning when my little brother joined the Army."

"Is that why she turned the company over to you?"

Kate nodded. "Basically." An image of her father fluttered to her mind, and she remembered she still needed to call him back. But what would she say? She didn't feel like arguing with him about a potential move to Charlotte.

"Well, I'll see you in the morning." Julia pulled up in front of Kate's hotel.

"Have a good night."

Kate got out of the car and headed to her room, eager to change into her jogging clothes. On a glorious day like today, the serene streets of Charlotte would be a pleasant change from the Upper East Side in Manhattan. And perhaps her run would help free her from the stress that had seeped into her body over the last week.

Her feet hit the pavement ten minutes later, and she found herself running faster than normal. Adrenaline burned through her as her fists pumped at her sides.

An hour later, Kate came to the conclusion that she was losing her mind.

Her skin prickled with concern as she rounded the next corner of the street. She slowed down to a walking pace before stopping outright.

Was someone watching her?

Of course, the idea was crazy.

But she had a strange, gut-wrenching feeling that she wasn't safe.

She looked around the street, but everyone seemed normal.

Her heartbeat elevated a notch as her phone vibrated against her arm. She unstrapped it and looked down at the text.

No words—just an image.

An image of her standing on the street looking around. Looking scared.

Her pulse climaxed as her jaw edged open.

What the hell? She gulped back the fear that trickled through her body. She spun around in circles, knowing that now she looked crazy.

But there was nothing for her to see. No one across the street looked like they had just snapped a photo of her.

It had to be a joke, right? Or was someone trying to scare her into leaving Charlotte? Maybe one of the dismissed event planners had discovered she was hired and was jealous? Her number wasn't hard to access. It was her business cell phone, the same one she used as her personal line.

She forced herself to believe her theory was credible and that she wasn't in danger. And she decided she wouldn't feed into whatever sick pleasure her mystery texter might get out of watching her look scared.

She tucked her phone back into the music case and strapped it to her arm. She refused to let some idiot rile her any further, and so she took off with an easy-paced jog.

And she kept running—running until the fear melted away.

CHAPTER FOUR

KATE TRIED TO ACT NORMAL AROUND JULIA AS THEY WORKED, TO mask the nervous energy that weighed her down.

"This is going to be doable." Julia looked up from her tablet. She shook her head, seeming a little amazed. "So, what do we have, officially?"

Kate opened her notepad. "Ten pieces of art. Box tickets to the Giants. Dinner with two Giants players. And your sailboat . . . but I still don't think you should give that away." Kate looked up at Julia.

Julia shrugged. "I can always buy a new one."

Rich people.

"So, do you have a boyfriend?"

"I, uh, don't have time to date. Every time I try the whole relationship thing, it doesn't seem to last." Kate perched her elbows on the table and rested her head in her hands.

She thought of the string of disasters that had plagued her after she'd signed up for an online matchmaker site a year ago. She hadn't had sex or been on a date in fourteen long months. At what point does one reclaim their V-card?

But Kate kept telling herself that this was what she wanted—

her new plan was to focus on her business and avoid men for a while.

"Was there anyone who ever really got to you?" Julia asked.

She was clearly more open than her brother. Well, from what Kate knew about him, anyway. He was notoriously tightlipped. And didn't that seem to add appeal for some women? The ones who were in it for the chase, to make the unattainable man theirs. Kate didn't have the time or energy for that kind of mess.

But Michael wasn't exactly the typical rich playboy.

He wasn't entitled. He was generous, but not for the sake of exposure. He was from humble origins, he'd served their country, he was a do-gooder and a genius beyond compare . . . but still totally off-limits. Even if he wasn't an infamous player, he was still her client. She needed to get the damn man out of her head.

She never dated clients, regardless of their numerous attempts. And now she just wasn't dating anyone period. Her lack of a sex life had to explain why she was lusting after Michael and visualizing him in a tux—she was trying to tell herself that, at least.

She wondered how she'd survive another week without her body blushing every time he was around.

Julia snapped her fingers in front of Kate. "You okay? Hey, did I make you think about some guy?" She smirked.

Kate contemplated an appropriate response but didn't have to come up with one. Instead, her phone rang. She reached into her purse and fished it out. She looked down at the screen and sighed.

"Not going to answer?"

"Just my dad. I'll call him later." Kate fidgeted with her notepad and pen and attempted to refocus, but she found herself unable to slide the mask back on.

It was getting harder to silence the pain that was seeping into her body.

* * *

"You're here."

Kate looked up at the cab driver and then out the window to the graveyard. "Could you wait here? I won't be long." She lifted the long-stemmed, red roses from her lap and opened the door.

"Sure," he replied, turning up the volume so that Sinatra's croon belted in her ears.

Kate exited the cab and began to wander through the maze of gravestones. "Where are you?"

Her breath caught in her throat when she finally found it.

Surprise flickered across her face at the sight of fresh white tulips nuzzled against the headstone.

Who visited you? Her eyebrows pinched together as she leaned down and rested the roses alongside the tulips.

"Hi, Mom." She traced her fingers over the name Elizabeth and kissed her fingers before bringing them back to touch the cool, arched rock.

She studied the second date on the headstone. September 9th. Today. The day her mom had given birth to her.

"I love you," she whispered.

* * *

"Got you a Cosmo."

"Thanks." Kate slid into a circular booth in the VIP area of the club. It was a different nightclub than the one Kate had visited a few nights earlier. "You look amazing."

Julia smoothed a hand over her short, black sequined dress, and smiled. "It's my go-to. I love your dress, though. Super-hot. Glad my brother's not here to see you in that. He has a weakness for gorgeous women, as you have probably heard."

"So, um, did Michael find a woman to auction off at the fundraiser?" *That sounds weird to say.*

Julia reached for her drink. "Yeah. Thank God we found someone on such short notice. You ever heard of Jamie Landon?"

"She's a model, right?" Kate wondered if she was one of the women on Michael's laundry list of sultry New York models that he didn't "date."

Julia nodded. "I hate her. Horrible bitch. Probably hooked up with Michael, too." She shrugged. "Should get a good price, though, which is all that matters."

"I'm surprised he goes by Michael, even by you," Kate found herself saying.

"He was always Mike when he was in the military, and I think it's too hard for him to go by that name now. He's different since he came home. A lot of people come back different." Julia stared into her drink and paused. "I—I lost someone close to me, because of that. He didn't die in the military—he died because he couldn't handle being out of the military. He wound up drinking and died in a car wreck. I was only in college when it happened. Michael was still in the Marines. I think his death was what inspired Michael's project. He wanted to set up a program that would help veterans find balance in the world as civilians."

Kate leaned forward. "I'm so sorry." She wasn't sure what else to say. She had never been good at dealing with tragedy. Look at her own life.

"I'm sorry to be laying this on you." Julia pinched the bridge of her nose and squeezed her eyes shut. Then, with a shake of her head, she flashed her blue eyes open, and her normal calm exterior was back. "Come on. We should be celebrating." She lifted her drink into the air. "Cheers to you defeating my brother."

"Um. Okay. You sure you're all right?"

"Of course." She clinked her glass against Kate's and tossed back the last of her drink. "Let's get shots."

Kate watched as Julia rose with perfect balance in her black strappy Manolos and headed toward the bar. Somehow, Kate couldn't imagine the refined and sophisticated Julia doing shots. But after the emotional day Kate had suffered . . . *why the hell not?*

When Kate approached the bar, she found Julia talking with a guy who was a little too pretty for her taste. His gel-spiked, coppery-blond hair and his waxed eyebrows screamed metrosexual. He was in khaki pants and a crisp, button-up top—Armani or something ostentatious enough to match his gold Rolex. Kate, of course, preferred a more rugged man. A man more like—*don't think his name.*

Julia was leaning in toward him, her hand resting on his chest. Her eyes shifted from the man to Kate. "Kate, this is my friend James. James, this is Kate. She's the miracle worker who managed to convince Michael to hold the fundraiser. I expect you'll be there next weekend?"

James reached for Kate's hand and plastered a smile on his face. "So nice to meet you," he said with a smooth voice.

"Kate, James is an investor, like Michael. He has deep pockets, so be sure to woo him next weekend."

"I don't think she'll have to try hard to woo me." His hazel eyes stared deep into hers before wandering toward her cleavage. "You feel like dancing?" He reached for her hand.

Kate looked to Julia, who encouraged her with a nod and smile. "What about our shots?"

"Here," Julia said, handing her a shot of tequila that the bartender had placed behind her. They downed the gold liquid, and both winced. "Now go have fun. I'll be out there soon." Julia waved her away.

James led Kate through the crowd of men and women, who all looked like they had stepped out of a fashion magazine. But the dance floor was even more impressive than the people. It was surrounded by dozens upon dozens of gorgeous strands of crystal, which dangled in thick, glinting rows. She brushed against them as James reached for her waist and pulled her tight against him.

She placed her hands on his chest, attempting to put some distance between them.

The music became almost a dull silence as her eyes shifted to see Michael walking with long strides toward his sister.

She kept her eyes on him as James moved them around on the dance floor, her body as limp as a rag doll.

Michael folded his arms across his chest and cocked his head to the side, staring at Julia.

Julia waved her phone in front of Michael before jabbing him in the chest with it. A moment later she started for the dance floor.

"Everything okay?" Kate asked, taking the chance to break free of James's grasp.

"Yeah. I forgot I was supposed to be having dinner with my brother." She rolled her eyes. "He tracked my phone to find me— he's a bit overprotective."

"Oh." *It's kind of sweet he cared,* Kate thought as she snuck another glimpse of Michael. His back was turned against them, and he was talking with the bartender.

"James, I think I'm gonna grab a drink. Maybe you and Julia could dance?"

"Sure," he responded, reaching for Julia's waist.

Happy to have secured a rescue, Kate made her way to the bar. She pressed her hands against the bar counter and waited for the bartender to notice her.

"You go dancing a lot?"

Kate shut her eyes for a brief moment. "Not as much as I'd like." She turned toward the man who had infiltrated her dreams the past few nights. "You look different."

An underdressed Michael was no less sexy than business-casual Michael. In fact, he looked even more appealing in jeans and a T-shirt. His tanned biceps swelled beneath the short sleeves.

His eyes focused on her glossy lips before he spoke. "We should dance. People know me here. I'm just thinking of your well-being. If you want to dance in peace, dance once with me."

Was he kidding? Was this really his line? She folded her arms and squinted one eye in a teasing manner. "What if I don't want other men to leave me alone?"

He tilted his head toward the dance floor and scoffed. "Come on." He grabbed her hand and led her toward the masses.

She should have resisted him, and yet, she hadn't found it inside herself to put up a fight.

Some of the men and women glanced their way as they passed, and she wondered who was more jealous—men wanting to be Michael or the women wanting to be Kate so they could be with the Man of Steel lookalike.

Kate glanced over at Julia and mouthed an apology to her—she didn't want Julia to think she was hitting on her brother. Julia smiled back and continued dancing with James. She didn't look mad. But the heated look James was directing toward Kate was somewhat unsettling.

Her heartbeat did a cowboy quickstep as Michael reached for her and held her as if he owned her. Somehow, having Michael's rock-hard body pressed against her was more than okay even though it shouldn't have been.

He rested his hand on the small of her back, and her chest pressed to his.

There was a shift in the mood of the room as the music changed to a low-tempo beat. The sound of the drums through the speakers thumped in her ears, matching the pounding of her heart.

Michael kept his eyes on hers as their bodies collided against each other in rhythmic movement to the music.

She breathed in his intoxicating smell, growing a little dizzy.

"You okay?" Michael pulled away.

How had he known she was stressed?

"Yeah, I just . . . you ever get the feeling that you're being watched?" Her thoughts, scrambling, had landed on the only other thing on her mind—the creepy text she'd gotten the other day.

"I'm sure a lot of guys in here are watching you." He reached for her waist in an almost protective manner.

"No, not like that. I mean . . . never mind. Sorry." Her cheeks burst red, as bright as fireworks on the Fourth of July.

"Is someone bothering you?" His eyes narrowed, and he began scanning the room.

"What? Um . . . no." She took a step back. "I should get going. My hotel's not too far."

"Come on, I'll take you." He placed his hand on her forearm. "There's no way I'm letting you walk alone."

"Relax. I don't need a babysitter." *Or do I?* The image from the text flashed into her mind again. But she was too pigheaded to take Michael up on his offer, despite her nerves.

He removed his hand from her arm, and she felt a few degrees cooler without his touch. She resisted the urge to stay with him and approached Julia. "I'm gonna get going. I'm tired, and there's a lot to do tomorrow."

Julia was dancing with someone new—Kate didn't see James anywhere. She had no desire to say goodbye to him, anyway.

"Okay, well, thanks for coming out." Julia air-kissed Kate on the cheek and Kate left the dance floor.

Michael caught her by the arm. "Please, don't be stubborn."

"Hey," a cute blonde said to Michael, coming up at his side.

"I gotta go," Kate said, turning her back on the scene, hoping Michael wouldn't stop her from leaving.

Once outside the club and two blocks later, Kate found herself analyzing a pair of street signs.

"Shit." *Wrong direction.* She began to backtrack toward the club, which was now on the way to the hotel, wishing she wasn't wearing stilettos.

"Kate."

She looked up to see James before her. "Hi. You decide to leave early, too?"

His eyes darkened, and he took a few steps closer to her. A little too close. She could smell the booze on his breath. "I was hoping you and I could get to know each other a little better." He brushed a strand of hair away from her face.

His touch was too intimate. "Sure. We can talk at the fundraiser next weekend," she offered.

"How about now?" He placed a hand on her hip.

She instinctively jerked backward. "I need to get going," she said with a weak voice and wished she had channeled more oomph to her words at that moment.

"Come on—let's have a drink together. My condo is a block away. I have a great view of the city that I'd love to show you." He touched her face with the back of his hand, and she inhaled. "I won't bite. I promise." He leaned in closer, and she turned her head.

"I'm beat and just want to get back to my hotel."

"You should probably back off." A deep voice blew over her shoulder a moment later, and she shifted around to see Michael.

Thank God.

With crossed arms and tight lips, Michael glared at him.

"Are you her keeper?" James guffawed.

"You need to go, man." Michael's voice dipped even lower than normal. "And I suggest you skip the party next weekend, as well."

James looked at Kate and back at Michael. He rolled his eyes and stepped away. "See you around, sweetheart," he said before walking off.

Kate exhaled the breath she'd been holding, relieved the stand-off was over. "Thanks. I guess I should've accepted your invitation to walk me home."

He nodded in agreement, and she pointed down the street. "I'm that way." She looked up at the sliver of the moon in the sky as they walked. "So, um, who was that girl at the club?" She knew she shouldn't ask, so why did the words tumble from her lips so freely?

"No one important." He stuffed his hands into his pockets.

"Thanks again for agreeing to host the party next weekend. You made your sister over-the-top happy."

He remained silent and kept his eyes on the street as they walked.

"This is me." She stopped outside the double door entry of her hotel and looked up at him. "Would you like a drink? It's the least I can do to thank you for rescuing me." *What am I thinking?*

"Sure."

When they entered her suite, she removed her uncomfortable heels, pulled her hair in a ponytail, and approached the bar by the window.

"Let me help," he offered from behind.

"Merlot okay?" she asked.

"Sure."

Her arm brushed against his as she moved away from the bar. The slightest contact had her body tensing.

She sat on the loveseat and stared at Michael as he poured the wine, appreciating how good his backside looked in well-worn blue jeans.

"How do you like Charlotte?" he asked when facing her, armed with two glasses of wine.

"It's okay," she said softly as he handed her the drink.

"Thanks." She raised it in the air, wishing the loveseat was a little bigger when he took a seat. "Uh, cheers."

His lips slipped into a sexy smile before he raised the glass to his lips.

The man may have been a notorious womanizer, but she was beginning to wonder if it wasn't his fault. Maybe women just threw themselves at him.

She'd never had a one-night stand before, but she had a list of men that she was willing to break her no-casual-sex rule for: Bradley Cooper, Brett Dalton, and Henry Cavill. Since Michael looked like Henry, maybe even better if that were possible, did that mean she could—

"You think you'll be able to pull off this party by next

Saturday?" Michael interrupted her thoughts, which was probably a good thing.

"I hope. Your sister's counting on me." She looked down at the scarlet-colored liquid. "So, do you like being a venture capitalist? Do you miss running your old business?"

He set his glass down and pressed his hands to his thighs. "I'm involved in running many businesses now. It's exciting bringing someone's idea or product to life. I never had any intention of creating my own company when I got out of the military, you know. I had ideas—a lot of ideas, and I needed help."

"You didn't want to become rich?"

"I didn't plan on selling my inventions to the military. I would've given them away. But to get my ideas from, well, an idea to a product, I needed capital. And investors want to make a profit." He reached for his glass again and took a sip of the Merlot. "After some time, I realized I couldn't morally justify selling my inventions anymore. They were saving lives. Catching terrorists. The original investors offered me a chance to sell my share of the company to them."

"And that's when you decided to use the money to help veterans?"

He nodded.

"You're amazing." She didn't mean to say that aloud.

He cocked his head to the side and smiled. "That's what I think about you."

She took in a breath, and her shoulders jerked at the sound of her phone beeping, alerting her to a text. "Sorry. Give me a second." It had to be important if someone was trying to reach her so late.

She stood and grabbed her purse, which she'd chucked by the door.

"Everything okay?"

She dropped the phone back into her bag a second later, her

hand trembling. "Um. Yeah, I'm fine," she lied. "It's—it's actually my birthday today, and I got a birthday message is all."

"Really? Happy Birthday. Julia didn't tell me."

"She doesn't know." She walked toward the wall of windows by the bar and folded her arms.

"You sure you're okay?" He stood and approached her, wine still in hand. He touched her shoulder, guiding her to face him, before tilting her chin up.

She prayed he wouldn't see her pain. "I don't ever celebrate my birthday."

"You don't like getting old, huh?" He released his hand from her face and tipped the remaining contents of his wine glass into his mouth. "How old are you today?"

"Twenty-seven."

"Well, you should at least continue celebrating your birthday until you get to be as old as me."

"And you are?" She already knew the answer since she'd done her research on the company before visiting, but she didn't want to come across as some creepy stalker.

"Thirty-three."

"Oh—you're ancient."

He grinned and glanced toward the windows. "What's going on? For real?"

She brought her hand to her lip and bit her thumb. Was she going to tell him? Somehow, she couldn't find it in her to stop.

"My mom died giving birth to me, so I feel like I'd be celebrating her death if I partied on my birthday." She looked back out the window, not wanting to see pity, which was the normal response delivered to her upon hearing her story.

After a moment, he spoke, his voice soft. "What happened?"

Where do I even begin? She shook her head, and her eyebrows quirked in surprise—who would have thought, three days ago, that she would be opening up to Michael Maddox?

"My mom was a student at UNCC. She got pregnant her junior

year. She was due in October, but apparently, some problems developed, and they had to do an emergency C-section. She lost a lot of blood. Too much." She cleared her throat and attempted to block the threat of tears. "My dad doesn't want me in Charlotte. He hates this place because of what happened to my mom."

"I can understand that." He walked away and sat back down on the couch.

Kate turned around and looked at him. He was leaning forward and resting his elbows on his knees with his eyes on the floor. He seemed . . . different.

"I was ten years old before he brought me to Charlotte. I never saw him cry until that day."

Michael looked up at her. "It's hard losing someone."

She studied him for a beat. His mood had definitely changed. The warmth that had radiated from him before when he had heated her body with his gaze was gone.

He was stone cold—steel.

"I should get some sleep," she whispered, feeling too heavy to speak anymore.

"You gonna be okay?" He stood and moved toward her and touched her cheek with the back of his hand. The soft gesture didn't match the now dark look in his eyes.

"You don't need to worry about me. You don't even know me."

The muscle in his jaw strained as he withdrew his hand from her face.

She moved back to the windows and looked out, arms crossed. "Goodnight, Michael," she said as their eyes met in the reflection of the glass.

"Happy Birthday." He paused in the open doorway for a moment as if unsure if he should leave her.

She sighed a breath of relief once the door closed, and she allowed her eyes to fill with tears.

CHAPTER FIVE

Kate glowered at her phone for the third time in the last minute. She was on the rooftop terrace of her hotel, trying to get some work done, but her brain kept drifting back to the text she had received the night before.

Who had sent it? It had been a photo of her standing before her mother's grave. No message, just like before.

There was no way she would be able to convince herself that the text was from a pissed-off event planner.

She stowed her phone and stared down at her tablet, trying to focus and do her job.

The sun was beating down on her back, but the shade above the table allowed her to see the image on her device. She didn't make it a habit of working outside, but the day was too beautiful to waste indoors, and she hoped the fresh air would help ease her suffocating anxiety. Still, she felt as though someone had a vise grip on her throat and was squeezing the life out of her.

She couldn't allow some crazy person to knock her off her game, though. She needed to finish the web design for the gala, hire a caterer and band, and wrap up many other details for the event. She was lucky the hotel had an in-house designer who could set up the ballroom at hyper speed, and in the way Kate had envisioned. But there was still so much more to do.

She didn't like weddings because they took too long—but hell, planning something in a week wasn't what she had in mind, either.

Kate had suggested to Julia to invite some of the veterans whom the Maddox Group had already helped to become success stories. She wanted some of them to speak about their experiences, hoping that the personal touch would entice more support from the deep-pocketed attendees. She thought it would also be a great opportunity for the veterans to network and meet potential investors.

Kate knew that auctioning off Michael was a little gimmicky, but she also knew it was a surefire way to maximize attendance and rake in the dollars.

A small smile wandered to her lips when she envisioned Michael in a tuxedo—for about the fiftieth time.

She knew she'd have the same reaction that all the women at the gala would have—butterflies. Just like last night.

Thoughts of Michael left her mind at the sound of her phone.

It was her dad again. "Hi."

"I've been calling you for days. You didn't even answer on your birthday."

"I'm sorry. I've been busy with a client."

"I want you to come back home. I don't want you in that godforsaken city." His voice sounded a little raw, or raspy. Had he been yelling recently?

"Dad, I'm fine." *Am I?* "I like it here."

Except for the fact that I have a stalker.

She cleared her throat. "I, um, visited Mom's grave yesterday."

Silence.

"There were fresh flowers on the grave. Who do you think put them there? Do Grandma and Grandpa visit?" It seemed unlikely, however. Her grandparents had abandoned their home on Lake Norman days after her mother died. They never bothered to pack their belongings or sell the house—they just left. They had been living in Savannah, Georgia, ever since.

It was all very . . . odd, to say the least. But anytime she would press the subject in the past her dad would brush the topic under the rug.

"Dad." Her eyebrows quirked with worry. "Dad?"

"I want you to come home. Now."

"The event is Saturday. I'll be home shortly after that." She exhaled a frustrated breath. "I understand why you hate this place. I know it's hard for you, but I think—I think I might like to open a third location here. It would be good for business."

"And I really just want you to come home. Please, Kate, for me. Please, get the idea of Charlotte out of your head."

The line went dead.

She stared at the phone in her hand, guilt twisting in her gut for upsetting him. But before she could even put her cell away, it began ringing again.

Unknown number. Great. "Hello?"

"Kate, darling. How are you?"

Relief flooded her when she recognized the voice. "Joseph, I'm so happy to hear from you." She stood and walked toward the railing, looking down onto the street twelve stories below.

"You'll be even happier when I tell you that my plans have been canceled for next weekend. So, I'm free to cater your event. What were you thinking? Duck? Filet? Lamb?"

Kate reveled in the good news. It was just what she needed. "I think duck and filet would both be great. I'll email you the details. Thank you so much. I owe you big-time."

"Anything for you." His heavy Italian accent added extra charm to the sentiment.

She'd known him since her first solo event upon taking over her stepmother's company. He had saved her then, and he was rescuing her from potential disaster now. She just hoped he wouldn't hit on her again. "I'll have one of my secretaries in New York arrange you and your team's flight."

"I look forward to seeing you soon. I hope to steal a dance with you, as well. I assume there will be dancing?"

"If I can get a band or orchestra in time." She only wished she was joking. "See you soon. Thank you again. Ciao."

Thank God for something. She immediately texted Julia the good news. A few minutes later, her phone rang with the number from the Maddox office. Kate was impressed—Julia at work, even on a Sunday.

"Hey, Julia. I'm so relieved we were able to get such a fantastic chef on such short notice."

"Looks like you're pulling this party off. I guess I'll have to wear a monkey suit after all," Michael responded, his voice light and friendly. The opposite of how he'd left her last night.

"Oh. Hi, Michael. Sorry, I assumed it was Julia."

"I was just checking in on you. Wondered how you were doing."

Why had she told him about her mom? "I'm sorry for diving into my issues with you. I don't normally share my personal life with people." She ran a hand through her hair and shook her head, wishing she could erase last night's conversation.

"You don't need to apologize."

"Yes, I do. I don't mix business with . . ." *Pleasure?*

"Let me take you to lunch. We can talk about the fundraiser."

Was he serious? For someone who professed to hate such events, he was certainly showing a lot of interest. "I have a lot of work to do, unfortunately. Maybe I can email you an update tonight?" She didn't want to come face-to-face with Michael again, not until she had to.

"Dinner."

He didn't sound like he was giving her an option, and she was beginning to think he wasn't used to hearing the word *no*. She pushed the heel of her hand against her forehead. "Where do you want to meet?"

"Pick you up at your room. Seven."

"Okay. See you then." She ended the call. *What the hell am I getting myself into?*

* * *

"HI," KATE SAID, OPENING THE DOOR. SHE RADIATED SENSUALITY no matter what she wore, but tonight, dressed in black pants and a white top that clung to her breasts, she made him feel a little weak. And weakness wasn't something he was used to.

"I wasn't sure where we were going." She hesitated as her eyes raked over his jeans and T-shirt. "If you give me a minute, I can throw on some jeans."

"You look perfect. I'm taking you to a little Italian place around the corner. Do you mind walking?"

"Sure." She reached for her bag and followed him to the elevator.

"How was your day? Productive?"

"Yeah, actually." She smiled. "I got a lot done."

As they stepped into the empty elevator, he took a deep breath and focused his attention on the silver doors. He didn't usually have such a problem keeping composed around women, but for some reason, he could barely control his desire to behold every inch of her body. "I'm glad you agreed to dinner."

"Thanks again for the offer," she said, and they remained quiet until they were outside.

He touched the small of her back, which triggered a small twitch from her body. "It's just a block away," he said before removing his hand.

They walked in silence to a drab brownstone building on the next street.

"It's quaint," she said when they entered the dimly lit restaurant.

"Mr. Maddox, so good of you to join us."

Michael looked over at the restaurant owner and smiled. "Frankie, Kate here is from out of town. I wanted her to have the best Italian food Charlotte has to offer."

"Nice to meet you." She shook his hand.

"What a beautiful woman." Frankie eyed Kate for a moment before he directed his attention back to Michael.

Kate's skin reddened at his compliment, which Michael found endearing. "Thanks for fitting us in." He patted Frankie on the back.

"Anything for you." Frankie looked back at Kate. "Hang on to this one. He's a good man. He helped me start my business. I began my restaurant at sixty-eight—two years ago. Can you believe it? All because this man believed in my vision."

"Oh—we're not dating," Kate responded, her cheeks blushing again. "But that's great about the restaurant," she added.

"How's Billy?" he asked Frankie.

"Pretty good. Coming home to visit soon." He must've realized he was still holding Kate's hand because he released it while speaking. "He's a Navy SEAL."

"Wow. Impressive." Kate smiled at Frankie and nodded. "Is he your son?"

"Yes," he answered while directing them to a small table near an exposed brick wall.

"You must be so proud," she replied.

"I am. And I look forward to running the restaurant with him someday." He gave one last look to Michael and Kate and grinned before leaving.

Michael pulled Kate's chair out and waited for her to sit before he took his own seat across from her.

"You help a lot of people, huh?" She reached for her black linen napkin and let it fall open and rested it on her lap.

He shrugged off her comment and slid into his chair. He remained silent, studying her face. Her glossy lips were parted, and her blue-green eyes were staring into his. He couldn't wait to taste her lips. "I highly recommend the eggplant parm." He broke their gaze and cleared his throat. His body was reacting to her way too fast, which wasn't the norm for him.

"Sounds great," she said. "I trust you."

God, that's the last thing you should do.

"So, tell me about your business. Do you like being an event planner?"

Before she could respond, a waiter appeared at their table and began to chat with them. "Anything particular you'd like to drink, or is there an appetizer you want?" Michael asked.

"You can pick," she said.

"Can we have a bottle of Barolo and an order of calamari, then?" Michael thanked the waiter and looked back at Kate. "So—your business . . .?"

"It's not what I originally planned on doing with my life, but my stepmom needed me. And since I'm a planner at heart, it works for me."

"Is she still involved with the business?"

"She helps out now and then, but she stopped focusing on the business when Alex, my brother, joined the military."

"I can understand that. My parents didn't handle my time in the service very well. It can be hard on family." The topic was darkening his mood, and he didn't want to face that side of him again. He didn't want to repeat the previous night's cold goodbye. "When you told me last night that I don't know you—well, it's true. But I'd like to get to know you."

Her eyes narrowed, and she leaned back. "Know me how?"

In bed, for starters. "I just want to know more about you." He tilted his head and mimicked her body language, moving back and concentrating his eyes on hers.

"Michael, I—I don't get involved with clients."

He noticed the tremble in her voice. "I'm not exactly suggesting a relationship. I don't get involved with people I work with, either."

Her eyes shifted from his face to his chest, as if noticing the steady increase in his breathing. "So, what are you saying?"

"I want you, Kate." He could see the shock flash in her eyes. Was he too candid? But he preferred to cut straight to the point; he never wanted to send a woman the wrong signal.

She stared at him for a moment. "Like I said, I don't get involved with clients. And I would never entertain the idea of being with you, regardless."

He didn't believe her. He could feel the way her body responded when she was around him. Had their conversation not turned so heavy last night, he would've made a move. But, as much of a dick as he could be at times, he wasn't about to come onto her right after he'd learned that she'd lost her mother.

Still, he couldn't get the woman out of his head and damned if he didn't need to know how she'd feel against him.

"Unlike you, I *only* do relationships." She released a breath. "Not that I'm even looking for one now."

He nodded with understanding. "I guess that settles it, then." He paused and quirked his eyebrows. "Friends?"

"Sure," she replied after a minute. She looked up at the waiter, who was standing by their table, uncorking the wine. "I could definitely use a drink."

He waited for the server to leave before looking back at her. She returned his gaze beneath long eyelashes, and his pulse jumped a notch. "So, why don't you want a relationship?" he asked, curiosity swelling inside him. She'd brought it up—the topic was fair game, right? Of course, he hoped to hell she didn't ask him the same question.

She tilted her head to the side and brought the wine to her lips. She took a sip, licked her lips, and set the glass down. "Why does it matter?"

"I just can't believe you're available." He took a swig of his drink.

"Most of the men I meet are either clients or guys from bars . . . guys who only want one thing."

He almost choked on his wine. *Guys like me.* "And I fit into both those categories, huh?"

She nodded and tucked her blonde hair behind her ear, exposing a small pearl earring. "Looks like it."

"Good thing we're just friends."

He studied her reaction. She was unraveling at the seams, just like him. He could feel the sexual energy radiating from her body, matching his own. But he knew it would be wrong for him to pursue her if he couldn't give her what she needed. That hadn't necessarily stopped him before, but there was something about this woman . . . she was already fragile. He didn't want to break her.

"You still haven't answered my question, though. Why don't you want a relationship?" He had his reasons, but what were hers?

"It's not in my plans right now. I need to focus on the business."

"Hm." He squinted a little, calling her bluff.

"What?"

"Nothing," he said with a smile as the waiter delivered their calamari.

"So, why'd you join the military? Was it because of September 11th? I'm always wondering what my life would be like if I had chosen a different path, if I hadn't taken over for my stepmom. I guess I was kind of thinking you might feel the same?"

"The military and the CIA pursued me when I was finishing my last year in college. They told me I could help them win the war on terror." He took a quick drink. "To be told at twenty-one that my designs could help locate terrorists and save lives was a little overwhelming."

"But you did it."

"I chose the military. I didn't want to be a spook." He stared into his wine glass. To his eye, the glass appeared to rattle with the sounds of war.

His eyes fell shut, and he tried to silence the memories, but they were too loud.

His erect posture waned for a moment as his shoulders arched forward.

"You okay?" she asked, her voice softening a touch.

"Yeah, sorry." He swallowed. "But yeah—yeah, I know what you mean about wondering if life would be different if I didn't join the Marines." He didn't regret his decision, but he knew he would never be the same.

"How about them Yankees?"

He looked up at her and smiled, her words surprising him.

"I always say that whenever things get a little too much."

He nodded. "I'm more of a Red Sox fan."

"Really? So am I."

"I guess we have more in common than we realize," he said. *God, you're sexy.* He forced his attention away from her as the waiter delivered the rest of their meal.

They chatted on and off as they ate, and he loved simply hearing the soft sound of her voice as she spoke. And he also enjoyed seeing a woman finish her entire meal—he was so sick of watching his dates only eat salad—with no damn dressing even.

"I'm going out of town tomorrow. Just for a night. But I assume I will see you in the office Tuesday?" He finished his last bite of eggplant parmesan and set his fork on the table.

"Business meeting?" she asked.

"I usually spend every other week in New York, but I didn't want to be away all week." *I want to get to know you more*, he thought as he looked up.

She cleared her throat and touched her lips. Her eyes remained frozen on his as her bottom lip slipped down at the touch of her fingers. "Must be tough to bounce back and forth each week."

"Not really," he said. "So, how'd you like dinner?"

She looked down at her empty plate. "It was delicious. And the wine was amazing. Nice choice."

He nodded, glad she'd been satisfied, but damned if he wished he could satisfy her in bed after, too.

"Thanks again for tonight. Sorry about—um—turning you down." She peered at him from the corner of her eyes. The dilation of her pupils and the slight tremble of her lips seemed to belie her words.

"Let's get going," he grumbled, worried his control would snap in half, and he'd say something over the line again.

He paid the check and said goodbye to the owner, and then they walked back to her hotel.

"I should say goodbye here," he said once outside her door.

"Thank you again."

His eyes drifted over the curves of her body before returning to her pouty lips.

He blew out a small but unnoticeable breath and leaned forward. He rested his hand on her arm and kissed her cheek. "Goodnight, Kate," he said gruffly and forced himself to leave, knowing if he stayed any longer, she just might bend to the desire they both felt for each other.

And for once in a long damn time, he didn't want to be an asshole and let that happen.

* * *

SHE COULDN'T BELIEVE MICHAEL'S ARROGANCE. DID HE REALLY proposition her for sex at dinner?

Why couldn't she get him out of her head, though?

Before she had a chance to get undressed, a knock at the door had her pulse racing.

Oh, God. Michael? Would she be able to keep up her thin veneer of restraint?

She rested her hand over the safety lock and shut one eye as she looked out the peephole with the other.

No one was there.

Had Michael changed his mind and left so soon?

She unlocked the door and stepped out into the hall, looking left and right. No sign of anyone, but she did hear the sound of the elevator doors closing down the hall.

He must have left. Maybe he realized his mistake and took off.

Thank God. She turned to go back in but noticed a red envelope beneath her feet.

She took a step back and stared down at it. Her lip tucked between her teeth.

She realized it wasn't Michael who had knocked on the door— in her heart, she knew whoever had been stalking her had just taken things up a notch.

She knelt down and picked up the envelope before returning to her room. She dead bolted the door behind her, then walked into the living area and tapped the crimson-red envelope against her leg, not sure if she should open it.

CHAPTER SIX

KATE HADN'T OPENED THE RED ENVELOPE SINCE SHE'D RECEIVED IT thirty-six hours ago. She had switched her hotel room within ten minutes of getting the envelope, and booked a room for the next night at the hotel where the gala was to be held. There was no way she was going to sleep one more night in a room where her stalker had been.

Her hand slipped into her large purse, which also served as her work bag today, and she felt the envelope between her fingers. But, at the sound of her phone, she let it go and scrambled to locate her cell.

"This is Kate," she answered.

"Hey, you coming into the office today?" Julia asked.

"Walking there now. I finished with the designer at the hotel."

"Perfect. Michael is back from New York, and he's asking for you."

Kate slowed down her pace, worried if everything was okay. "Oh really? Does he want to check in on our progress?" *Or fire me for turning him down?*

"I have no idea. Just head on over to his office when you get here. See you in a bit."

Kate tossed her phone back into her bag, thoughts of the envelope far from her mind now.

Michael. He was all that was in her head.

When she got to the office, she nodded and smiled at Cindy, then started for Michael's room.

Julia's office was empty, giving her no reason to stall now.

She toyed with the strap of her bag as she forced her black pumps to move, one step at a time.

When she arrived at his door, she popped her head in, but her mouth closed when she saw he wasn't alone. He was sitting on his couch next to an auburn-haired woman. His hand rested on her shoulder, and the woman's gaze was cast down.

She took a step back, attempting to duck away before Michael saw her, but it was too late. His eyes captured hers, and he gave her a slight shake of the head.

She put her hand up, motioning she'd catch him later and quickly left. It was obvious she had come at a bad time.

"Kate," Julia called out on approach.

"Hey, I was going to set up shop in your conference room. Is that okay?" Kate pointed to the room that adjoined Julia's office.

"Of course. I was hoping to catch you before you saw Michael, anyway. He got a visitor right after we hung up, but I'm sure he'll find you after."

"Sure."

"You okay?" Julia arched a brow.

Kate shrugged her purse off her shoulder and allowed it to drop to the ground. "Yeah, just a little tired. I've been working like crazy on this gala." It wasn't a total lie.

Julia smiled. "Thank you. I'm so grateful." She sat down at the conference room table and folded her hands. "I have great news. I followed your advice, and I have a special guest speaker for the ball."

"That's awesome." Kate started to sit but seeing Michael through the glass wall caught her off guard. He was walking down the hall next to the redhead, his hand on the small of her back. He managed to avoid looking into the conference room, and Kate forced herself not to overthink anything. Besides, what did it matter? She'd said *no* to Michael the other night. What difference did it make to her who he dated—or whatever he did with women . . .

Julia cleared her voice, which had Kate glancing over at her.

"Maybe we could order some lunch to the office while we work? I'm starved—my treat," Kate suggested.

"Let's go grab some food instead. I know a great place."

Kate nodded, preferring Julia's idea. She'd been in the building for five minutes but suddenly felt like she was suffocating.

She kneeled down to grab her purse off the floor, but a large hand beat her to it. She followed the black dress shoes to slacks, which stretched all the way up to a trim waist. She inhaled as she straightened, taking in with her his cologne and the smell of clean linen.

"On your way out?" Michael handed Kate her bag.

"We're going to lunch." Julia looked at him. "Care to join us?"

"I'd love to."

The way Michael's eyes traveled the length of her body before settling on her face made her buzz to life with excitement. Her body betrayed her as her nipples hardened beneath her silk blouse.

"Michael? Kate? You two ready?" Julia asked.

"Yeah." She swallowed. "You, Michael?"

"More than ready." His words were like satin, wrapping around her every limb—and she hated that he was able to create such an intense reaction within her so easily.

She diverted her attention, unable to look at him any longer without giving away her thoughts.

Once they all entered the elevator, she stared at her heels and clutched her bag with both hands, hanging onto it like a lifeline.

"Is Mexican okay?" Julia asked as they stepped into the lobby.

"Yeah, I love anything with spice." Kate spotted a quirk in Michael's lips as he held the door open for them.

The restaurant was around the corner in one of the most popular areas of Uptown Charlotte. They sat at a table out front, and Kate found herself too close to Michael, even though they were across the table from each other.

Kate looked at the menu, pretending to have no idea what she wanted, buying herself some time before she'd have to get lost in his blue eyes again. She'd decided on their color, anyway. *Navy blue.* For today, at least. It depended on what he was wearing tomorrow as to what shade she'd get lost in.

"So, how was New York?" Kate stole a look at him above her menu.

"It was fine. But what I'm really interested in is to find out how the planning is coming along."

"Bullshit," Julia said almost immediately and reached over and slapped her brother's chest. "Don't be an ass."

He reached for his collar, popped open the top button—tie already removed—and smoothed his hand over his shirt before resting it in his lap. "No, seriously. I've taken an interest," he said casually as Julia stared at him with parted lips.

"Ohh." Julia straightened and looked at Kate.

"Well, we're wrapping up the details—fine-tuning everything," Kate finally answered, but she was worried about what Julia was thinking right about now.

Julia's phone began to ring a moment later, helping diffuse the awkward tension that had begun to ping-pong back and forth between Kate and Michael.

"Sorry," Julia muttered and glanced down at the caller ID. "Shit. It's Aiden calling."

"That can't be good," Michael responded. "Why's he calling you instead of me?"

Julia rose to her feet, gripping the phone. "Business stuff he doesn't want to trouble you with."

"Well, tell him to call me later, okay?"

Shit, don't leave me alone.

Kate watched Julia walk away with the phone pressed against her ear.

"Eh, so, who is Aiden?"

"A friend of mine in Boston. We served together in the Marines, and then not too long ago I invested in his pub. Apparently, Julia's been helping him out more than I realized." Michael's hand wrapped up around to the back of his neck, and he squeezed.

A thick band of tension had cut between them, and he hardened before her eyes. *What is with you?* Was he worried that his friend might be hooking up with his sister? Julia had said Michael was overprotective . . .

Julia returned to the table after only a minute, thank God. "Ugh. Kate, I'm so sorry, but I need to fly to Boston today. I might need to be there for a little bit." She lifted her purse and hung the strap over her shoulder. "Don't worry—I'll be back in time for the gala. I'm so sorry I have to bail on you right now."

"Why does Aiden need you in Boston? Something wrong with the pub?" Michael pressed back in his seat, worry spreading across his face.

"He's fine, but he says he's not business-minded, so he calls me when he needs help. It's nothing to stress about." Julia came over next to her brother and patted him on the shoulder. "Really, I've got this. You can help Kate since you've developed such an interest in the ball."

"If you say so. But that also means you're going to miss our monthly poker game again. The guys are going to be so pissed." Michael reached beneath the table and produced his cell phone a moment later.

"Looking for my replacement so fast, huh?" Julia chuckled. "Well, I'm sorry to exit in the midst of lunch, but I need to go book a flight and pack. I'll call you later."

Michael looked up from his phone and nodded. "Have a safe flight."

"We'll be fine. No worries." Kate hoped, at least. She gave Julia a reassuring smile and waved goodbye, then focused on Michael as he stowed his phone back into his slacks pocket. "So, Julia plays poker?"

"I taught her a long time ago."

Kate smiled as she drew up images of her own past. "I taught my kid brother to play before he went into the military."

"You play?" He stared at her, and his lips parted. "What got you into the game?"

Kate fiddled with the drink menu. "One of my boyfriends at Harvard liked to play. He used to compete in tournaments all of the time, and so I asked him to teach me. I fell in love with the game and continued playing even after we broke up. He had a bad gambling problem that I later discovered . . . but I thought the game was fun, and I even won a couple of local events." She sighed. "I haven't played in years. Ever since I began running my stepmother's business, I never have time to have fun anymore."

"You played in tournaments?" Michael scratched at his jaw. "I'm having trouble believing that you would sit at the table with poker sharks, and—" He stopped himself and shook his head, a smile threatening his lips. "Actually, I think you must be great at the game. All you need to do is bat your eyes and smile, and the players are putty in your hands."

"What? Can't a girl have real poker skills? A woman has to use her looks to win?"

"No, but I—"

"I do have talent, by the way. There is no eye batting. I wear my Red Sox hat and a pair of sunglasses."

"To hide your tells?" he taunted, his eyes glinting with amusement. "I would still be able to read you."

Kate's chest constricted at his words. "There's only one way to find out." *What am I doing?*

"You want to be Julia's replacement?"

"Nah. I can't play you. It wouldn't be fair. I'd take all your money."

"I think that sounds like a challenge," he responded, the deep baritone of his voice reminding her of the dangerous turn their conversation had taken.

Poker, with Michael? With Michael's friends? Am I out of my mind? She wet her lips and reached for her water.

"Come on, don't back out now." He leaned over the table, trying to get her attention. "It's tomorrow night at my friend's loft. Starts at nine. And don't use work as an excuse."

Shit. Spending more time with him was definitely not part of the plan. "Okay." Her answer surprised her as it dropped free from her lips.

"Great." He sat back and looked up at the outdoor entertainment system, which was nestled in the corner of the building overhang. An English translation of a Spanish love song poured through the speaker, and he directed his attention back on Kate, his eyes resting on her mouth.

With an unsteady hand, she reached for her water again, feeling the need to cool off. She forced her gaze away from him and out onto the nearby street.

The unnoticeable shakiness of her hand turned into an obvious tremble as her eyes fixated on a man sitting on a bench along the street. He was on his phone and looking at her. Blond. Athletic. Middle-aged. Was it the same man? The man who'd given her the chills at the club on her first night in town?

It was impossible to remember exactly what the guy had looked like. It had been dark in the club, and she hadn't taken a close look at his face. But for some reason, the same gut-wrenching feeling was climbing its way through her system.

"Kate? You okay?"

The man was watching her. There were no flashing lights like at the club to cast doubt on his gaze. And it wasn't the stare of a man checking out a woman. This was different. She could feel it.

She inhaled as she watched the man rise to his feet, phone still at his ear. He gave her one last look as his lips pressed together, and then he walked away.

"Kate?" Michael waved his hand in front of her face.

"Huh?" She shook her head, freeing herself from the spell of fear that sliced through her. Had she laid eyes on her stalker? If so, who the hell was he? And why was he following her?

"What happened?" Michael asked, his voice registering concern.

"Nothing. I'm fine. Sorry." She pushed a fake smile to her lips, but she doubted he was buying it. "Just thinking about my mom." She noticed his body ease and grow less rigid.

"Oh. Sorry."

The waiter appeared at their side. *Thank God.* He couldn't have come at a better time.

* * *

THE RED ENVELOPE SAT ON HER HOTEL BED, TAUNTING HER—again. She rubbed her hands together, balling them into fists, hoping to calm her nerves and release her tension.

Kate looked at her watch. It was almost eleven at night.

She had decided to head back to her hotel after lunch with Michael. She wasn't sure if she was afraid he would sense her worry, or afraid he would sense the desire she couldn't seem to curtail.

She'd told Michael some lame excuse about needing to bounce around the city and run errands tomorrow so she wouldn't have to see him until the poker game. Avoidance—her only way to stifle her body's craving of the man. Sex would be good with him, though, wouldn't it? More than good, she was sure.

She blew a hair out of her face and looked back at the blood-red envelope.

Maybe she should've been more worried about some creep following her—wanting to kill her, or whatnot, instead of fixating on Michael's ass or the sound of his deep voice.

"Just do it." She unclenched her fists and reached for the envelope. She held her breath as she opened it, as though some deadly powdery substance might drift from its folds.

Surprise flooded her system when she found herself staring down at a picture of Michael and an unknown woman. He was embracing a raven-haired woman on a dance floor. Their bodies were pushed together, and his mouth appeared to be nuzzling her neck.

She shuffled through four more photos, all of Michael. All the images were of Michael with different women. But the fourth photo was of a woman Kate recognized—the redhead from the office. Michael was sitting at a dinner table with her. White linen. Fancy. Half-empty wine glasses between them.

But the last photo . . . it was of Michael and Kate dancing at the club Saturday night.

"What the hell . . ." She dropped the photos on the bed and rubbed her hands over her tired face. Her emotions were spiraling in all different directions, and she couldn't make sense of anything.

When she looked back down at the photos, she squinted in surprise, picking up one of the photos that had flipped over. There was writing on the back.

"Go back to New York." She re-read the words a dozen more times, trying to figure out the motive of her stalker, and why whoever was following her not only wanted her out of Charlotte, but possibly wanted her away from Michael, too.

CHAPTER SEVEN

MICHAEL STUDIED KATE AS SHE STOOD ON THE OTHER SIDE OF THE door at his friend's apartment. She was dressed in a pair of faded blue jeans and a loose-fitting, yellow T-shirt that made him wonder if she was attempting to hide her sexuality. She was failing, in his book.

"I can't believe you tried to back out on me."

"Well, you know, I don't have my lucky Red Sox hat. So, I thought maybe I shouldn't come," she answered with a smile in her eyes.

He moved out of her way and allowed her to enter his friend's loft. "This is Jerry's place. He teaches at a school north of Charlotte." He shut the door, and she turned toward him.

"Don't take this the wrong way, but I love that you don't play poker with, um, millionaires. It means I can afford to play."

God, he loved her smile. The way her eyes lifted in perfect time with her lips made something in his chest hurt, in a good way. He could tell she was nervous, but he doubted it was because of the poker game. "I wasn't always rich. And having money doesn't mean anything," he said, low enough so his friends wouldn't hear him. His buddies were impatiently waiting in the living room where the poker table was set up.

"Money means something when you use it to help others as you are." She winked and walked down the narrow hall like she knew exactly where she was going.

He stood still at her comment and watched her disappear. When he heard a loud grumbling of voices, he knew his friends had just laid eyes upon her. He rubbed his jaw, grinned, and hurried toward the living room.

"Michael. Seriously? You think we're going to be able to concentrate with Kate at the table? You know we have a hard time with Julia—and she's like family," Brett joked as he folded his arms across his chest and leaned against the back of the oversized white couch. Most of the furniture was pushed against the walls to make room for the long, oval poker table.

The entire apartment was no greater than eight hundred square feet, but a nice loft in the city came with a price. Michael and his friends rotated the game among their houses. There were eight players in total, including Julia, when she was able to make it.

"You better continue thinking of Julia as a sister," Michael warned. He tapped Brett's shoulder and looked at Kate. "This is Brett—he's a pediatrician. And married, by the way." *Did I really invite Kate to a poker game with a bunch of sex-charged guys?* He studied his friend, Jerry, watching the way his eyes raked over Kate's toned body.

"The only one of us who is married," Jerry added. "Hi, this is my place," he said, stepping up to Kate.

"Hi," she said.

Michael observed Kate, noticing the way her jeans hugged her ass as she reached forward for Jerry's outstretched hand. He glanced at his friends who were lined up next to him, looking somewhat ridiculous as they waited for their introductions.

They'd met plenty of Michael's dates in the past. Half of them had been models. Some famous. And he'd never gotten sensitive about his buddies checking out whatever woman he was with at the time. But tonight, it felt different, and he didn't have any damn idea why it bothered him. He had no claim over this woman.

"You remind me of a young Denzel Washington," Kate said when she released Jerry's hand.

Jerry exposed his white teeth when he grinned. "I've heard that a couple times."

Michael introduced Kate to the rest of his crew before they settled in at the poker table. "Want a beer? I think that's all we have."

Kate shook her head no as she took a seat across the table from him. "I don't drink when I gamble," she said before giving him the gift of her gorgeous dimples.

He set his Corona down and reached for his wallet.

"How much? Is this a tournament or a cash game?" she asked while dipping a hand into her purse.

"Cash game. You can put in as much as you want. No limit," Michael responded.

"Hell no. There is a limit—a thousand. We aren't all drowning in cash like this one," Brett said while poking at Michael, who was sitting on his left.

"Okay, sure. A thousand. But you can buy back in if you run out of cash," Michael added.

"And you've done that plenty of times," Jerry said before cracking a smile. "Welcome to the game." He raised his Corona in the air to Kate, who was sitting next to him.

"Thanks," she said, placing two hundred dollars on the table.

"High card is the dealer," Jerry said while shuffling the deck of cards. He flipped a card face-up to everyone at the table. "Looks like you, Michael." He pushed the cards to him and sunk back in his chair.

"Not going to put your sunglasses on?" Michael asked Kate while deftly shuffling the cards.

"I don't think I'll need them."

I think you do. Your eyes tell me everything, Michael thought as he dealt.

After several rounds of Texas hold 'em, Kate proved to be a legit player, but Michael had yet to go head-to-head with her. His cards were always shit whenever she was in the pot, and so he spent his time watching Kate, reading her, studying the way her eyes looked down, and her lower lip would sometimes catch between her teeth. It was a nervous habit of hers that he had picked up on during their first meeting. She always won the hand when he saw her do this. She was trying to appear worried, to dupe his friends into thinking she was bluffing.

It was the longest hour he had ever played poker. Sitting across from Kate killed his focus on the cards. He could smell the sweet, flowery fragrance of her perfume, and since she was wearing barely any makeup, Michael noticed a slight dusting of freckles across the bridge of her nose.

God, he wanted to kiss her.

"Michael?" Jerry was waving his hand in the air as if pushing away a cloud of cigar smoke.

Michael looked up. "Sorry. My turn?" He glanced at his cards. Pocket kings. Finally, a decent pocket pair. He placed his bet and leaned back in the black folding chair, which was a bit too small for him.

"I'm all in." Kate looked up at Michael and tilted her head.

He kept his eyes on her as his friends to her right bowed out of the game. When it was back to him, he studied her, checking for tells. She swallowed and adjusted back in her seat. That was new. Was she bluffing?

Or was he just feeling sexual tension from her? The magnetic pull between them was making it hard to breathe. He reached for his chest, ready to loosen a tie that was strangling him, only he was wearing a T-shirt. "Is it hot in here?" he found himself asking as he stood.

"Come on, you afraid of a challenge? A duel of the sexes?" Jerry joked.

Michael tried to focus, but he found himself consumed by his past, by the memories he had tried to silence. Why was this happening now?

The rocky terrain as his boots slipped on the climb.

Gunfire.

IEDs.

Torn flesh.

Blood.

He turned away from the table, not wanting Kate to see him like this. His throat constricted, and he wondered if he was choking. He opened the patio door and walked outside. He braced the railing and closed his eyes, trying to shut out the steady stream of images that exhausted his mind.

"You all right?" It was his friend Jerry.

His civilian friends didn't understand what he'd been through. It was hard for anyone to get it unless they served. So, he lied, "Yeah, I'm fine."

"Kate wanted to check on you herself, but I figured you'd prefer not."

Good call. He inhaled a sharp breath and opened his eyes.

He tucked the painful memories back inside and rubbed his hands over his face. "Be right in."

After a few moments, he sat back at the table and reached for his beer. He took a swig of his drink and studied Kate. Her mouth was angled down, and her shoulders drooped forward. Was she worried about him? Or worried he might call?

Perhaps she was playing him.

"I fold." He set his beer down and watched her cheeks flush.

The two players to Michael's left also folded, leaving only Kate in the hand. She began to gather in the pot. "So, what did you have?" he asked as he leaned back in his chair, feeling more relaxed.

"A good player never reveals," she said as she stacked the chips in front of her.

And then she winked at him.

God, she was the perfect distraction to ease the pain away from his mind.

You're killing me. He straightened in his seat, feeling overwhelmed by his desire to kiss the edges of her mouth as her lips shifted up into a sexy grin.

* * *

"YOU'RE REALLY NOT GOING TO TELL ME, HUH?"

"No way," Kate said, swatting his chest. "What if we play again?"

He stopped walking for a moment. "Can it be just us next time? And maybe . . . a different kind of poker game?"

She studied his eyes as they focused on her mouth, wondering what sinful albeit delicious thoughts he was harboring. "In your dreams." She couldn't help but crack a smile. *And only in my dreams, too.*

Michael cleared his throat. "Why'd you change hotels?"

I think I'd rather go back to talking about strip poker. She started to walk again, not sure what lie to spin. "I thought it would be more convenient to be here for the gala." *Totally plausible, right?* And true, in part. It would be a lot easier to stay at the same hotel as the ball.

"Miss Adams?"

Kate looked away from Michael and toward the concierge, who was approaching her. The staff had become well acquainted with her from her work on the ball. "Yes?"

"We had a delivery for you earlier this evening." He was carrying a glass vase of at least two dozen white tulips.

Michael tilted his head and studied Kate. "Secret admirer?"

Kate swallowed the lump that had formed in her throat. The

memory of the flowers that had been laid upon her mother's grave flashed to her mind.

Michael removed his hands from his shorts pockets and reached for the vase when Kate didn't move. "You okay?" he asked, nodding toward the concierge and studying her.

She stared at the vase in his hands as her heartbeat escalated.

"Kate?" Michael gripped the vase with one hand and rested his other hand on her shoulder.

She looked up into his eyes, not sure what to say. "Yeah, I'm okay. No note?" She kept her hands to her sides, not eager to touch the flowers, which were no doubt from the man or woman who was following her. She had started to believe it was a jealous ex-lover of Michael's who was trying to scare her away, but now her mind reeled, trying to come up with alternate theories.

"I don't see a message," he replied as he held the vase up. "I'll ask the concierge."

She watched him head to the desk, and she rubbed her hands against her thighs, unconsciously sucking her bottom lip between her teeth.

The texts had made her nervous. The red envelope had tripped her up a bit, making her more alert. More cautious. But the flowers —the flowers felt different. Perhaps it was the connection to the grave, to her mother, that was making her ready to run to the bathroom and throw up.

"No note," Michael said upon approach. "Any idea who sent them?"

"I don't know. It's no big deal." *Only it really is.* She started for the elevator, but Michael grasped her arm.

"Kate, what's going on?"

She gulped and turned to face him. "The flowers are probably from someone who knew my mother. Someone left the same white tulips at her grave when I visited last weekend."

His hand slipped from her forearm to her wrist, and he pulled her closer to him. The gentleness of his grip, despite his massive strength, surprised her. "You're going to drop those," she said, her gaze drawn to the vase, although she wanted it nowhere near her room.

"Do you want me to leave the flowers down here?"

They were close. Their bodies would have been touching if it weren't for the massive vase between them. "Yes, please," she whispered while looking up at him, unable to hide the emotion brewing inside of her.

He released his grip on her and walked to the nearby lounge area. He set the vase down and quickly came back. "Let me take you to your room." It was a statement, not a question.

She stared at the floor in silence as the elevator moved to the top floor.

"Will you let me inside and tell me what's really going on?" he asked once they reached her room.

She searched her bag for the keycard. "I'm fine." She turned to open the door but shuddered when his hand touched her back.

"I may be a bit coldhearted when it comes to women, but I'm always there for a friend." His voice was low and raspy.

"Are we friends?" she asked, her back still to him.

"I think so."

"Then I'd better say goodnight now."

She had no idea what she would do once inside her room. She knew it would be easy to lose herself in his arms. To forget her confusion and fear.

But then wouldn't Michael become just another problem?

She grew cold when his hand left her back.

She pushed open her door, nervous she'd change her mind. "Goodnight, Michael." She turned to face him.

"See you tomorrow?" He pressed a palm against the wall outside the doorframe.

Kate hesitated for a moment. "Probably not until the gala. I'll be working in the ballroom to make sure all the preparations are complete."

He shoved his hands back into his shorts pockets. "Okay. Well, goodnight, then."

Like wings breaking from a crystal butterfly, she found her body shattering at that moment as she watched him walk away when all she really wanted was for him to stay.

CHAPTER EIGHT

IT WAS FRIDAY AFTERNOON. KATE HADN'T SEEN OR HEARD FROM Michael since he dropped her off at her room, and she also hadn't received any other messages or deliveries from her mystery stalker. Of course, her father had called her numerous times—she assumed to push the topic of her return home—but she always put him to voicemail. She felt guilty, but she needed to focus. Besides, she would be going home soon.

She'd spent the last day and a half working nonstop on the Maddox Gala. And everything for the ball was about as perfect as it could be for such a last-minute event.

Kate walked around the ballroom, making sure everything was decorated as spectacularly as she had imagined. And it was. The designer had done a fantastic job. The room looked sleek and sophisticated. The ballroom had a baby grand piano, large crystal chandelier, two stages (one for the orchestra and another for the auction), and plenty of room for dancing. Thirty tables surrounded the dance floor. The ice-blue linens with metallic overlays and silver chairs would be enhanced by the vases of fresh, cream-colored roses that would be placed tomorrow as centerpieces. Kate's favorite part of the ballroom were the two terraces. On each,

French doors opened out onto a romantic and cozy overlook: one of the city, the other of the hotel's massive rose garden. Kate could picture the band playing with the doors open, the fresh September air ventilating the room.

It would be perfect . . . she hoped.

She smiled and took a seat at one of the tables. She was waiting for her friend Joseph, the caterer. He'd arrived early that morning but had been busy shopping for his menu. She tapped her short, pink nails on the table in front of her and reached for her phone. With it, she began to research Michael on the internet.

Kate scrolled down the page of web hits until she found an article that had been published in GQ a few years earlier. Next to the article was a photo of Michael in his Marine uniform. He looked like a man not to be reckoned with in a business suit, but in his military uniform, he looked downright dangerous.

She averted her eyes from the photo, needing to still her pulse, and began reading the article.

MICHAEL MADDOX IS A REAL-LIFE SUPERHERO. HE IS A MAN WHOM men dream of becoming and women fantasize about. He is an American military hero.

But today? Today he is dressed in a custom-fitted Ralph Lauren three-piece suit and sitting across from the board of directors for a company he just sold for three hundred million dollars. Today, Michael Maddox is a multimillionaire.

But before the brawny man became a superhero, before he received the Purple Heart and Silver Star, before he became a superrich entrepreneur—who was he?

He grew up in a small town on the outskirts of Raleigh, North Carolina; his parents were both teachers. According to his parents, Michael was a gifted child. A prodigy. He enrolled at Duke when he was only sixteen and completed his bachelor's in engineering by his eighteenth birthday. Then he went on to earn master's degrees in computer science and business at Yale, graduating at the top of both classes in 2001.

But when the tragic event of 9/11 occurred, Michael found himself pursued by government agencies and both the Army and Marines. They wanted him for his genius and his athleticism. So, Michael decided to serve his country and place his entrepreneurial desires on hold for the greater good.

He enlisted in the military as an officer and quickly worked his way up to first lieutenant. He served in both Iraq and Afghanistan, completing several tours of duty for his country.

In 2005, a pre-unified command plan to fight against global terror networks was proposed, and in February 2006, in Camp Lejeune, North Carolina, the Marine Corps Forces Special Operations Command (MARSOC) was activated. Michael became a member of the elite Special Forces after completing seven months of training at Camp Lejeune. In addition to the rigorous military training he'd already received, he trained in reconnaissance, maritime navigation, foreign internal defense, survival evasion, asymmetric warfare, close-quarter combat . . . and the list goes on. After his training, he was deployed to Afghanistan on several reconnaissance missions, which was when Michael began working on building and refining his intelligence software and technology. He improved the tactical remote sensor system to better monitor enemy activity and helped develop more advanced SATCOMS.

But it was in 2010 during Operation Knife—

"KATE!"

Kate stopped reading the article and looked up to find Joseph approaching. She stood, feeling like she had one too many to drink.

He planted a kiss on both her cheeks.

"It's so nice to see you. How's everything going?" she asked as they began walking toward the hotel's industrial kitchen.

"Fantastic," he remarked. "I procured all of the fresh food we need for tomorrow, and we're good to go. My team is practicing the menu as we speak. The hotel servers seem competent and professional. Everything is going smoothly."

"That's great news. Anything I can do for you? Anything else you need?"

"We're good. I'm just looking forward to seeing you in an evening gown tomorrow. You will dress for the occasion?" His green eyes widened with his smile.

"Yeah, of course. I'm torn between red and navy. You know . . . I want to dress in our country's colors since the fundraiser is for veterans." Navy would match Michael's eyes, though.

"Red," Joseph said. "Definitely red. With your long, golden locks, you absolutely must wear red."

She smiled then looked around as they entered the busy kitchen. "Smells fabulous."

"Then my staff is doing an excellent job," he replied. "I was wondering, instead of waiting until tomorrow to see you, maybe we could catch up over a drink tonight?" He reached for her hands and held them in his own, keeping his eyes on her.

His touch suggested he had yet to give up on dating her, even though she'd lost count of how many times she had told him she wanted to keep their relationship professional. "One drink won't hurt, I guess." She squinted one eye at him, and her lips puckered, giving a playful warning that she suspected his intentions.

"I'll be on my best behavior. Chef's promise," he said before leaning forward and kissing her hand.

* * *

"I should get back to the hotel." Kate looked at her watch. It was close to ten, and she wanted to get an early start on the day tomorrow. Plus, she didn't want to traipse around the city at night if someone really was keeping tabs on her.

God, she was eager to leave Charlotte on Sunday and carry on with her normal life.

Her father would be pleased when she told him she wasn't going to consider Charlotte for a third location for the company. She had no intention of telling him why, but he wouldn't care, as long as the topic had been shelved.

"One more drink."

Kate looked up from her empty wine glass, feeling a little lightheaded from the alcohol. She had nursed only two glasses of Chardonnay in the last two hours, but the pours here were absurdly deep. "I need to get some sleep. I'm beat," she said before faking a half yawn.

Joseph shifted on his barstool and motioned for the bartender. They were in the Epicentre, at a restaurant that turned into a nightclub around eleven. "Come on, Kate. I rarely see you. And one more glass will help you fall asleep that much easier."

His Italian accent sounded thicker than normal. Perhaps it was the whiskey he was drinking. "Fine," she agreed, wrinkling her nose. "You win."

He clapped his hands together before tapping her on the shoulder like a sister. Good. She hoped he would start treating her like one more often.

"Another round," he said, waving his hand in the air. He adjusted his seat so he could better face Kate. His dark brows lifted as his attention shifted to something or someone behind her. "Did you invite Maddox?"

Kate's hand rushed to her throat as if she was going to choke, and she shifted in her seat to check if Michael was, in fact, on approach.

"Isn't that the supermodel, Jamie Landon?" Joseph arched his shoulders back in obvious excitement.

"Yeah," she answered under her breath.

The sight of Jamie with her arm wrapped around Michael's as

they walked toward the bar like a power couple had her stomach flipping, which was ridiculous, she knew.

How many times did she have to remind herself that she was the one who turned him down? It was her fault that she'd never experience his hands on her body, or discover the way his mouth would feel on her skin.

She needed to keep her heart guarded, to keep her plans intact.

Business first.

Boyfriend later.

And preferably fall for a man who actually wanted a relationship.

She shut her eyes for a second, hoping she could blink the two of them away. When her eyes opened, Michael was staring back at her, shy of her by a couple feet.

"Kate." Michael said her name while giving her a curt nod.

She stood and closed the short gap between them. "Hi. This is Joseph, the caterer for the gala. I didn't expect to see you here." She looked over at Jamie, who began to touch her bottom lip with a bright red fingernail as she tilted her head slightly.

"So, you're the one who managed to get Michael to throw a party. Thank you," Jamie said.

"And thank you for participating in the auction." Hoping to hide her annoyance, she motioned her hand, inviting Michael and Jamie to sit at the bar.

Michael glanced at the empty barstools before his gaze swept back to Kate. "We have reservations. Late dinner. Jamie's flight arrived an hour ago. But thank you for the offer."

Kate shot him an awkward smile, hating the stir of jealousy inside of her. She wished for one night she could let go of her principles—her plans . . . and be with Michael. But it was the morning after that had her entirely too fearful of being so daring.

"Well, you two have a good night. We'll see you at the ball tomorrow." Michael shook Joseph's hand and looked back at Kate with narrowed eyes.

"Bye." The word had brushed from her lips almost like a coo. *What is wrong with me?*

"Wow, she's gorgeous." Joseph sat back at the bar.

"Sure, if you like long legs, big boobs, and flowing brown hair."

"Do you have a thing for Maddox?"

She waved a hand and smiled. "What? No way."

He reached for his whiskey. "Yeah, and I don't want to see you naked."

She playfully slapped his arm once seated. "Joke around with me one more time, and I'll deck you." Her lips quirked into a smile, but it slowly dissolved as she caught sight of Michael from over her shoulder.

He stood near the entrance to the hall that led to the restrooms, and he cocked his head to the side as if beckoning her.

She glanced at her drink for a moment. "I need to use the ladies' room. Be right back."

"Don't get lost," he quipped as she stood.

"I'll try not to." She patted him on the shoulder then moved slowly toward Michael, unable to pull her eyes from his intense gaze.

"Something wrong?" she asked once near him.

He folded his arms and leaned against the wall outside the restroom. She hated how casually sexy he looked in black slacks and a polo shirt.

"You and the chef on a date?"

Her brow creased in surprise. "You're kidding, right?"

"I thought you didn't date at work."

"Aren't you here with a supermodel?"

His eyes dropped to her mouth briefly. "You know you're the one I want."

"And you know how I feel."

"You want to be with me as much as I want to be with you."

The arrogance in his tone was mind-blowing. "Don't lie to yourself."

She swallowed her nerves and leaned into his frame. She pressed up on her toes to find his ear while resting her hand on his chest. "This routine of yours might work with other women, but you need to understand . . . I'm not one of them."

She forced herself to walk away without looking back, too worried he'd see the lie in her eyes—that she did, in fact, want him.

CHAPTER NINE

K ATE STOOD BY THE AUCTIONING STAGE, TRANSFIXED BY THE warm, romantic lighting and the silky sounds of the saxophone. The night was going as planned, except that Michael hadn't shown up yet.

"You look positively ravishing. Glad you listened to me," a voice said behind her. She turned around. It was Joseph, of course. He leaned in and kissed her on both cheeks.

Kate wore a strapless, red taffeta mermaid gown with a sweetheart neckline and origami pleating. The seams of the dress hugged her curves, and her exposed back showed her toned and tanned body. Her hair cascaded over her one shoulder in soft, shimmering waves. She wore more makeup than usual, having enhanced her eyes with black liner and charcoal eye shadow.

"Thank you," she replied. "But you'd better get back to the kitchen."

"Save me a dance," he reminded her before hurrying away.

Kate looked around for Julia, who had managed to get an earlier return flight to Charlotte so she could go over the last-minute details with Kate.

She finally spotted her standing in a crowd of men who were donning military uniforms. She looked polished and exquisite in her long, flowing white gown with shoulder ruffle. She admired the way Julia carried herself. Her confidence and success probably threatened many men—perhaps that was why she was still single. Either that or she had been too heartbroken to move on when her ex died years ago.

Where are you? She scanned the room, knowing that when Michael arrived, he would be hard to miss.

And then she saw him. He was wearing an impeccable single-breasted tuxedo. Could the man get any hotter?

Yes, she realized when she saw him tilt his head back and laugh with one of the veterans to which he was speaking.

She wanted to approach him and say hello but found her feet frozen. She stared across the room at the enigmatic man and wondered what he looked like beneath the suit. She mentally harangued herself for having such a thought, yet again.

It was getting exhausting beating herself up all the time. But, she couldn't be just another woman—she couldn't give in to the temptation of him.

Michael's attention switched from the Marine to Kate. He patted the serviceman on the back before stalking with purposeful strides toward her, ignoring several other people who attempted to catch his attention as he passed.

"Kate." His voice was husky. His eyes flickered with an intensity that doubled her heart rate. He didn't look pissed over last night's rejection. That was a relief.

"You clean up nicely." She rubbed her hands against the sides of her dress, not sure what to do with them.

"And you look . . ." He paused and ran a hand through his hair. "Well, you shouldn't be dressed like that."

"Gee, thanks." She peeked over his shoulder to see Julia heading their way. She took a few steps forward to meet her.

Michael caught Kate by the elbow. "I won't be able to think straight tonight with you in that dress," he whispered.

Kate flushed. How were things still stirring between them?

The man was relentless. And why did she feel a bubble of excitement that he hadn't given up yet? "Hi, Julia." She noticed the frown on her face. "What's wrong?"

Julia looked at Michael with an expression of pained irritation. "I just got a call from Jamie Landon. She's not coming, and she said to tell you to go to hell."

"Shit. I didn't think she'd take it so damn personally."

"What did you do?" Julia asked.

"It doesn't matter. What's done is done," he said, stuffing his hands in his pockets and looking around the dance floor as if nothing earth-shattering in the world of event planning had happened. "We don't need her, anyway."

Kate bounced her attention between Michael and Julia, trying to mask her concern.

"Yes, we do," Julia snapped back. "We can't just auction you." She scanned the room, but then her blue eyes widened. "I got it." She rested her hand on her brother's arm.

"What?" Michael asked.

"We have Kate," she exclaimed. "Every man in here has been gawking at Kate since the gala started. I guarantee they'd be more excited to have her in the auction than Jamie, anyway."

Kate stared at Julia and raised her brows. *No way.*

Michael crossed his arms and shook his head before echoing Kate's inner thoughts. "No."

"I agree with Michael," Kate said.

"Please. Kate's a respectable and successful businesswoman—practically famous from that piece in *The New York Times*. And she's undeniably stunning. Come on." She pressed her hands together in prayer pose, standing before her brother, not Kate, as though his answer was the final say.

"I don't think anyone will bid much on me. I'm not a celebrity." Kate felt a little annoyed at being left on the outskirts of the conversation.

"No," Michael said again, ignoring Kate's comment.

"Why not?" Julia asked, placing her hands on her hips. "What do you care?"

"What about you, Julia?" Kate interjected.

"Thanks, but . . . I think it would be a bit weird having a brother and sister auction," she said. "This gala is your baby, Kate. Do you want to see your vision fall apart?"

At least Julia was talking to her and not to Michael. She almost wanted to say *yes* just to spite him. "My flight is tomorrow."

"Leaving so soon?" Julia asked.

"Yes, I . . ." *Damn.* She didn't want to burden Julia with the knowledge of her stalker or tell her about the feelings she was juggling for Michael. "Okay. Maybe I can come back, or the winning bidder can come to New York."

Michael held his hands up in the air and stepped in front of his overeager sister. As he started to speak, Julia stepped around him.

"You can work out the details with your date. So, it's settled." She looked up at her brother, her nostrils flaring a little. She reminded Kate of a large red flag waving in the wind—and Michael was the bull.

Michael didn't charge, though. He shook his head and stood in silence as Julia thanked Kate and left to circulate among the guests.

"I understand that you probably don't think I'll raise enough money, but I guess I don't have a choice. Sorry." Kate looked away from him, too afraid to look him in the eyes.

He reached for her face and tilted her chin toward him, demanding her attention. He stared into her eyes for a moment, and his lips parted, but no words escaped his mouth. A few awkward and silent moments ticked by before he took a step away and removed his hand from her face. "You'll raise a lot of money. Thank you." He gave her a slight nod and walked away.

You're so confusing. She released a breath, trying to control the panic that was now sweeping through her as she faced the harsh reality that she would have to stand in the spotlight while men bid on her. She wasn't one to be self-conscious or shy, but she also hated being up in front of a crowd.

She forced herself to swallow her anxiety about the auction—there were more pressing matters. She spent the next two hours working the room, making sure everything was in order, that everyone had a delicious meal, and that all the guests were having a fantastic time.

As the hour for the auction drew near, Joseph appeared at her side. "May I have this dance?"

Kate couldn't help but smile at him. He was a charming and adorable guy, and she liked him, even though he was always flirting. "I guess I could take a break." She looked over at the dance floor and saw that Michael was with a beautiful young woman.

"Do you waltz?" Joseph asked and took Kate into his arms.

"I can try," she replied.

Joseph moved around the dance floor; his arms angled up, his elbows pointed out, holding onto her hands, clearly skilled in the art of formal dancing.

She, on the other hand, felt stiff, hating the constraints of ballroom dancing. As Joseph swirled her, Kate caught sight of Michael. His eyes were pinned on her, and she could feel the warmth and energy from his body directed toward her, even from across the dance floor.

Her mind reeled from the jumble of sensations that surfed through her body every time he looked at her.

"May I cut in?"

Kate stopped dancing and turned her attention to the man by her side. Despite being in his early fifties, he was still attractive. His hair was rich black, a touch of silver at the edges. He was tall, trim, and in great shape for his age. She studied his green eyes before turning back to Joseph.

"Thanks for the dance." She nodded to Joseph and redirected her focus back to the mystery man.

"I heard you're the woman who put this whole thing together," the man said as he placed one hand on the back of her shoulder and reached for her hand with the other.

"Yes."

His green eyes focused on hers as a warm smile gathered over his face. "Would you be interested in working for a law firm? We host many corporate events." He twirled her around before she could answer.

She wondered whether he was sincere or leading her on. The way he looked at her suggested he was more interested in her body than in her talents as an event planner, despite the fact he wore a platinum wedding band. "Is your wife here?"

"Unfortunately, no. She's out of town. But she would love your work, I'm sure."

Okay, maybe he's normal. But I'm not moving here. I'm wasting my time. "I had been thinking of opening a location in Charlotte, but I've changed my mind. I'm sorry."

"Oh, well, I have offices in New York, Boston, and Chicago."

She smiled. "I would be happy to assist you with any event planning needs you may have in New York and Boston."

This was exactly what she had wanted to happen, although she'd hoped the networking would be to drum up business for a new Charlotte location. "When you're in New York, please give me a call. I run Marissa Adams Events. I'm Kate Adams." She took a step back from the gentleman to hold out her hand and shake his.

"I just have to ask you a question," he said while reaching for her hand. "Are you related to Elizabeth Merrill?"

She pulled her hand away from his without thinking and took a step back. "How do you know about her?"

"You look like her. I was a pre-law student at UNCC years ago. Elizabeth and I were classmates." He rubbed his hand over his jaw while shaking his head a bit. "I'm sorry. I just can't believe the uncanny resemblance."

"I'm her daughter." She placed her hand on her chest, wondering if her lungs and heart were still functioning in proper order.

His eyes narrowed, and his lips parted. "I'm so sorry for your loss. She was an amazing woman." He gripped the back of his neck, and she could see the look of pity in his eyes. It was such a familiar look.

"Are you okay? I'm so sorry."

She cleared her throat and found her voice. "No, that's okay. It's nice to meet someone who knew my mother."

"I'm Erick Jensen." He reached into his back pocket and retrieved his wallet. "Listen, I would love to get together sometime. Perhaps I can share some funny stories about our college days."

Kate reached for the business card he held out in front of her. She wasn't quite sure what to say. She felt like so much of her mother's past was a blank page because her father hated talking about her. She only knew stories of her mother's childhood, which had been told by her grandparents. "I think I would like that."

"I'll be in Boston next week, working out the details with the mayor for this season's winter ball. I'm one of the main sponsors for the event. Perhaps I might be able to interest you in throwing the event this year?" Erick was offering her the gig of a lifetime.

Kate longed to bite her lip, to do something to release the tension of paddling through such deep waters. But she resisted. She held her cool and remained professional, wishing she could do the same around Michael.

"So, what do you think?"

"Yes, that would be incredible."

"Great." He patted her arm and smiled. "How's your father, by the way? I've seen him a few times in the New York courtrooms, but it's been years."

Of course, he would know her father. Her dad had been a pre-law student, as well. "He's good. Busy."

"Well, until we meet again." He tipped his head and walked away, blending into the crowd.

She needed a distraction—something to ease her mind from the heavy thoughts of her mother. She looked around the dance floor for Michael but noticed he was gone.

"You good?" she asked Julia, who was near the stage. "Speeches are about to begin."

"I'm ready," Julia said with no evidence of nervousness.

"Perfect. Go ahead up on stage." She looked over at the clock. The timing was flawless. The band stopped playing, and the spotlight lit on Julia. Kate gulped down a wave of nausea as she realized she would soon be under the same shining light. What had she gotten herself into?

She watched as Julia stood with poise behind the microphone. She began speaking with obvious passion about the foundation, gesturing toward Michael from time to time. He was standing across the stage from Kate, hands in his pockets—and he was looking at her, not his sister. She wet her lips and forced her gaze back to the center of the stage, away from the man who was making her shake with desire.

"I would like to present Johnathan Reese: a former, and highly decorated, colonel in the Marines," Julia said, motioning toward the man in uniform who stood behind her.

He smiled at Julia and walked toward the microphone. "I've known Michael Maddox for many years," Johnathan began. "He's like a brother to me. He had my back in Iraq and Afghanistan, always putting his life on the line to save a fellow Marine. As I'm sure you all are aware, Michael doesn't like to talk about himself. I'm amazed we're even here tonight." He grinned and looked over at Michael as the room murmured in agreement. "But I'm very grateful to this man. He saved my life not only in combat but at home as well. I felt empty after my military life ended. I felt hopeless. But Michael refused to let me drown. He threw me a lifeline and helped me through some of the most challenging times in my life. His organization is why I am now the successful business owner of eight fitness centers in New York City. And I'm able to help other veterans as well, now. Paying it forward."

The audience stared at Johnathan, their attention fixated on the man as he spoke, hanging onto his every word.

"Michael invested in me financially and mentally, and his organization has truly been life-changing for so many people." He paused for a moment. "Now, Michael may look like Superman. God knows he's built like him and is even bulletproof, I think." He paused, grinned at the few chuckles from the audience, and continued, "But he needs help. It's not about money—we all know that Michael is one of the richest men in the room." Everyone laughed. "It takes more than that to transform the way our society embraces veterans when they return to civilian life. What Michael's foundation needs is more people who will invest their time. He needs real people who care. He can't do it all alone . . . although he's been trying." He smiled again at Michael.

Maybe you are Superman. Kate's lips curved into a smile at the mental image of Michael in a pair of tights. She shelved the image to the back of her mind as Julia shoved a microphone in Michael's hands.

"I really don't know what to say," he remarked while placing the mic in the stand and pushing his hands into his pockets.

Kate observed Michael, noticing he had a habit of putting his hands in his pockets. She wondered if it was his way of dealing with nerves. What was his kryptonite? What was he afraid of— other than relationships?

"I appreciate the kind words that have been spoken about the organization. I truly believe in the work we do, and I hope you all have learned more about it tonight and will open your checkbooks at the auction. More importantly, I hope you'll volunteer to help connect our veterans with the right people and invest your time and energy into making a difference for them. That's what matters. Thank you all so very much for coming." Michael's comments were short and direct, which was consistent with his personality.

Julia patted her brother on the shoulder before stepping back up to the microphone. "Now, it's the moment you have all been waiting for: the auction. As you know, we've decided to do a good old-fashioned verbal auction, rather than a silent one. All proceeds will go to the foundation, of course. I thank you all in advance for your support." She took a moment to glance at Kate before fixing her attention back toward the audience. "I'm sure everyone was very surprised to hear that I managed to rope my brother into auctioning himself for a date, as well as model Jamie Landon. But we've had to make a change to the lineup."

There was some groaning in the audience from women, who probably assumed Michael was backing out.

"Unfortunately, Jamie Landon was unable to attend."

Now the men griped.

"We do have a replacement." Julia waved her hand toward Kate, motioning for her to approach.

Kate had to remind herself to breathe as she walked to the center of the stage. The spotlight shone brightly in her eyes.

"This is Kate Adams, the woman who not only planned this event but got my stubborn brother to agree to be auctioned. I have begged her to step in for Jamie Landon, and I assume you gentlemen are not disappointed?"

The men in the audience applauded, and Kate's cheeks turned red.

"Once the other items in the auction have been sold, we'll bring Michael and Kate up here. And remember—the dates are for the foundation, so don't be stingy with your wallets."

The second Julia finished speaking Kate fled the stage so fast she almost tripped over her dress. "You ready for this?" she asked Michael, who was now standing dangerously close to her. It was never a good idea for her to be within arm's length of him.

"Are you?" he quipped.

"I hope these people realize they're bidding on a dinner date and nothing more," she answered.

Had she effectively become a high-priced prostitute in the eyes of the bidders? What had she been thinking when she suggested auctioning dates? Now that she was thrown in the middle of it all, she couldn't help but worry.

"I'll have a talk with your date to make sure he understands," Michael said, clenching his jaw. He touched her shoulder before moving his hand to her cheek, staring deep into her eyes. He mesmerized her with his look and touch. "Looks like we're up."

And just like that, the intimate moment between them was gone.

She shook herself free of his spell and followed him out before the crowd. She was to go first, and Michael would follow. It had been her idea—to save the best for last.

She rested her hands at her sides, trying to mask her nerves, as she stood before the auctioneer. A herd of men had gathered around the stage, their faces upturned and bright from, no doubt, the copious amounts of champagne that filled the room.

She had figured most of the men in the audience were married and would be unable to bid, and yet, they were circling the stage like a pack of hyenas. The lawyer she'd met, Erick, was there, as well as a few other married men she'd encountered during the evening. Even Chef Joseph was standing in the crowd.

Her heart was beating fast, and she was grateful she didn't have to speak because she'd never be able to utter a clear word.

As Kate's gaze perused the audience members, her eyes fell upon James, the man who had harassed her outside of the club last weekend. Michael had warned him not to come to the event, but there he was.

The loud voice of the auctioneer boomed in her ears, and she focused her attention on him.

"Fifty thousand."

Kate looked at James, who had yelled out an obscene number, increasing the bid from ten thousand.

She glanced over at Michael. If the spotlight weren't on the stage, she wouldn't have been able to notice the slight twitch of muscle in Michael's jaw. Was he jealous, or was he pissed at James for showing up?

Kate exhaled a noticeable sigh of relief when a stranger placed a much higher bid. She was in no mood to see a showdown between Michael and James because the way Michael was eying him made her wonder . . .

"Eighty thousand," James countered, his voice sharp.

"Ninety," the mystery bidder was quick to respond.

Freaking seriously? Kate couldn't see her mystery bidder. His voice was deep, but not too gravelly.

"A hundred thousand." James wasn't ready to give up. It was some kind of game to him, wasn't it?

"One-twenty."

Kate stared, open-mouthed, at the audience. Thank God the money was going to a good cause; otherwise, she would have assumed the men were outright delirious. She bit her lip and looked over at James. *Please, don't bid. Please, don't bid.*

"We have a winner," the auctioneer announced.

Relief spiraled through her body when she realized the mystery bidder won.

"Michael, it's your turn." Julia stepped out front on stage and beckoned her brother. He kept his eyes trained on Kate, following her with his gaze as she backed away from the center of the stage to stand off to the side.

Kate fought back the unwarranted envy as she watched the women swarm in front of him.

There were fewer women than men, as most women at the gala

were married. Unlike the men, they were not about to piss off their husbands by gawking at Michael in the way the men had admired Kate. Regardless, all twenty women who had gathered at the front began fighting tooth and nail over Michael, jostling each other as if he were about to toss a bridal bouquet.

Kate found herself tuning out the bidding. She was in no mood to watch the women fight over a man she'd never have.

Two hundred thousand was the winning bid for Michael. Kate recognized the twenty-one-year-old as the daughter of a rich Dallas oil tycoon. *Sure, what's two hundred grand for the chance with Michael Maddox?* She cringed and looked away from the woman who had won herself a one-night stand with Maddox.

She looked over at Michael, who was now off stage and approaching James. *Oh, God.* She moved close enough to overhear them.

"What the hell do you think you're doing here?" Michael asked.

"You were serious about not showing up, huh? I thought you were kidding." James grinned. "What, you got a thing for your event planner? I didn't see you bidding on her."

"Get the hell out. Now."

"Fine. I came for the auction anyway. I thought there was supposed to be a famous model up for bid. I was surprised to see your planner on the block, though. I was hoping to win her, but she's definitely not worth that much."

"If you don't get the fuck out of here, I'll remove you myself." Michael's voice was low enough to avoid turning heads but deep enough for it to register warning to James.

James shook his head, but thankfully, he backed down and turned away. Before she could feel relief—she caught sight of someone familiar, which had her stomach turning.

She shuffled across the floor and back onto the stage to get a better view.

It was him. The guy from the club. The guy from the street

outside the Mexican restaurant. Blond and muscular. And he was watching her again from across the room.

Was he the stalker?

He started for the exit.

She got off the stage and hurried after him. But in a sea of black tuxedos, she lost him.

She needed some air. The room was closing in on her.

She rushed away from the main exit, back toward the rose garden terrace. She drew in a deep breath as she exited the ballroom. She walked to the railing and gripped it until her knuckles turned white. She bent over, squeezing in on herself, thankful to be alone. There was only so much she could handle in one evening.

"You did a great job tonight."

Kate turned to see Michael standing outside the entrance to the terrace.

He removed his bow tie and shrugged off his jacket, throwing both on a nearby table. "This is just not who I am." He stopped a few feet away. "You okay?"

"I—I don't know." She turned away from him and looked back out over the city.

He closed the gap between them. "Did James say something to you?" The muscles in his arms tensed as he gripped the railing. He looked over his shoulder, holding her gaze. His face was almost as taut as his muscles, as concern radiated from his body.

"What?" She shook her head. "No."

"I have seen you look startled—maybe even scared—on a few occasions now. You're sure nothing is going on?" He released his grip on the railing and faced her.

"I'll be fine. The party is about over. I'd better wrap things up. You heading out now?" She rubbed her hands together and smoothed on a fake smile.

"Soon. There are a few people I still need to chat with," he replied. "Let me walk you back to your room when you're done."

He wasn't buying her act. Clearly. "If you're still around. Sure." Before he had a chance to respond, she walked off the terrace and back into the ballroom. She gave one last look around the room for the muscular blond man. When she didn't see him, she forced herself to complete the job she had been hired to do.

CHAPTER TEN

KATE WAS SAYING GOODBYE TO SOME OF THE FEW LINGERING guests when the man with the winning auction bid called out her name. She looked over at the handsome man and feigned a smile. She wasn't in the mood to be friendly to this pseudo-date, but what choice did she have? "Hi. Ethan, right?" She reached for his hand. "Thank you for the donation. It will help a lot of people."

His gray eyes lit up when he reached for her hand. "Will Friday work for you? *The New York Times* and *Charlotte Observer* want to take a few photos of us during our date. They approached me after the auction ended." Unlike most of the men at the gala, he wasn't wearing a tuxedo. He was sporting a sleek, gray, three-piece suit with a bright red necktie.

He was handsome and seemed nice enough, Kate thought. *Could be a lot worse.* She hated herself for wishing the date was with Michael, though. "I was planning on leaving for New York tomorrow. Is there any way you could come there? If not, I can fly back for the date." But she wasn't sure if she wanted to come back to Charlotte ever again.

"I would, but I'm making a quick trip to China this week, and I won't be back until Friday afternoon. We could change the date if you would prefer?"

At least he was agreeable. "No, that's okay. We can meet here." *Just change the date. Meet him in New York.* Before she had a chance to voice her change of heart, he was leaning forward and pressing a kiss on her cheek.

"Until Friday." A grin touched his lips, and he walked away.

"I hate that guy," Michael said. He'd walked up beside her after Ethan left.

"Oh yeah? Why?" Kate asked, fighting back a smile.

"Because I know what his intentions are. Don't worry, I'll talk to him," he said as he crossed his arms.

Was he acting like a brother, or was he jealous? She had no clue at this point. And it shouldn't matter to her.

"His intentions can't be any worse than yours." Kate watched the corner of his lips quirk as his eyes moved over the length of her body. The things he could make her feel with one look. *God, help me.*

She forced her attention away from Michael and looked around the almost empty ballroom. She had already said goodbye to Julia, who had walked a few prestigious guests out of the hotel. "You can head out. Everything is all set here."

"I'm walking you to your room. Remember?" He held up his hands. "My intentions are honorable, I swear." There was a tone of mild amusement dancing in his eyes, which had a hint of steely gray in them tonight.

"Okay." She found herself agreeing not because she felt sure that she could control her feelings, but rather because she was more afraid of her stalker than of making a mistake with Michael.

She looked down at the elevator floor once they stepped in, toying with her keycard on the ride up. "Thank you again for allowing me to put this event together. You've helped a lot of people, and the work you do is important." She could feel him watching her. She forced her eyes up to meet his, and neither of them moved to exit the elevator when the doors opened. He looked so broody and contemplative—what was he thinking about?

The doors began to shut, and he thrust his arm out to stop them.

"I'm this way," Kate said, tipping her head to the left as she exited.

"I remember," he said before grinning. They walked the short distance down the hall to her room. "I guess this is goodnight." She could hear disappointment echo through his voice.

"And goodbye," she added. She unlocked and pushed the door ajar before turning back toward him. "I probably won't see you again until we launch the next event. I was thinking we might try the Hamptons at New Year's? I mentioned it to Julia, and she loved the idea."

Michael studied her for a moment. "I'm not a Hamptons kind of guy. Too many rich, uppity people there."

She smirked at him. "And you are?"

"Not uppity."

Was that a schoolboy smile? "Okay, no Hamptons, then. I'll see what I can come up with."

"And no auction."

She laughed. "Definitely no auction. Although I have to say, we raised quite a lot of money tonight. So, nice job."

"Won't you be in town all week now?"

"I'm still going to leave tomorrow as planned. I'll just fly back down for the date Friday."

"Maybe we could get dinner when you come back. Or the next time I'm in New York?" His eyes darkened, and he took a step closer to her. "You know, maybe hash out some of the details for the next event."

"I don't know," she replied, although her body screamed *yes*. "I told you I'm not like . . ." She let her voice trail off as she grew hot and a little dizzy in his presence.

And then she did something stupid.

She pressed up and touched her lips to his, but pulled away almost immediately, her heart racing in her chest.

Before she could mutter an apology, Michael reached for her hip with one hand and cupped the back of her neck with his other as he pulled her back against him. His mouth found hers, parting and coaxing her lips open. It all happened so fast. He swung around, so they were both inside her room and kicked the door shut behind them, never losing his grip on her body, her mouth.

He kissed her with tenderness at first, but as his tongue roamed her mouth, he seemed to lose control. His hand wandered from her neck and through her wavy blonde locks. His other hand held her tight against him.

When Kate broke contact, she struggled to catch her breath. The desire she'd felt from that kiss had been like nothing she'd ever experienced before.

"I'm sorry." Fear of tomorrow, of the unknown, settled back inside of her. "That shouldn't have happened." She ran her hand over her face and slipped off her strappy heels and walked toward the bar. "I haven't had a drink all night, but I think I might need one now," she said, reaching for a cold bottle of Riesling.

Michael moved up behind her and touched her shoulder. "Sorry, Kate." He pushed his hands through his hair. "I told myself I would leave you alone after last night." He crossed his arms and leaned against the window.

She set down the unopened bottle of wine and turned to him in surprise. "Michael, I . . ." She stopped talking when she saw the open bedroom door. "I know that I shut that."

"Maybe a cleaning person came up here."

"At night?" She walked to the bedroom and stopped at the sight of her bed. A stone sank in her stomach, and she fought the urge to let go—to break down and cry.

The stalker had been in her room. Pictures were splashed all over her bed.

"Kate?" Michael came up behind her.

"No, don't." She held up her hand, almost too afraid to take a close look at the photos herself.

"What in God's name?" He grabbed a handful of pictures and looked back at Kate. "There are so many. And they're all of you sleeping."

She approached him and reached for the photos he was holding. "He was in here while I was asleep?" How had she allowed this to happen? Who could have gotten so close?

"Who is 'he'?" Michael demanded.

"I need to get out of this. I can't breathe," she mumbled while tugging at her dress. She stumbled toward the bathroom and slammed the door shut behind her.

Kate slipped out of her gown and pulled a T-shirt over her head as Michael burst into the bathroom. "Michael," she shrieked as her face flushed with embarrassment. She was standing there in only a pink T-shirt and red thong.

"Fuck." He practically hissed the word and left the bathroom. "Sorry, I wasn't thinking," he hollered out. "But what the hell are these pictures all about?"

"Nothing. I mean, I don't know," she answered when she stepped back into the bedroom. She had paired gray yoga pants with her T-shirt. As she walked toward the bed, she began to yank her hair into a ponytail. She sat down beside him on the bed, careful not to look at the pictures.

"Well, I'm worried." He rose to his feet and tossed the handful of pictures back onto the bed. He crossed his arms, making it clear he wasn't going anywhere without answers.

"I don't know what to say. Some creep has been stalking me. Ever since I got to Charlotte, I think. I don't know why." She bit her thumb and looked at the ground.

"You have a stalker? Does Julia know about this?"

She shook her head.

"Aside from these pictures, what else has happened?"

"I've seen someone watching me. Once at a club, and then

again at the Mexican restaurant, and tonight at the ball. And—"

"Shit. You should have told me."

"Why? I barely know you." She stood and started for the living room. She needed more space to breathe. Michael had a way of absorbing all of the oxygen in the room.

"Who cares how well you know me? You should've asked for help if you were—are—in danger." He followed her into the living area and pulled out his cell phone.

"Who are you calling?"

"The police."

"No," she cried, grabbing his phone and tossing it on the sofa. "I don't want to make this a big deal. I don't need the police getting involved. This is my life. I'll handle it."

"You can't be serious. You think I'm just going to let you handle this?"

"Let me? Yes, you are going to 'let me' handle this. Thanks for caring, but I'll be fine." She rubbed her hands over her arms to calm her sudden chill.

"You're so damn stubborn." He heaved out a deep breath. "I have a friend in the FBI. I'll ask him to do me a favor. Off the books."

Why do you care? But she nodded. "Seems extreme." But, maybe she'd been an idiot for even letting it continue for as long as it did without seeking help? "Okay." She nearly sighed the word.

"Anything else I should tell him?"

She pursed her lips together, deciding how much to divulge. "Yeah. I got a few texts from him as well." She retrieved her phone and showed him the messages. She wasn't sure if she wanted to show him the photos inside the red envelope. "I think he sent me those flowers the other night."

"Is this the real reason you changed hotels? You were scared?" he asked after viewing the texts.

"Yeah. And there's more." She walked over to her purse and

reached inside for the envelope. "Here," she said, handing it to him.

He opened the envelope and removed the photos. "I don't understand," he said after looking through the images. "What the hell does this have to do with me?" He grimaced and took a seat on the couch.

"The one of us dancing—turn it over."

He read the message and looked up at Kate. "There's no way you're going back to New York."

"Of course I'm leaving Charlotte. Are you kidding?" She shut her eyes and pinched the bridge of her nose.

"Did it ever occur to you that this person wants you back in New York for some godforsaken reason? Maybe running back to Manhattan would be even less safe than staying. You just don't know." He rubbed his hand over his clean-shaven jaw and tossed the photo on the coffee table. "I don't know why in the hell your stalker is sending you pictures of me with other women, but I do know the situation is out of control."

"I don't know what to do."

"You need a bodyguard until my friend catches the bastard who is following you," Michael said while lifting his eyes to meet hers. "And you need to cancel your date on Friday."

"What? No way. I made a commitment . . . for the foundation. I can't back out now. I will not let some psycho scare me out of doing the right thing," she said, vehemently shaking her head. "I don't need some bodyguard following me around—I'm already being followed enough."

"That part is non-negotiable," he said as he rose to his feet. "Listen, I may not know you that well, but like it or not I'm going to help you. I'm not about to let someone hurt you. I won't let it happen." He placed his hands on her arms and slid them down to her wrists.

"Okay, fine. But I've got the bill."

A smile slipped to Michael's lips. "Go ahead and pack your bags." He pulled away and picked up his phone.

"Why?"

"Because you'll be staying at my place."

"Now you're out of your mind." There was no way she could stay under the same roof as him.

"Julia's going back out of town for a few weeks, so you won't be secure at her place. I can keep you safe. If you're worried I'll try to . . . you don't need to worry about me, okay? I can restrain myself. Just don't go walking around naked or anything."

Before Kate had a chance to rebut, Michael was on the phone with the concierge, requesting that the hotel retrieve her luggage and bring the bags down to his car. He collected the photos from her bed during brief lulls in the conversation, and this suited Kate fine. She never wanted to see the pictures again.

She watched Michael move around her hotel room as if she were a bystander, watching a scene unfold. The sheer dread and panic that had caught in her throat when she saw the pictures on her bed had faded, and she felt numb and a bit chagrinned. To think that someone had stood by her bed and watched her sleep, having access to her to do God knew what . . . the thought brought a bubble of pure horror back to her throat. If she didn't stop the train of what-ifs that were trammeling her mind, she would lose her sanity.

Fortunately, Michael distracted her. He all but scooped her into his arms and carried her out of the hotel. She slid into his black Audi R8 Spyder and clasped her hands in her lap. She had been rushed out of her room and to his car so fast that she'd had no time to think. What was she getting herself into? Would she truly be safer with the man around whom she could barely breathe?

Michael ignored Kate's feeble protests as he zipped down the streets and into the garage of his uptown penthouse. Without uttering a word, he parked, opened the door for Kate, and grabbed her two suitcases. He motioned for her to follow him to a nearby elevator. He punched in a key code—*oh, a private elevator*—and they jerked upwards.

The doors opened directly into the foyer of his home. Kate entered with caution echoing in every footstep. She looked around, first noticing the high ceilings, wooden beams, and exposed brick. His place screamed uptown New York much more than it did Charlotte, but she liked it. The large living space was decorated in warm, neutral colors with oversized, plush furniture. It was nothing like the modern bachelor pads she'd seen from other rich men, whose décor was cold and simple—all right angles and black and white. The handmade oak coffee table and light brown throw rug in front of the fireplace made her want to curl up with a glass of wine and a good book. God, she wished that was what she could do right now—and not be the protagonist of some thriller movie.

She pushed away her fears and refocused on his loft. "I love the rustic look of the place. I mean it's modern and all, in terms of the features." She scanned the sophisticated kitchen, its top-of-the-line appliances. "But it's also so inviting." She dropped her purse on the marble countertop in the kitchen. "This is very different from your office."

"My sister decorated the office. Our styles are polar opposites."

She stifled a yawn. "I don't know how you managed to talk me into coming here."

"I didn't give you much of a choice," he remarked. "Something to drink?"

"No, thanks. I should get some rest."

"Okay. Follow me." They exited the kitchen, and he retrieved her luggage before they walked down a long hall that held a series of doors.

The guest room was like the rest of the house—decorated in warm tones, with soft lighting. The king-sized bed was perched atop a dark walnut, sleigh-style frame and adorned with creamy silk linens. Hanging over the headboard was a photograph of a still lake surrounded by mountains. A breathtaking view.

"Did you take that photo?" she asked, seating herself on the bed.

"Yeah," he replied. "It's my place in Boulder. A place to escape when the world gets a little too loud." He was looking down at the floor.

She smiled and waited for him to bring his eyes back up. Was he okay?

"Anything I can get for you? There are towels and stuff in the bathroom," he said, pointing to the adjoining door.

"I think I'm good." Well, as good as she could be in her current situation.

"Okay. Well, I'm going to call my friend tomorrow morning about your stalker. We'll see what he comes up with." Michael reached for the doorknob.

"I hate to say it, but what can he do with only a few texts and photos? I'm sure there are no prints."

Michael grinned. "If anyone can find this guy, it's Jake," he assured her. He stared down at her as if fighting the impulse to join her on the bed. "Goodnight."

* * *

MICHAEL WALKED AWAY FROM KATE'S ROOM AND TO THE MASTER suite, which was on the other side of his house. There were guest rooms closer to his, but he preferred to keep her as far away as possible. He needed to put some distance between them. She'd be the first woman who wasn't family to sleep over. As much as he wanted to keep her safe, the idea of having her here made him nervous.

He hurried into his bathroom to take a shower, needing to cool off.

After washing up, he tried to dull his senses by reading the news on his tablet, but he only tossed around in his bed, ruffling up the sheets.

Around two in the morning, he wandered into the living room. He rubbed his jaw and moved toward the long wall of windows that overlooked the city.

"What are you doing up?" he asked when noticing Kate's reflection. He turned to face her, which probably wasn't the best idea.

She was wearing a flimsy silk nightgown that stopped a few inches above her knees. She hugged her arms, out of nervousness or perhaps to conceal the fact that she wasn't wearing a bra.

"I can't sleep," she replied before sitting down on the oversized, brown suede sofa.

He inhaled a sharp breath, feeling the painful discomfort of unsatisfied lust as she sat there before him, wearing barely any clothes. He had restraint, but he was still a man. He looked away from her and back out the window, trying to calm his erection, which seemed to grow more demanding every time she was near.

"Do you always sleep in sweatpants?"

"I sleep commando, actually." He couldn't see her response in the reflection, but he assumed he'd made her blush. At least her thoughts weren't on the stalker.

"How come that model Jamie didn't come to the gala? The real reason."

Her question took him by surprise. He gripped the back of his neck with his left hand, working out a kink. What was he supposed to say? His tension eased somewhat, and he turned back toward her. "I wouldn't worry about Jamie."

"Did you sleep with her?"

He cocked his head to the side and stared at her. "I turned her down last night after dinner, which was hard for her ego to deal with."

Kate looked at him with hooded eyes. Surprise swallowed the features of her face.

"Are you cold?" he asked, trying not to notice her nipples poking through the silk nightgown.

"I'm okay." She rose from the couch and approached him, her eyes focused on his. She stopped just out of reach.

His pulse ticked up a notch as she wet her lips. "Kate." The deep sound of his voice was meant to serve as a warning. "Do you know what you're getting yourself into?"

"We shouldn't, I know. I have a crazed stalker. And I know I've told you no, but—"

His mouth crashed down over hers, and his hands moved up her arms and slid under the silk straps of her nightgown, moving them from her shoulders. The material slipped to her feet. His body pressed against hers; his full cock charged and ready. His hands roamed over her breasts, which swelled beneath his fingertips. God, she was perfect.

Kate threw her head back as he kissed her neck.

He caressed her skin until his own was on fire. And then he took a step back and looked at her, taking her all in.

She did something he didn't expect. Without a hint of modesty, she slipped out of her red thong and let it fall to the floor. She stood before him wearing nothing more than a look of deep hunger in her eyes.

A look of acceptance—giving herself over to the moment. To their need for each other. A need that had thrown him off guard the moment she spilled her drink on him.

A blazing need that went beyond his normal primal desire to screw.

He groaned before lunging toward her, his hands practically ravaging her body, wanting to touch every inch of her. He grazed her lips with his teeth and tugged at her bottom lip. "I want you so fucking much," he said with a throaty voice. He swooped her into his arms and carried her to the master suite.

The room was dimly lit, the curtains closed, and the comforter lay rumpled at the bottom of the bed. He set her down on the black silk sheets. She lay before him, naked and ready. He hastily peeled off his T-shirt and removed his pants and boxers, freeing himself.

He positioned himself over Kate, staring down at her body. "You're so sexy."

As he leaned in to kiss her again, he felt her soft fingertips touch his chest.

"Oh my God," she whispered. She ran her fingers over his pectoral muscles and abdomen, circling each of his three bullet wounds with her fingertip.

Reality was settling, heavy and thick. Michael's pulse ticked at his neck, and the muscles in his face strained.

He had been in such a hurry that he'd forgotten about his scars. They were scattered over his chest: one just below his ribs, another by his shoulder, and a third dangerously close to his heart. Kate seemed fixated on the last.

He cursed under his breath. His friends had died in battle, and yet, women thought these bullet wounds were hot. He usually wore a shirt during sex to hide the evidence of injury. But tonight, with Kate, he had forgotten. He looked down into her eyes and was surprised to see them glistening. Was she going to cry?

"I didn't realize it was that bad. I didn't know you were hurt like that."

He rolled off her and squeezed his eyes shut.

He could hear the gunshots splicing through the air, loud and sharp. He balled his hands into fists.

He tried to silence the memories, but they assaulted him with deadly force. His heart hammered in his chest when her hand rested on top of his. His eyes flashed open, and he stared at her.

"I'm sorry." He pushed off the bed and grabbed his sweats and pulled them on.

She reached for his bedsheet and covered her body. "Did I do something wrong?"

He looked down at the gorgeous woman in his bed, wondering why he was thinking of Afghanistan when he should have been thinking of all the ways he was going to get her off. "No, of course not, but I let myself get carried away. We shouldn't do this." Did he sound convincing? "I don't want to be an asshole," he bit out.

"I don't understand." She rose to her feet, pulling his bedsheet with her.

"You're being stalked. The timing of this—it's not right." He folded his arms and leaned against his tall, mahogany dresser. He forced his eyes to look past her, pulling armor down over his sight.

"And maybe I need this. Maybe I was wrong before. I need to forget for a few moments that I'm Kate Adams, the woman who doesn't do one-night stands and has to have everything planned down to the minute. I'm not Kate Adams, the woman who is being stalked—who lost her mom at birth." She raised an eyebrow. "Can't I just be Kate tonight? The Kate who wants to sleep with you?"

He looked away and toward the double doors that led back into the hall. He was trying to remain steadfast, but he was losing his resolve. "I had no intention of sleeping." He directed his eyes back on hers.

The mood in the room shifted as his concern over her stalker found its way to the back seat, and his desire fought to resume control. He beheld her with heavy-lidded eyes, but he remained firm in his stance, arms crossed.

"We can't." His indecision was making him ready to claw at his skin in frustration.

"Shouldn't it be me who decides what I can and can't handle tonight?" She tilted her head to the side and bit her lip.

"I don't do relationships, Kate. Nothing has changed. Don't make a mistake by being with me." His eyes narrowed and focused on her mouth . . . but she was making him forget the gunshots. Forget Afghanistan. "I don't normally care. I go for what I want—I've been after you all week. But tonight . . . what's happening to you is a game changer."

"So, let me get this straight. Up until the discovery of my stalker, you were willing to screw me with little regard for my feelings and the aftereffects, but now—now your moral compass is suddenly pointed in the right direction?" She arched her shoulders back, and her mouth opened, but no further sound came out.

"Basically."

Kate took a step closer to him. "You're a jerk," she said, glaring at him. "At least when it comes to women, that is." When she left his room, the dark sheet trailed after her, swishing against the floor.

He forced himself to look away. His hard-on was growing painful, and he had been seconds away from ignoring his brain and grabbing Kate. He could still smell her delicious scent on his body. He had to find a way to forget the way her mouth tasted and ignore the way her body had felt beneath his.

She was staying with him so he could help protect her from a stalker, after all. The last thing she needed was casual sex and a broken heart.

He groaned, slipped off his sweats and headed back to the shower. How many more cold showers would it take before he washed away his need?

CHAPTER ELEVEN

KATE WANDERED INTO THE KITCHEN AROUND NINE THE NEXT morning. She saw Michael perched on a barstool with his cell phone pressed to his ear.

"See you in a bit." Michael placed his phone on the kitchen counter. "Hi."

She studied his messy bedhead hair and the dark stubble that gave him a rugged, dangerous look. She hoped they could put their close encounter with sex behind them and move on and act normal. But was that possible? She still couldn't believe she'd broken her rules last night.

"I, um, planned on taking a run this morning, but I figured I wouldn't be able to get back in the building afterward. Is there a key or code I could have?"

Michael guffawed. "You have got to be kidding." He rose to his feet.

She took a nervous step back as he approached her. "What?"

"You can't go out alone."

"I didn't come here to be a prisoner." She folded her arms. She was still feeling the bitter taste of rejection. Part of her was angry at him for turning her down, but she was mostly relieved.

"My friend in the FBI will be here tomorrow morning, and I have someone who will be your bodyguard starting tomorrow, as well."

"That's fast." Her shoulders sank a bit, and she decided not to argue with him about going for a solo run. He was stubborn and headstrong, and also trying to protect her. He was right not to let her go. She sighed. Why was he helping her, anyway?

"We'll get this straightened out and soon."

Kate walked over to his fancy espresso machine. "Is this for coffee?" Puzzled, she turned toward Michael, her eyes pleading.

"What would you like?"

"Just coffee."

He opened the cupboard and pulled out a white mug. He pressed a few buttons on the machine, and warm black liquid began pouring into her cup.

"Thanks."

He nodded and leaned against the counter, crossing his arms. "You shouldn't dress like that when you're around me."

She dropped her unopened sugar packet on the counter and whipped around to look at him. "Like what?" She looked down at her clothes, confused. She was wearing pink stretch pants and a white tank top. What was the big deal? "I'm in workout clothes."

"Well, you look hot." He cleared his throat. "If you want to run, you can use my gym." He broke his gaze and motioned for her to follow. "I rarely use it. I belong to a gym near the office, but it should have what you need."

She grabbed her coffee and followed Michael out of the kitchen and down a different hall, the one that led to his bedroom.

"I converted a guest bedroom into a workout room a few months ago, in case I ever felt like working out at home. Although I haven't used it much." He pushed the door open, and she was pleased by the amount of equipment the room had to offer. There was a treadmill, elliptical, bike, rower, large punching bag, and a speed bag, as well as a full set of free weights. Two large and long windows allowed in plenty of natural light, which brightened up the room.

"This should work." She took a sip of her coffee and realized she'd forgotten to sweeten it.

"You should eat before you exercise."

She nodded.

"I have some work to do in my office. I'll be in the room next door if you need anything," he remarked as he walked back out into the hall.

"Um, Michael. Thanks. Thanks for helping me with my problem." She gulped. "I don't think I said that, did I?"

"Well, now you have," he said. "It's no problem, but, uh seriously, if you have some less-sexy workout clothes . . . and more modest pajamas, for that matter . . ."

A smile snuck up on her. "I'll see what I can find."

Michael left, and she went back to the kitchen to grab a piece of toast and sugar for her coffee. While dumping the sugar into her mug, she remembered that her father was expecting her home.

She had texted him before the ball that she would be returning home and had no plans on coming back to Charlotte. What would she tell him now? She couldn't tell him about her stalker. He would demand that she return home, and if she said *no*, he would fly down and drag her back to New York.

Then again, wouldn't she be safer in New York? Or was Michael right?

"Kate?"

Michael came up behind her in the kitchen and she turned to face him. "I have to leave. I have to take an emergency call with the DOD."

"Department of Defense?"

He nodded. "I can't do it here, or else I would. I may be gone all day. I need you to promise me that you will not leave the house, under any circumstances."

"Yeah, I'll stay here," she mumbled and brought her coffee to her lips.

"I have security cameras inside the place. I don't want to have to turn them on."

"Can you see in my room?" She set her coffee down and crossed her arms.

"No. They're only in the main living areas. And they only work if I activate them. So . . . don't make me activate them."

"No way. I don't need another person spying on me."

"I would feel better knowing that I could check up on you from anywhere," he mused. Then he shook his head. "Please, just don't leave. I can't be on a call with the government talking about ISIS and—"

"Wow. You're helping the government with ISIS? That's a bit intense." She tilted her head and looked down at the floor, realizing her problems were rather minuscule in the grand scheme of things.

"Be good and stay here," he said. "There are cold cuts in the fridge. Help yourself to lunch, and I'll bring some Thai food back with me for dinner."

"Thanks." Once he was out of sight, she glanced down at her drink, no longer hungry or thirsty.

She needed to run. Do yoga. Do something to distract herself before she lost her sanity altogether.

* * *

"WE NEED YOU BACK. AT THE VERY LEAST, WE NEED YOU OUT IN the field to train the men directly. We appreciate that you've been helping out at Camp Lejeune, but we need more from you. Your country needs you," General McKinsey said, leaning back in his chair.

Michael stared at the general, whose image and audio was live-streamed via the secure internet at the office. He tried not to betray his shock. He looked down at the pen he was tapping and let it go. "I need some time to think about it."

"I know you left because of your injuries, but—"

"That's not why I left. I left because my family couldn't handle the pain of worrying about me anymore." *That, and because I just don't know if I can kill again . . . and stay sane.* He shifted in his seat and ran his hands through his hair.

"Your family needs to understand that you're keeping them safe with your time in the service."

"I'll think about it." He glanced over at the family portrait that he had taken with his parents at Hilton Head. "I'll be in touch." He ended the call and hung his head low.

They had spent hours discussing military tactics in relation to his intelligence designs, which were currently used to locate terrorist cells. Then bam! The old man had tried to rope him back into service. It wasn't enough for him to be one of the leading experts in observation technology—what his sister called spy shit —they wanted him back in the Middle East, too.

I can't think about this right now, he decided. He checked the clock. It was already close to six. He dialed up his favorite Thai place and preordered the food before leaving the office. He had left Kate alone for far too long.

He called her name as he walked into his living room, but there was no answer. Panic had begun to grip his throat, but he noticed a flash of blonde hair on the balcony. He set the bags of food down on the coffee table and walked toward the double glass doors to the terrace. "Kate."

She rose from the lounge chair. "Hi."

"I thought we agreed you would stop dressing like that." He was joking. Well, sort of.

His eyes combed over her white shorts and yellow halter top. "Okay. You need to get your eyes checked," she teased. "I am completely covered."

"I think a baggy T-shirt would be good," he said, eying her

chest. "And loose-fitting pants. Maybe a pair of my sweats." He grinned.

"Well, that's not going to happen." She clasped her hands together and peeked inside the house. "You bring food?"

"Yeah, I got sushi, Pad Thai, and red curry chicken. I remembered that you like spice." He smiled again as she walked past him and into the house. His eyes followed the sway of her hips as she moved.

He shut his eyes for a moment, hoping to quell his desire for her, and he took in a deep breath and stepped inside. He looked over at Kate as she sat on his couch, and he reached for the remote to turn on the radio.

"Lady Gaga's *Poker Face?*" A smile slipped to her lips.

He was about to change the channel but stopped when he saw the bright look in Kate's eyes. "You like this song?"

"Just reminds me of playing poker with you." She was beaming, which he preferred to sulky and depressed. Most people would have tended toward the latter if they had a shadow creeping after them.

He set the remote down, leaving the song playing, and he took a seat next to her. He watched her shut her eyes and move her shoulders a bit. There was no way he'd survive the week.

They dipped back into their food, and he tried to ignore the odd feelings that swirled inside his gut.

"How'd your call go?" Kate asked a few minutes later.

He looked at her as he brought a piece of sushi to his mouth. After he had finished chewing, he responded, "It went well, but there's only so much I can do from here. It's hard to help when I'm not out in the field."

"I don't get it. Why do you need to be in the field? Can't you just make the technology here?"

"Sometimes they need a little guidance in the field, with use and installation. Especially right now, with this new platform I've built." He paused. "They want me back."

Kate froze. She placed her chopsticks on her paper plate and looked up at him.

"I don't know what to do. I got out after I was injured because my family begged me not to sign up for another tour of duty, but I feel so guilty about not being more involved. I feel like I could help so much more if I were at least there to assist with the reconnaissance missions. ISIS is getting out of control. Something has to be done." He stared at his food in a daze.

"But you've built a life here. People need you. The veterans need you. You're helping so many." She paused for a moment. "And you were shot. I don't think going back is a good idea."

"You don't know me." His eyes landed back on hers, and he grimaced.

"I know that your sister loves and adores you. She needs you." She kept her eyes on his.

"A lot of people need me. Our country needs me. At least that's what the general just said."

"You don't need to hold the weight of the world on your shoulders. I know you want to save people, but you can't save everyone. It's not your responsibility."

He looked away from her and rubbed his hand over his clenched jaw. Why had he even said anything to her? He never opened up to anyone, not even his sister. What the hell was wrong with him? "Listen, can we drop it? I'm sorry I got so tense." He rose to his feet and picked up his almost empty plate.

"Fine." She closed up the containers with leftover food and brought them into the kitchen.

"Wine?" he asked when she entered.

"Um, sure."

He poured a German Riesling into two large Riedel glasses. He offered her one and leaned against the counter in his usual stance. He pushed one hand into his jeans pocket while bringing the cool, crisp liquid to his mouth with the other.

Kate sat on a nearby barstool, and her eyes scanned the length of him as if assessing his mood. "Should I leave you alone?"

He looked over at her, studying her tanned and shapely legs. "No."

"So, where'd Julia have to go this time?"

Finally, something he could talk about with ease. "L.A. Her flight left this morning."

"Um, does she know about me being here?"

"I didn't want to worry her."

"Good. Thank you."

He wasn't exactly itching to tell his sister Kate was staying at his place. He knew she'd freak.

"So, your friend will be here tomorrow? And the bodyguard, as well?"

"Yeah. The sooner this is over with, the better."

"I hate to be such a burden. I can stay at a hotel starting tomorrow since I'll have a bodyguard."

She had taken his words the wrong way. "No. Hell no. You're staying with me." He walked over and stood in front of her. "I didn't mean that I wanted to get you out of my house. I want the creep caught, so you're safe." He tilted his head and stared into her eyes, which were a little more green today than blue. "Of course, you being here is a challenge for me." Pure temptation.

"You're the one who turned me down," she reminded him.

He touched her face with the back of his hand and set his wine glass down. His heart hammered in his chest as the proximity to her almost filled the void inside him. But she was off-limits.

He quickly removed his hand from her cheek and picked up his wine, taking a step back. "So, how about them Yankees?" He echoed her joke from their first dinner together.

"Red Sox, remember?" She raised her eyebrows as her eyes widened. "You never fail to surprise me." And then her face changed. "Please, don't go back to the Middle East."

Instead of responding, he poured more wine into his glass and left the kitchen.

He couldn't think about the desert right now. The men he'd lost. The people he'd killed.

"Michael, wait. I'm sorry."

Outside now, he leaned against the railing, looking down at the city sprawled below. So many people were off enjoying their lives, with little idea of how dark the world could really be. He'd be damned if he wasn't sick of the darkness.

But when he looked at Kate, she was like this bright orb glowing. She was pure. Real. And it scared the hell out of him.

"I don't want you to get hurt. I may not know you well like you said, but you don't know me, either, and that hasn't stopped you from trying to protect me. So why can't you understand that I want to help you?" she said over his shoulder, her fingers splaying over the center of his back.

"Your life is worth saving. Mine's not." It was the truth. The things he'd done—witnessed. There was no forgetting. No redemption. Memories of the fallen would always haunt him—from his friends who'd died to the lives he'd taken. Maybe the people he had killed were enemies of the state, but wasn't it still murder?

"Why would you think that? Clearly, you're needed. What good would you be dead?"

He faced her in one quick movement, his hand slipping to her wrist, holding it tight. His jaw strained as the past pulled at him. "I should've died in Afghanistan." He heaved out a deep breath and released his grip. "Almost my entire platoon died. I shouldn't have survived."

"I don't know what happened, but you're here for a reason." She placed her hand on his forearm, not backing down, even though he was doing his best to scare her away. "How many lives have you saved since that day? With the technology you've designed . . . how many people are alive because of it?"

He gripped her shoulders and pulled her against him. He slanted his mouth over hers, kissing her with an intense fierceness, a desperate need. But it was also a punishing kiss—forceful with anger that she'd made him remember, made him feel . . .

He felt a slight tremble in her body, and he pulled away.

"Michael," she whispered.

His eyes widened just slightly before he tore off the balcony without another word.

It was for the best. The sooner she came to terms with the fact that he was a prick, the better.

* * *

THE SOUND CAME AS A SHOCK TO HER. IT STARTED SLOW AND guttural, but it grew louder.

Kate left her bedroom and went to the living room, searching for the noise that had awakened her from her dreams.

He was screaming.

A blood-curdling yell.

Kate picked up her pace and ran to Michael's room. She opened his door without thinking and darted to the bed. Tangled in his sheets, his naked body jerked in convulsive movements.

He was having a nightmare. *Jesus.*

"Michael." She whispered his name, afraid to startle him.

No response.

He continued to flail on the bed.

She moved toward him and sat on the edge of the bed. She touched his chest and said his name again, a little louder.

And then she was on the floor. Breathless. And he was on top of her, his weight punishing her chest, making it difficult to breathe. His eyes were dark and unrecognizable. "Michael, please."

Realization must have hit him; he jumped off. "What the hell?" He kneeled down and helped her off the floor, scooping her into his powerful arms and set her on his bed. "Shit. Are you okay?" He brushed the back of his hand down her cheek, standing naked before her.

It took her a moment to process everything. One minute she was trying to help him, and the next she'd been pinned beneath him. "I'm okay."

"What happened?"

"You were having a nightmare, I assume. I heard you all the way from my room. I tried to wake you."

"I'm so sorry." He sat beside her and reached for her hand, but she jerked it away. She couldn't even look at him. His body was hard—rock hard. And glistening with sweat. Greek gods had nothing on this man.

He rose to his feet and grabbed a pair of boxers from his dresser.

Kate attempted to rise to her feet. Her knees buckled, and she sat back down.

"I thought your room was far enough away so I wouldn't wake you." He leaned against the nearby wall, placing some distance between them.

"Does this happen often?" Her eyes landed on his hard chest, and she tried not to obsess over the scars there.

"I don't want to talk about it."

She attempted to flex the muscles in her legs. Would they hold her if she tried to stand again? "What are the nightmares about?"

His eyes narrowed. "I said that I don't want to talk about it."

The grit in his voice should have served as a warning—leave him the hell alone. The man was cold, bitter, and angry.

But she ignored the warnings in her head and rose, crossing the room to where he stood.

She reached out and touched his chest, and his pectoral muscles flinched beneath her fingers. Without thinking, she leaned in and kissed the bullet wound near his heart.

His hands came down over her forearms as if he were trying to push her away from him.

But she resisted. Instead, her fingertips glided over his six-pack, and then she brushed her lips over another scar.

"I want to take your pain away," she said, looking up into his eyes.

He stared at her for a beat, and then lifted and carried her to the bed. His gaze was intense, focused. It burned through her as he laid her down.

"Michael."

He joined her in bed, and he gently pulled her on top of him. He cupped both sides of her face and brought her lips to his.

She moaned against his mouth, and he parted his lips, his tongue dipping inside—twining with hers. Her body rubbed up against his, and she hated the feel of her clothes as a barrier to his skin. She wanted to be naked. To have his skin touching hers—she needed to feel him. She couldn't lose this moment.

Their lips parted as he grabbed the hem of her tank top and lifted it. She sat up a little, her groin pressing against his erection, her center throbbing as her breasts became tight and heavy beneath his stare.

He cupped her breasts as she lowered back down, her mouth running over his jawline, down the side of his throat.

The feel of his thumbs hooking each side of her shorts had her gasping, and she pushed back up to help him rid her body of them.

She stood in front of him, and he sat up, resting on his elbows as he stared into her eyes. His gaze was steady on hers, even though she was naked before him. He was the one sinking his teeth into his bottom lip.

Suddenly he rose and lifted her into his arms, and she wrapped her legs tight around his hips. Supporting her weight with one hand, he pressed a palm to her collarbone and then spread his fingers up to the base of her throat. He gently tossed her back, and she landed on the plush comforter.

She sucked in a breath and eyed the man before her. He was toned and beautiful, rugged and strong.

She was going to break her rules. Damn her plans.

Michael's eyes smoldered as he shoved his boxers off, freeing his hard length. "Are you on the pill?" he asked with a throaty voice.

"Yes, but I always use protection."

He gripped his shaft, barely taking his eyes off her as he grabbed a condom from the nightstand drawer. After, he unrolled it down his hard length and placed a knee on the bed, his hand above her shoulder.

He slowly lowered himself over her, his hand sliding to her smooth center. She was so damn wet. She moaned and bucked her hips when he slid two fingers inside of her.

He rubbed his thick fingers there for a minute until her nipples hardened with want. Then he positioned himself on top of her, and she released a pent-up breath as he eased into her, resting his hands on either side of her body.

He held himself up and looked into her eyes as he edged himself inside of her—it had been so long since she'd had sex—it was almost painful at first. She inhaled a sharp breath, but then relaxed against him as she took every inch of him. He fit inside of her like she'd been made for him—at least it sure as hell felt that way at the moment.

Their breathing became more rapid as their bodies moved together. The feelings of pleasure he elicited with each and every touch, with every thrust, had her spiraling out of control.

It was ecstasy.

Sex with Michael was sheer bliss—a precipitous climb that resulted in the most amazing orgasm she had ever experienced.

Once her desire was satiated, he began to move faster, which heightened her already raw body to feel entirely new sensations.

After a few more minutes, he groaned and bowed his head in release.

He rolled to his side, a lazy smile on his face, looking drunk with satisfaction. He pulled her against his sweaty body, tightening his grip on her waist.

"Oh, are we done?" She drew her eyebrows together into a false pout. God, this was so not like her—and it felt so damn good.

"Give me a few minutes, and I promise you there'll be more." He pressed his mouth to hers and lifted her on top of him.

* * *

KATE WOKE A FEW HOURS LATER TO FIND THE BED EMPTY. THEY'D had a marathon of sex, and she must have fallen asleep after. Sex with Michael had proven spectacular and addictive.

The night had been amazing—what she needed to take her mind off the heavy stuff.

But, when she had decided to sleep with him—well, more like her body had told her mind to pull over and let it drive for a while —she knew that she would need to accept him as he was.

And that meant accepting that he would be rid of her soon. Maybe he was already done with her, which should've been fine— she didn't want anything heavy, either. Hell, maybe she needed to rethink her rules. Maybe casual sex was the solution to staying out of a serious relationship while she was building her career.

But thinking about Michael sleeping around created an unwelcome tightness in her chest, and that was a pretty strong indicator that Kate wasn't really up for casual sex. Sleeping with Michael had been incredible, but now her heart would pay the price.

She stepped out of his mammoth bed and retrieved her silk tank top and shorts from the floor, wanting to find him and assess his mood.

She walked down the hall in search of him.

He was standing out on his balcony, dressed only in a pair of sweats despite the slight chill of the September night. Her breath caught in her throat as he turned toward her. In spite of her drowsy soreness, she found herself growing hot with desire just looking at him.

She doubted any woman would ever get enough of that man. He was gorgeous, and yet there was so much more to him than that. But he didn't want anyone to see—he didn't want to let anyone on the inside. Those emotions trapped inside of him— she'd felt them, with every thrust. It was like he was sharing himself with her in the most pure and honest way he could since they'd met.

It didn't take a rocket scientist to know that Michael was hurting. But why? Because of what happened when he was in the military? The people he lost?

The shadow of the moon was cast down on him, making him look somehow unreal. His chest moved with each slow breath. She noticed for the first time his slight dusting of chest hair and the dark trail of hair at his navel. His five-o'clock shadow from yesterday had grown even darker.

"Are you okay?" she asked upon approach. Her shoulders sagged a little as she rubbed her arms, feeling a bit cold, and waited for him to reply.

"Yeah."

She closed the gap between them and rested her hand on his forearm. "Why aren't you in bed?"

He pushed a strand of hair behind her ear. "I'm not great at sharing a bed." He looked away and fixed his gaze on the hotel across the street.

Was he worried about the nightmares?

"Michael, I always encourage my brother to talk about what he's going through when deployed. He shouldn't keep things locked up." She raised her right shoulder and released a breath. "I know it's hard, but . . ." She paused. "Sorry, I feel nervous for some reason, and I'm beginning to ramble."

"You don't need to be nervous."

She wasn't going to come away from this unscathed . . . was she?

He cleared his throat and stepped back, turning away. "You should get some rest." He was closing himself off. Of course, what else did he do when things got real?

She looked over as his hands swept up to the railing. He gripped it and bowed his head, and she noticed the muscles in his back tense.

"If you change your mind about talking, well, I can be a friend. I can listen," she said with a slight tremble in her voice.

Without turning around, he answered, "Thanks."

And like that, the icy mask slid back into place, and the Man of Steel was back.

CHAPTER TWELVE

MICHAEL WAS STANDING IN THE KITCHEN COOKING AN OMELET when he looked up to see Kate. Although she'd only gotten a few hours of sleep, she looked rested. He was relieved when she had left the balcony to sleep in her own room. He didn't want to send her any more mixed messages. Besides, what if he'd had another nightmare? What if he hurt her?

The sex had been amazing with her, but she was too good for him. So sweet and innocent that she should have come with a warning label.

"Hi."

She stood at the edge of the kitchen, and he could already see the damage he'd done.

"Morning." He focused back on the frying pan, unable to look into her eyes, afraid of what else he might see.

"A man who can cook. Smells good. Can I help?"

He turned back around, not wanting to be rude, even though he knew he shouldn't be nice. She wouldn't fall for him if he acted like a dick, he hoped. Hell, but what if she already had?

He tilted his head to the side and studied her for a moment. He couldn't stop himself from appreciating the sight of her.

She was in her gym clothes again, and he'd be damned if he ever saw someone wear workout clothes better. A fitted, bright orange tank top showed off her curves, and her tiny workout shorts revealed defined legs and hinted at an equally toned backside.

"I'm just about done. Have a seat." He grabbed two plates and slid the food onto them before sprinkling a dash of salt and pepper.

"Looks good. Thank you," she said when he set the food in front of her.

He sat on the stool next to her, and then he did something stupid. His hand came up over the top of hers. "Are you okay, Kate?" When he looked up at her, her eyes were focused on his hand, her mouth in a tight line.

Shit. What am I doing?

"I—ugh . . ." she started.

He lifted his hand from hers and pressed it to his lap.

"Michael." She kept her eyes trained on her dish, and that was fine with him. He didn't want to see pain on her face. He didn't think he could handle it if he did. "I don't think I'm cut out for this. I'm sorry." She stood and came around behind the stool. "Thank you for the food, but I don't have much of an appetite."

He rested his elbows on the edge of the counter. He wasn't sure what to say.

"Last night was amazing. I mean, like, amazing with capital letters. But we have been thrown together under unusual circumstances, and that would never have happened otherwise." She paused and rubbed her hands against her sides, fixating on the floor. "The girl in the bedroom with you last night—that's not me."

He swallowed as he turned to face her and stood, his eyes studying her high cheekbones and full mouth. She could have been a model or an actress, but he was immensely relieved that she wasn't. Not all celebrities were pretentious and shallow, but most of the ones he dated were—and that was just the way he liked it, usually. That way, he was in no danger of falling for anyone.

But Kate, she was the entire package, wasn't she? And while

he adored every new detail he discovered, each thing pricked him with the pain that he would have to lose her.

"When I walked into the kitchen this morning, and I saw you—"

"I'm sorry." He couldn't let her continue. He couldn't hear what she'd say. "I enjoyed last night. It was great. But I can't be anyone else—this is me." He dragged a palm down his face, hating himself right now. "I can never give you what you need—what you deserve."

"And why is that?"

He looked at the hardwood floors and stepped back, needing some space. "I just can't get into this right now." *Or ever.*

He paused and forced his attention back to her eyes. "Listen," he began, reaching for her hand, but she stiffened and pulled away. He deserved that. "I promise I'll keep you safe. I promise I won't let anything happen to you—that is something you need that I can give you."

Before she had a chance to respond, Michael's phone began ringing. "That's probably Connor, your bodyguard." He reached for his phone. "Yeah, come on up. I'll buzz you in."

He went to the foyer and tapped at the keypad by the elevator doors.

Connor stepped out a moment later, wearing faded blue jeans and a dark green T-shirt. He'd clearly stopped shaving, Michael noted when assessing his scruffy beard.

Michael felt strangely uneasy as he watched Kate's eyes wander over Connor's body, before adjusting to meet his green eyes.

A muscular arm extended toward Kate. Her dimples were exposed as she smiled back at Connor. "Hi, I'm Kate."

"I wish I were meeting you under different circumstances, but it's nice to meet you. I'm Connor." He flashed her a bright smile.

"Thank you for coming," Michael said and looked back at Kate. "Connor was with me in the Marines—he joined the year I did. He's been out of the military for about as long as me." Michael motioned them into the living room.

Connor studied Kate's long legs as he followed behind her, which Michael observed with pained annoyance. "How do you know each other?" Connor asked before taking a seat on the suede sofa next to Kate.

Michael stood by the fireplace and trained his attention on Connor. Now that he noticed how captivated Connor seemed to be with Kate, Michael was beginning to question his choice of bodyguard. Connor was thirty-two, single, and a handsome guy. He'd have to be blind not to notice Kate.

God, what is wrong with me? He shouldn't care if his friend checked out Kate—she wasn't his.

"I planned the ball for Michael. I didn't see you there the other night, did I?"

Connor shook his head. "No, I just got back from London yesterday. I was working on a special assignment so I couldn't make it."

"Do you, um, keep people safe for a living?" she asked, her eyes widening with curiosity.

Connor smirked. "When it pays well," he joked. "Michael explained to me the situation. I'm glad to be at your beck and call until he finds the bastard who is following you."

"I don't think we'll need you today," Michael found himself saying, deciding he could protect Kate today and skip his meetings. "I'm not needed at the office today." So maybe he'd piss off about ten different people by not showing, but at the moment, he didn't give a damn.

He had another meeting with the DOD tomorrow, though. He'd have to go in for that one. "If you could be here by eight tomorrow morning that'd be great."

Connor nodded. "I'm staying at the hotel across the street, so I'll be close by."

"Thank you. I think this is all a little extreme, but Michael insists, so I guess I have no choice." She smiled at Connor and rose to her feet when he stood.

"We'll keep you safe. Don't worry."

"Let's talk for a minute," Michael said. He motioned for Connor to follow him into his office.

"It's good to see you, man." Connor patted Michael on the shoulder. "How are you?"

He knew Connor would see the truth behind any lie, so he said, "Same as always."

Connor tipped his head in understanding.

"How's your brother? Mason on his last tour of duty?" Michael folded his arms and stood in front of his desk.

"He signed up for another one, and then I think he's done. Dad wants to groom him for the family business." Connor rubbed a hand down the side of his head before he swept it to the back of his neck.

"When are you going to stop running around—risking your neck?" Michael chided gently. "You could work at your dad's place, too, you know."

Connor shook his head. "Fuck no."

Michael didn't press. Instead, he filled Connor in with all the details.

"And Jake managed to get time off to come help tomorrow?" Connor asked as they made their way back to Kate a few minutes later.

"Yeah, fortunately."

"Good. Well, see you guys in the morning." Connor smiled and said goodbye after they chatted for a few more minutes.

"So, what do you think of him?" Michael asked after the elevator doors closed.

"I like him," she said.

Michael's jaw clamped shut for a brief moment. "Good." He looked down at his watch. "We have a few hours before Jake gets here. I was thinking that maybe you could try and sketch a picture of what the guy looked like—the one you saw watching you at the club, restaurant, and ball."

Kate released a small laugh. "Me? I can try, but I doubt it will do us much good. Drawing is not exactly my forte."

He gave her a slight nod. "Come on, I'll let you use my office." After providing her with paper and a pencil, he left without saying another word. He didn't want to be alone with her. He couldn't breathe around her right now. She smelled too good—looked too good.

And he had promised to keep her safe.

"YOU'RE GORGEOUS." THOSE WERE THE FIRST WORDS THAT JAKE uttered to Kate. Not "hi," "how are you," or "nice to meet you." He opened with, "You're gorgeous."

Michael pushed his fingertips against his right temple. "Jake," he muttered in a low voice.

"So, some asshole has been following you, huh?" Jake released her hand and smiled.

Kate decided that swear words sounded sexy with a Texas drawl. "Unfortunately."

"Perhaps we could sit and get acquainted and discuss what you already know," Jake replied before heading toward the living room.

"Sure. Let me just grab something." She left and went to the office to get her drawing.

"You could have warned me about Kate before I met her." Kate paused in the hallway on her way back at Jake's comment.

"Warn you about what?" Michael asked. She could just imagine Michael rolling his eyes.

"She's an incredible-looking woman. And with no makeup on . . . she looks like that? Tell me you're not screwing her. Tell me she's available."

"Jake, you're a good friend, but if you even think about making a move on her . . ."

A small pebble of hope bounced around her stomach.

She must have made some small sound because Michael looked up and found her standing still in the doorframe of the hall. "Kate."

Kate glanced at Michael as she made her way to Jake. "Ugh. Here," she said, handing her drawing to Jake, playing off the weird tension in the room by offering a forced but tight-lipped smile. "I can't draw well, but that's the best I could do. I saw this guy a few times. I don't know for sure if he's the one following me." She sat down in a nearby armchair.

"This will help. Thank you," Jake replied. "So, tell me what's been going on."

She studied Jake as she thought about what to say. He had short, dirty-blond hair. He was tall and muscular, but a little leaner than Michael and his warm brown eyes seemed to smile whenever he flashed his dimples at her. Like Connor, he was handsome. Did Michael only have good-looking friends?

"Show him your phone," Michael said when she hadn't spoken.

"It's over there." She pointed to her phone, which sat on the coffee table just in front of Jake.

Jake nodded and grabbed it. "Michael said your stalker started off by sending text messages, right? I assume they're from the blocked number in here." He scrolled through the images. "What else do you have?" He put the phone back down and looked at Michael, and then to Kate.

The red envelope was sitting on the end table by the armchair, alongside the dozen or so pictures that had been on the bed at the hotel. She reached for them, noticing her fingers trembling slightly. "Here," she said, trying to steady her hand.

Jake flipped through the photos and opened the envelope. If he was worried at all, his face didn't show it. In fact, she couldn't gauge any type of reaction from him whatsoever. He was an FBI agent, she had to remind herself, and her situation probably didn't even rank on the weird meter to him.

He set the photos and envelope on the table next to her phone and leaned forward, perching his elbows on his knees. "Stalkers generally send messages and photos for one of a few reasons. Sometimes the stalker actually believes that he or she loves the person that they're following, and the messages are meant to serve as a token of appreciation and love. Sometimes a stalker sends messages because they get off on the fear. They like seeing your face when you receive the message and the person enjoys your reaction."

Kate pulled the side of her bottom lip between her teeth for a moment before realizing it. She shifted her focus to Michael, who rose to his feet and walked to the wall of windows. The cloudy sky was growing darker, matching their somber mood.

"But it may not be either of those reasons," Jake announced.

Her shoulders slumped as her brows lifted. "What else could it be?"

"The person might not be obsessed with you in an infatuation sort of way, but rather just wants you to think that he is. Considering your stalker demanded you go back to New York suggests the motive of the texts and photos was to frighten you out of the city."

"But why?" she asked, her voice cracking a little as she spoke.

He sunk back into the couch and clasped his hands together. "I have two theories. Your stalker wants you back in New York for whatever reason, maybe to do you harm there. Or, there's also a chance this is somehow connected to your mother's murder."

"I'm sorry, what?" she snapped.

Michael turned away from the window, zoning in on Jake as though he had a grenade in hand.

"I did some research on you after Michael called me yesterday," Jake said.

"Apparently, your research sucks because my mom wasn't murdered." She closed her mouth and pushed to her feet, walking to the fireplace, where she stared down at the fake, gray logs.

"Kate, I'm sorry. But what do you know about your mom's death?" Jake asked.

She turned around and looked at Michael. He was beholding her with the same worry that rippled through her own body.

There was no way she could deal with this right now. No way. "She was eight months pregnant and went into labor early. They had to do an emergency C-section. There was a lot of bleeding. Her blood pressure spiked. She died."

"Shit, I didn't expect to be the one to tell you this. I assumed your father—or, at least someone, would have told you the truth." Jake reached into the duffel bag by his foot and retrieved a folder.

"Your mom was murdered in her parents' home on Lake Norman, in your grandfather's office. She was shot in the chest."

Kate trained her eyes on the FBI agent, who was killing her on the inside with tiny little knife jabs of unwanted truth.

"Your dad arrived on the scene right after it happened—your mom was still alive, but barely. The medics couldn't save her, but the ER doctors were able to save you." He took a breath.

Jake might as well have put a gun to her heart. It felt like her life was seeping from her. She looked down at her chest to see if there was blood.

Jake continued, despite the fact that Kate was ready to collapse into an abyss of darkness. "The police decided it must have been a robbery gone bad, that maybe the burglars expected the home to be empty, and your mother confronted them with her father's gun. Perhaps they took the gun and shot her . . . and then when her boyfriend—your father—showed up, they took off."

She was touching her chest now. There was real pain there. She could feel it. She couldn't possibly be imagining the feeling—her heart was constricting against her rib cage. Her nails clawed at her chest as she struggled to catch her breath.

"Kate?" Worry lit across Michael's face. "Are you okay?" He darted toward her, holding her arm as if she might fall. He guided her back to the armchair.

She sat down for a few minutes in silence.

Murder?

No, it wasn't possible.

"My dad would have told me. I don't believe it," she mumbled.

Jake let out a breath and continued to speak with a steady but softer voice. "Your father took you to New York as soon as the hospital let him. And your grandparents abandoned their home after the shooting. Either it was too painful for them to be in Charlotte or they suspected the murder was more . . . personal . . . than the police's explanation."

Her legs felt heavy, even though she was sitting down. "My dad left Charlotte because my mom died here. He left because this city was a painful reminder of her existence. Not because she was murdered."

"Kate, I'm sorry, but it's true. I can show you the police report if you'd like," Jake said.

Michael's eyes narrowed on Jake as he held up his hand. A warning.

"She needs to know this," Jake insisted. He stood and walked over to Kate.

Her attention shifted up to meet Jake's eyes. "Go on," she whispered.

"DNA evidence was brand new back then, and forensics didn't reveal much. There was evidence of a break-in at the door to the back entrance. Your father reported that a family necklace your mother always wore was missing from her neck. Since your father saw no sign of a vehicle, the police assumed the robbers had parked down the street and approached the house on foot. Because your father worried there was more to the story, the cops interviewed friends and classmates of your mother, but they came up with a bunch of loose ends."

Kate wasn't sure how she would manage to stand. "I need to make a call. Excuse me." She stood, but her legs had that weird, rubbery sensation as she walked. She didn't remember how she got to her bedroom or dialed her father's number, but she was now listening to him say her name for the third time.

"Are you okay? Kate? Say something."

She shut her eyes. "You lied to me. Why?"

"What in God's name are you talking about? What's going on?" Her father's voice had lost its cool edge. It broke with stress.

"Mom was murdered." The words sounded strange as they rolled off her tongue.

Silence greeted her on the other end of the line.

"Why did you lie to me?" Her eyes flashed open, and she gripped the phone tight to her ear.

"Who told you this?"

"I just want the truth. What happened to her?"

"I'm taking the next flight to Charlotte. I'll call you when I land, and then I'm picking you up and taking you home."

The line went dead.

She continued to hold the phone to her ear as though answers would pour forth from it.

"Kate?" Michael rapped at the door. "Are you all right?"

"Go away." It was her turn to blow him off. To close herself up and hide behind a fortified wall of steel.

"I can't do that." Michael opened the door, and she regretted not locking it. She dropped her phone on the bed and focused her attention on the plush carpet beneath her toes. *Don't cry. Don't break down in front of him.*

"Kate."

She shifted to lie down. Turning away from him, she pleaded, "Please, leave."

But he ignored her, damn him. She felt the weight of the bed shift as he joined her, and when he wrapped an arm around her, tugging her flush to his body, she cried, "Let me go. Leave." She started to struggle, to shift her shoulders, to move away from him, but he only tightened his hold.

"I'm here for you. Let me be here for you."

"Damn you." He had no right to be her savior right now. To be the friend she'd tried to be to him.

But as he nuzzled his face to her neck, sweeping his hand down the side of her face, she gave in to the warmth. To the comfort and feeling of safety.

And tears began to stream down her face as she remained tucked against the one man who could possibly hurt her more than her stalker. The man who was slowly possessing her heart.

CHAPTER THIRTEEN

SOMETHING HEAVY PRESSED AGAINST HER STOMACH, AND THE NEED to take a deep breath forced her awake. Kate's eyes fluttered open, and she looked down to see Michael's arm resting on her abdomen. His long, dark lashes lay against his bronzed skin. His chest gently rose and fell.

She wanted to shut her eyes and stay next to him for as long as possible. To will away the truth of what she'd learned earlier.

But she couldn't hide forever.

She stared at the ceiling and swallowed as she processed her thoughts. Learning the truth was like losing her mom for the second time.

"How are you?" His palm cupped her chin, and he nudged her face close to his.

Their lips were only inches apart as she practically breathed out his name. "Michael."

His brows pinched together, his eyes like blue glass. "I—"

"My father's on his way here," she cut him off, worried he'd try to dance around the moment and turn into an ass—and right now she couldn't deal with that. "He plans on taking me home."

Michael's head snapped back, and he immediately sat upright

and rubbed a hand down his face. "Hell no. You're safe here, with me."

Sure . . .

His voice softened a fraction as he said, "I don't think going back to New York is a good idea, especially if that's what your stalker wants."

She scooted to the other side of the bed and stood. "I don't know where I'll be safe—maybe nowhere. But my father is an attorney; he knows people who can protect me." She paused, and her shoulders shrank. "But I'm so angry at him for lying to me all these years. I don't know if I can face him right now." She looked down at the floor.

Her life had been a lie.

"Can I ask what he said to you?"

She ran her hands up and down her thighs, trying to slow her rapidly beating heart. "He didn't say much of anything other than he was taking the first flight here. But it's strange, huh?"

Michael came around in front of her and reached out, cupping her cheek. The gesture was sweet. And so damn confusing it hurt.

She sucked in a breath, taking note of his eyes, which were not as dark and appeared more like the Gulf of Mexico on a summer day. Or maybe her vision was off from all the crying.

"I don't know who killed my mom, or if it's the same person who is after me, but I kind of want it to be the same person," she softly admitted.

He stared at her in silence, his eyes narrowing.

"I—I need it to be the same person because I want to bring my mother's killer to justice. I have a better chance of finding her killer if he has already found me."

Michael's hand fell. "It sounds to me like you want to be bait."

"Not bait . . . not any more than I already am." She crossed her arms. "I have to find out who killed my mom."

He wrapped a hand around the nape of his neck and stepped back. "Fine." He cleared his throat. "We'll find your stalker and your mother's killer—even if they're two different people. But we're not using you as bait. Period."

* * *

MICHAEL SLID OFF THE BARSTOOL WHEN HE SAW KATE approaching. She looked refreshed and energized after her shower. She had applied a little mascara and lip gloss and had thrown on a pair of blue jeans and a pink, Victoria's Secret T-shirt.

"You look better."

"My dad sent me a text. He said he couldn't get a flight until early tomorrow morning." She approached the fridge and opened it. "I texted him the address of the hotel where I was staying before. He thinks I'll be meeting him there at eight. He has no idea about you." She peeked around the fridge door. "Could you meet him instead? I can't face him."

"Of course." He preferred to have a one-on-one with her father anyway. "I'll push my meeting until a little later."

"I'm starving. Mind if I ransack your fridge? I stress eat."

God, it was wonderful to be around a woman with an appetite. Someone who ate actual food. Not lettuce and carrot sticks.

Was there anything he didn't like about her? He was trying to think of something as they finished their food awhile later. "You amaze me," he said.

She finished her last bite of bowtie pasta and looked up at him. "What?"

He hadn't meant to say that, but he couldn't turn back now. "You just amaze me." And that was all he would say. He stood and grabbed a bottle of wine. "Want any?"

"Sure."

"While you were in the shower, I spoke with Jake," he said as he poured the wine. "He asked me to email him the guest list of the ball. He's going to see if any of the guests had a connection to your mom."

"Oh."

When he handed her the glass, she briefly closed her eyes. "I didn't mention this before because I didn't think it was relevant, but I met someone at the ball who knew my mom. He told me I looked just like her. They were classmates." She looked up at Michael. "I'm sure he has nothing to do with my stalker. I mean, we don't even know if there is a relationship between her murder and what is happening to me."

"Do you remember his name?"

"Yeah. He gave me his business card."

"Okay, I'll let Jake know." He took a sip of the wine. "Jake also got the official police report of your mother's case while we were sleeping earlier, and he'll visit with one of the detectives who was on your mother's case tomorrow. He's retired, but he'll see if the detective remembers anything."

"Wow. He moves fast."

"Like I said, he's one of the best. He normally deals in counterterrorism, but—"

"Jeez. I hate taking up his time then . . ." She shook her head and looked down at her glass. "I've completely disrupted your life. Thank you for helping me, though."

He set the glass down on the kitchen island and moved toward her. "You don't need to thank me, and I don't want anything in return," he said in a low voice. "I'm helping you because I care about you."

She bit her lip and her gaze averted to his mouth. "Why do you care about me? Even before you and I, um, hooked up, you wanted to help me. I don't get it. Is it because you were in the military? You have some desire to help people in need?"

"I like you, Kate. You know I do. I can't help but care about your safety." He rubbed his forehead and grabbed his wine again. "But I shouldn't want you the way that I do. It's selfish of me to still want you, especially now. Especially after the day you've had. But damned if I do." He poured the remaining contents of his glass down his throat and swallowed. "I'm going to call Connor and have him come over."

"What? Why?" She moved closer to him.

"I need to go out. I can't be here right now." He didn't trust himself. And, although he hated the idea of Connor spending the evening with Kate, he knew it would be worse if he spent any time with her. He was still sending her mixed signals, and it wasn't fair. She needed protection, and all he'd ever be was pain if he got any closer to her.

"I thought we were going to come up with a plan."

"Jake's working on the plan. Don't worry." He reached for his cell and left the kitchen before he could change his mind.

"Where are you going?" she asked, following him into the living room. "To a bar? A club? To find someone else to be with? Someone that's not me?"

He jerked around to face her, his chest moving up and down as he tried to control himself—to stop himself from taking her in his arms right now and showing her that she was all he wanted. All that he needed.

And then he turned his back and strode from the room—getting as far away from her as possible.

* * *

MICHAEL BROUGHT THE JACK AND COKE TO HIS LIPS AND STARED in a daze at the row of liquor bottles that lined the wall. The bar was dead. It was a Monday night, after all, and closing time was in fifteen minutes. He was on his fourth drink, and he was still unable to digest his feelings for Kate. The last few days had taken him by surprise. Kate had gotten under his skin in a way that no one else had. He was trying to keep his wall up, but she was like a sledgehammer. All she had to do was smile.

He'd thought he would get her out of his system once they slept together. But he only wanted her more. He'd never done drugs before. But for the first time in his life, he felt like he could understand the dilemma that drug users faced. Once they felt the high, they wanted more of it. They knew it was wrong. They tried to stay away. But when temptation was near, their mind would ignore the sin and only remember the pleasure it could bring.

Kate was becoming his drug, and he couldn't trust himself around her. He was growing weak.

He'd faced terrorists eye to eye. He'd gone to bat with men who strapped bombs to their chests—and yet, he couldn't be in the same room with Kate without needing her so much that it risked his self-control. What was happening?

He took a sip of his almost empty drink and tried to remind himself of all the reasons that a true relationship was not an option for him. The memories came hurling back with such force that he almost spat out his drink. He shut his eyes and bit back the pain that was now gathering like a storm in his chest. He reached into his pocket and threw a few twenties on the counter.

His legs felt heavy as he exited the bar and walked the few blocks back to his place. When the elevator doors opened, and he entered the living room, he saw Kate curled up asleep on the couch, with Connor sitting beside her. An action flick was playing on the television, and Connor appeared engrossed in the movie. He jumped up when he saw Michael.

"Thanks for looking after her, man," he said as he kept his eyes fixed on Kate asleep.

"Sure." Connor arched his back, and then stretched his arms out in front of him. "Are you okay? You seem more tense than normal." He laughed a little. "If that's possible."

Michael nodded. "I'm fine," he answered as he finally looked at his friend. "Thanks again. See you in the morning."

As soon as the elevator doors closed and Connor was gone, Michael reached for Kate and picked her up in his arms, trying not to wake her. He carried her down the hall and to the guest bedroom, staring down at her, mesmerized by the sleeping beauty in his arms. Relief struck him upon noting she was still in her jeans and hadn't put on one of her flimsy nightgowns for Connor to see. Gently, he laid her on the bed.

"Michael . . ."

Hearing his name, even mumbled, caused him to stop in the doorway.

She was dreaming. About him.

He pressed his palm to the inside of the doorframe and bowed his head as he stifled the sudden stiffening between his legs.

He glanced over his shoulder at her, wishing he could sleep next to her. To feel her in his arms again. But the nap they had earlier today was the closest he'd come to sleeping with someone since he'd been out of the Marines. And even that had been a mistake.

CHAPTER FOURTEEN

"DAVID ADAMS?"

The man was not who Michael would have expected. He knew David Adams was a powerful defense attorney in New York City, but he wouldn't have pegged him for a shorts-and-wrinkled-T-shirt kind of guy. He decided that Kate's looks must have come from her mother—her father had dark cropped hair, brown eyes, and a plain, oval face. Something about him screamed lawyer, though—or maybe it was that Michael didn't trust lawyers, and he definitely didn't trust Kate's father, who had lied to his daughter all her life.

"Michael Maddox?" David closed the distance between them but didn't meet Michael's extended hand. "Where's my daughter?" He looked around the busy lobby of the hotel and back at Michael.

"How'd you know who I am? I didn't think Kate mentioned me." Michael shoved his hands in the pockets of his black business pants and trained his attention on David's brown eyes, trying to get an accurate read on his character.

"Doesn't everyone know who you are?" He echoed Michael's pose. "Besides, you're the reason my daughter is here, right? She planned your event. And I want her to come back to New York."

"You don't even know what's going on," Michael said with a

deeper-than-normal voice. "We need to talk. I'll take you to my office."

"I have no intention of going anywhere without seeing my daughter. This is her hotel, correct?"

"It was. She's staying at my place now."

David took a step back from Michael and removed his hands from his pockets. "What the fuck is going on?" His tan faded, replaced by bright cheeks. "If you think you're going to manipulate her—I know your reputation, you son—"

Michael held his palms up. "Hang on, man. I'm trying to help Kate. She's in danger." And that was all he had said before he made for the exit, assuming David would follow.

"What's going on? I want to see my daughter," David demanded as he trailed after Michael.

Michael spun on his heel and motioned toward his Audi. "Get in. I'll explain."

David huffed out an exasperated breath and shook his head, but at least he followed instructions.

As soon as Michael was behind the driver's wheel and pulled out into traffic, he spoke. "Kate has a stalker. Someone began following her the minute she arrived in Charlotte. It looks like he's trying to scare her away." He glanced over at David out of the corner of his eye. He was pressing his palms against his knees and staring out the passenger window. "I called in a favor from a friend of mine in the FBI. He told Kate about her mother's murder."

"This is crazy." David looked over at Michael as they stopped at a red light. "Jesus, I told her not to come to this city. I told her."

"My friend in the FBI doubts the stalker is connected to her mother's murder, given that the police think Elizabeth's murder was the result of a burglary, but he wants to pursue every possible angle."

"I didn't want her to find out. I didn't want her to know that her mother was shot. Do you blame me?" His face pinched together as anger, or maybe guilt besieged him.

Michael pulled off to the side of the road and parallel parked a few blocks from his office. He looked over at David again, studying him, but found himself unable to get a read on the man. Had he lost his touch? "It's between you and Kate as to why you lied, but I need to know if you think there's a chance that there's a connection between her mother's murder and her stalker."

David looked like a man who had just lost a child. Or a wife. Sadness replaced his hollow stare, and the muscles in his face sagged, as though gravity had become heavier. "I don't think there's a relation," he said at last.

"Why'd you run away from Charlotte when her mother died? Why the hell did her grandparents abandon their home—sadness? Or fear?"

David straightened his slouched shoulders and wet his dry lips. He wondered if Kate received her nervous energy from her father. How could a powerful attorney be so weak? Maybe it took having a child to understand what David was feeling.

"Tell me the truth," Michael said with a flash of warning in his voice.

"I don't know if her mother's murder was premeditated." David rubbed his forehead. "Her mother, Elizabeth, told me that she felt like she was being followed. She couldn't prove it, though, and I—a pre-law student to the core—demanded evidence. I wanted to help her, but I said that without proof there was nothing to go on. Soon after she told me that, she died."

"What did the cops say?"

"Same as I said to Elizabeth. Without proof . . ." He shifted in his seat and pulled his wallet out of his back pocket. His hand fumbled inside before retrieving a folded photo. He handed it to Michael.

It was a headshot of Kate's mother, Elizabeth. The photo was creased in the middle and worn at the edges, the color faded, but the resemblance between Kate and Elizabeth was astounding. Michael studied the photo and touched the necklace in the picture.

The white gold chain was simple, but the pendant in the middle was exquisite. He didn't know much about jewelry, but he guessed that the center diamond was, at least, two carats, and there were also small diamonds encrusting the large stone.

"That was her grandmother's necklace—the one the killer took." David's brown eyes grew dark. "Where's Kate? I need to see her."

"Right now, she doesn't want to see you." He was beginning to feel sorry for the guy. Would he have done the same thing if he had been in David's shoes? Would he have silenced the past?

"I need to protect her."

"I have that covered."

"I'm her father." David slammed his hand against the dashboard as he glared at Michael.

"I'll talk to her. I'll see what I can do." He opened the door and got out of his Audi. "Check into a hotel, and I'll call you later." Michael opened the trunk and retrieved David's small suitcase. "Can I hang onto this photo for a bit?"

"Yes," he answered as he met him on the sidewalk and stared at Michael, disbelief etched in the lines of his face.

"Here's my number." Michael handed him his business card. "I'll call this afternoon. I promise."

David knitted his eyebrows together as he took the card. "I have to see her. Please, tell her I'm sorry."

Michael nodded and walked away, uneasiness building into a full storm that swirled inside him, threatening to break free.

* * *

"MICHAEL MET WITH YOUR FATHER EARLIER, AND HE'S AT A meeting right now. He'll fill us in when we see him later," Connor said, peering up from his newspaper. "I made coffee. The real kind of coffee. I didn't know how to use his fancy-schmancy gadget."

Kate tried not to feel disappointed by the fact that Michael wasn't there. It was after nine, though. She was the one who'd asked him to meet with her dad because she was too cowardly to face him, but she wished she and Michael hadn't left things the way they had the night before.

She wondered if he had slept with someone last night. Her stomach clenched tight, and she almost felt ill at the thought of him having sex with someone else.

But what had she expected—flowers and a proposal after they'd hooked up?

She couldn't believe this was her life now.

"Uh, you okay, Kate?" Connor waved his hand in front of her face before handing her a cup of coffee.

She hadn't even realized he was standing in front of her. Was she so blinded by thoughts of Michael that she couldn't even see the hot man before her, holding her favorite beverage? "Sorry." She smiled at him, took the coffee, and slid onto a barstool. "Thank you." She brushed her hands over her sundress and tucked a strand of hair behind her ear.

Connor responded with a grin that she was sure would make most women quiver with excitement. "Jake called and said he'd try and be here by two. Michael promised to be back by then, as well." He sipped his coffee. "Would you like to get out of the house today? We could walk around the city. I assume you must feel a little claustrophobic being stuck inside."

The man had a point. Fresh air was exactly what she needed. "I could almost kiss you for suggesting that," she exclaimed, promptly rising to her feet.

"I would take you up on that, but Michael would kill us both," he said before flashing her a knowing smile.

"Michael and I are just friends."

Connor nodded. "Uh huh. Okay. So, Michael didn't look like he wanted to snap my neck when he saw you asleep next to me on the couch last night . . .?"

Kate turned back around. "Oh. What time did he get in?"

A slow grin met his lips. "We should go," he said instead, which deflated her a little. Did he not want to shred her with the truth? Or was he purposefully trying to get her to admit her feelings for Michael?

He tilted his head and motioned for her to follow.

"Connor, has Michael always been—"

He stepped into the elevator and cocked his head to the side. "An ass?"

Kate's lips twitched with amusement.

"He's a good guy. Give him a chance," he said and then winked at her.

He waited for her to enter the elevator and crossed his arms, showing tanned biceps that bulged from beneath the sleeves of his gray T-shirt.

"Did Michael mention to you that I have a date on Friday?" she asked as they rounded the corner of the street and headed for a local coffee shop.

"Yeah, I heard about the auction."

"The thing is, I don't want my date to know about any of this, and it might be kind of hard to explain why I have a, um, bodyguard." She fidgeted with her fingers as they walked.

"Well, you know that Michael will never let you go alone. If he even lets you go at all." He opened the door to the cafe so she could enter. "I could keep some distance from you. I could be out of sight but always there. Would that work? Maybe Michael will be okay with that."

"He better be okay with it, because I'm not giving him a choice. Thank you."

After finishing their breakfast sandwiches and lattes, they exited the cafe, but Kate stopped in her tracks before they made it more than a couple of feet outside the door. She had forgotten how close they were to Michael's office building.

And there Michael was, standing on the other side of the street. He was talking to the slender auburn-haired woman she'd seen at his office last week. The redhead was touching his chest, and then she reached up and pressed her lips to his.

A city bus zipped by, blocking her view for a moment. When it was gone, she saw Michael looking over at her.

Michael's eyes left Kate's and returned to the redhead. He took the woman by the elbow and led her inside his office building.

"You okay?"

"Do you know her?" Kate asked while looking up at Connor.

There was a sudden darkness, or maybe a pain, flickering in his irises.

He stared at her for a brief moment and then shook his head as if he were shaking free a thought. "Come on," he said instead of answering. "Let's take a walk."

CHAPTER FIFTEEN

"MICHAEL'S CALLING." KATE LOOKED DOWN AT HER CELL PHONE. Connor and Kate had been roaming the streets of the city for about thirty minutes after Kate had witnessed Michael's kiss. "I don't feel like talking to him right now."

Connor's cell began buzzing as soon as Kate's had stopped. "I have to answer it. He's the boss." He shrugged. "What's up?"

Kate bit her thumb and took a seat on a nearby bench. She tried to ignore the pain that pooled in her stomach, ready to crash down like a tidal wave, to knock her off her feet. She looked up at Connor, who had stepped away to talk to Michael in private.

Connor was grimacing when he approached her. "He wants to see you," he said, shoving the phone into the back pocket of his board shorts.

Kate jumped to her feet. "No. I don't feel like seeing him right now. Come on, let's get a drink."

"It's eleven in the morning." He reached for her arm. "Kate, Michael isn't the guy you say 'no' to." He tilted his head in a beckoning motion. "Please. You don't want me to get in trouble, do you?" A small smile threatened his lips, though.

He was trying to manipulate her. There was no way this ex-military badass was afraid of Michael. "Connor, I—I can't face him. Okay?"

"He won't be happy about this." He reached for his phone and sent Michael a text. He grabbed her hand and pulled her toward him. "You win. It'll be my head, but I aim to please you, madam." His eyes lit up like those of a mischievous young boy. "I have an idea. Follow me."

The touch of his rough hand against hers made her feel unfaithful. But she knew that was totally crazy. What was there to be faithful to? Frustrated with herself, she tightened her grip on Connor's hand and allowed him to lead the way.

"There's a great dive bar a few blocks away. We can throw some darts and drink a few beers. They should be opening about now."

He was definitely right about the dive part, she realized when they stepped inside. The bar looked like something out of the Blue Lagoon. It wasn't her typical hangout place, which was why it was perfect. The last thing she wanted was to be typical Kate. Of course, ever since she'd come to Charlotte she'd become almost someone different.

"I love it," she exclaimed as they sat down at the bar.

"Two Coronas with lime," Connor ordered.

"I don't drink beer . . . but what the hell, first time for everything."

"This will be your first Corona?"

Kate decided the shock on his face was rather cute. "Yes." When he handed her the bottle, they clinked them together, and she took a sip. She attempted to hide her obvious distaste for the gold liquid, but judging by the huge smirk on Connor's face, she failed.

He grinned and motioned for the bartender. "Can you make a mimosa for the lady?"

Kate's cheeks warmed. "Thank you," she said. "That's a little more my speed."

"You should do that more often," he said before raising the bottle to his mouth.

"Do what?"

"Smile," he said over his shoulder and drank his beer.

"You, too. You have a great smile." When her drink arrived, she took an eager sip and looked around the bar. "So, tell me about yourself."

He ran a hand over his short brown beard, and his pale green eyes turned a shade darker. Kate waited for him to speak, but she wondered if she had hit some invisible mute button. "Connor?" She reached for his shoulder and rested her hand on it. "You okay?" she whispered, sensing the unspoken tension in his body. She never expected that such a casual question would prove to be such a difficult one.

He cleared his throat and looked up at her. "I don't have much of a story." His voice gave her a chill colder than the Arctic. Gone was the carefree, charming companion—in his place was now an aloof stranger. He reminded her a little of Michael, in that way. Warm one minute and steel the next. Of course, steel could get hot pretty quick. "Connor, you don't need to tell me anything. You don't owe me your story. I was just making conversation." She released her hand from his shoulder and looked down at her drink.

"Kate, Michael trusts me to keep you safe, but I think most of us—those who spent a lot of time in the Middle East—well, we don't like to talk about our past. We don't like talking about ourselves all too much. Michael and I are kind of fucked up, to tell you the truth. Afghanistan was the breaking point for us." He took a swig of beer. "I think he's a bit more messed up, though," he said with a smile, attempting to lighten the mood. "I try to be a happy-go-lucky guy, in spite of everything, but Michael, well he . . ."

She was curious to hear more, but Connor was looking at something behind her. She swiveled around to see what had grabbed his attention.

Michael, wearing his powerhouse, three-piece suit, was

standing at the entrance of the bar. He looked even more out of place than she did.

He crossed the room in a few long strides. "Kate," he gruffly said. "We need to talk." His eyes were focused on hers, ignoring Connor's presence.

"How'd you find us?" Kate mumbled as she stood.

"Never mind that." He directed his heated gaze Connor's way. "What were you thinking having her leave the loft?"

"Oh come on, she's fine." Connor stayed seated and finished his beer.

"I'll bring her back to my place. Jake will be there at two—come over then."

Kate looked up at Michael, a shiver darting up her spine. "Bye, Connor. Thanks for the drink."

Connor raised his brows and grimaced in apology. Did he feel bad for getting her into trouble?

Michael rested his hand on the small of her back and nudged her forward. She wouldn't normally allow a guy to boss her around, but he was trying to help her, so she let it slide this time.

Kate had to blink a few times as they exited from the dim bar and burst into the bright, sunlit outside.

"It's not a big deal that we're out." She leaned against the brick building next to the dive bar.

"Kate." He ruffled his hair, pieces sticking out, making him look a little disheveled, and she had to assume that was a new look for him. She was sure he was used to being in control and composed at all times. "I'm trying to keep you safe."

"I know, but . . ."

"And about what you saw earlier—"

"Was none of my business."

She pushed away from the wall and attempted to walk away, but he grabbed her wrist and spun her to face him. "What?" she rasped, hating that she was, in fact, hurting from seeing him kiss that other woman.

"Kate." His voice was a plea. "Come on, let's talk at my place." He motioned for her to follow him, and she agreed. Where else did she have to go?

* * *

THEY WALKED THE SIX BLOCKS BACK TO HIS HOME IN SILENCE. When the elevator doors opened, she rushed out.

"What's your problem?"

She pivoted back around and walked toward him, failing to mask her look of total madness. "I don't have a problem. I was perfectly fine having a drink with Connor until you showed up, looking like the Hulk."

If he weren't so angry, he would have laughed.

He chucked his keys on the hall table. "Can we talk?" He took off his blazer and tossed it on the recliner as he moved toward the living area. He unbuttoned his black vest and threw it off, as well.

She ignored his question and went out onto the balcony.

"It wasn't what it looked like," he said, taking a seat on one of the lounge chairs. He crossed his ankle over his knee, his slacks stretching over his quads. He rolled up the sleeves of his black collared shirt and drummed his fingers on his knees.

She finally turned around so he could chance a look at her eyes —to see the expression on her face. She was hurting. This is exactly what he didn't want happening.

"You don't owe me any explanations."

"It sure as hell feels like I do," he bit back. He shut his eyes, trying to calm the hot thread of frustration that spun through him, winding him up.

He was pissed as hell Connor had taken her out for a casual stroll in the city with what was going on. And then for Kate to stumble upon him and Trisha . . .

"Michael, I don't care about some pretty redhead. Kiss whoever you want."

He let out a slow breath as he opened his eyes. His attention wandered to her lips. She was the only one he was in the mood to kiss. Didn't she know that? "*She* kissed me. I didn't expect it, and I didn't want it."

September. He fucking hated this month.

"Who is she?"

He wasn't sure why he felt the need to reassure her. They both knew they couldn't be together. They couldn't play by each other's rules, so why were they even having this conversation? Why did he need to explain himself, to show her . . . what? That he'd been faithful? He groaned and looked over her shoulder and at the hotel across the street.

"She's no one of concern to you." And he sure as hell wasn't going to talk about this anymore, that was for damn sure.

"Because women kiss you on the street all the time?" She paused. "Or do they? Damn you and your superhuman good looks." Her shoulders slouched forward as she turned away from him. "I remember her from your office," she added a few moments later in a somber voice. "And she was in one of the photos my stalker sent me. She must mean something to you. I thought you never got involved with—"

"She's an old friend. Now, let's drop it." He stood and came up alongside her, joining her at the railing. Together, they stared down at the street. "I don't feel like getting into all of this with you. I want to help you find the bastard who is stalking you, and I promised I would help you find your mother's killer. Can we focus on that for now?" *Please, for the love of God.*

"Fine. I can forget the way you feel inside me. If you can," she commented as her blue-green eyes dipped south of his hips, before slowly moving back up to his face.

She started to turn, but his arm banded around her waist, and he pulled her back. Her body was an inch from his, and her face so close. "You're making me lose my damn mind. You know that, right?"

Her pink lips parted, her eyes still holding his. He swept his hand to the back of her head and brought her mouth to his.

And she returned his kiss, allowing his tongue entry to her mouth.

Without thinking, he lifted her up, and she wrapped her legs around him—where she belonged.

With his lips locked onto hers, he carried her into the house before slamming the glass doors shut.

He would never make it to a room. Still holding her, he tapped a button by the door, and the automatic blinds began to close. "God, I need you," he hoarsely said as he set her down.

And she must have wanted him, too, because she lifted her dress over her head and tossed it in one fast movement.

She was standing in nude panties and a beige lace bra, her nipples poking through the thin material. He came at her so quickly that she stumbled back and landed on the couch. A smile met her lips as she looked up at him, sinking her teeth into her lip. The woman was torturing him.

He knelt before her, his fingers skirting up the sides of her toned thighs before reaching for her hips, pulling her closer to him, to his mouth.

She braced each side of his shoulders when he pushed her panties out of the way, his tongue darting to her wet flesh.

"Jesus Christ," he muttered a second later as the elevator buzzed.

"Oh, God," she shrieked.

He released his hold on her and stood.

"Perfect timing." She rose to her feet, still in heels, and slipped her dress back over her shoulders.

"Tell me about it." He shifted the material of his pants, hoping to calm his hard-on. "Thank God I didn't give the guys access to my place yet. I'd have to kill them if they saw you naked." He grimaced at the thought.

"Last time I checked, you don't have exclusive rights to my

nudity. Just an F.Y.I." She smirked, but the realization of her words hit him hard. "Will you kill every man who sees me naked?"

"I wouldn't test me," he grumbled.

CHAPTER SIXTEEN

KATE TUCKED AWAY HER NERVOUS SMILE AND ATTEMPTED TO LOOK professional in front of Jake and Connor.

Michael was standing about as far away from her as he could get while being in the same room. He'd gone behind his own personal Berlin Wall again. Damn him. "I almost forgot. What did my dad have to say?" she asked as they sat down at the large farmhouse table in the kitchen.

Michael shifted in his seat to face Kate, who sat to his left. "He said he was sorry." He cleared his throat. "Your dad said your mother thought she had a stalker. Not long before she died, she told him she felt like she was being watched."

Like me. Oh, God. "Does he think there could be a connection?"

"He doesn't think so. Or at least, the cops ruled out the idea of a stalker." He pressed his palms against the table and looked at Jake. "What do you think?"

"I have two suspects in mind if there is a connection to your mother. Two people at the gala went to school with her. And one of them looks like the man you drew."

Kate's lips twitched as her nerves pulled at her heartstrings.

She reached for the folder that Jake slid to her. With a shaky hand, she opened it and looked at the first photo. "That's him." She stared at the picture of the muscular, blond man. The anxiety that coursed through her body made her feel like she had taken four shots of espresso.

"That's Nathan Williams. He's a real estate attorney. He has several offices, including one in New York," Jake responded.

She moved Nathan's photo aside to view the other.

"Erick Jensen." She ran her fingers across the image of the face. She had danced with him at the gala.

"Michael tells me that Erick admitted that he knew your mother." Jake looked down at the photo and back up at Kate.

"Yeah. He even asked me to help out with the winter ball in Boston." Kate pushed aside Erick's photo to study the image of the blond man, who now had a name. "Given that this Nathan guy has a connection with my mom, do you think there's a link between her murder and my stalker?" She tried not to feel a pinch of hope at the possibility of getting justice for her mother.

"We have to keep in mind that your stalker may have nothing to do with your mom at all. This Nathan guy might be following you, but it may be sheer coincidence that he went to school with your mom." He rubbed his hands together as if attempting to dispel the nervous energy that was hanging above everyone's heads. "The detective on your mother's case was adamant that it was a robbery gone wrong. I need you to understand that I might not be able to help in regard to her murder. My main focus is catching your stalker."

"But if someone was following my mom, too . . ." Kate stared down at Nathan's picture, desperate to confirm that he was the killer and the stalker. She wanted to get this over and done with. She wanted the man behind bars who murdered her mother, stealing her chance to know her—to feel her love.

"Your father told the police that, but the cops said there wasn't any evidence of stalking. No notes, pictures, or anything like that.

Remember, she wasn't living in the times of social media and cell phones."

"I think I need to sit down."

"You are sitting." Michael reached out and touched her arm, which was surprising.

"I'd like to go meet with Nathan and Erick soon." Jake stood.

"Well, Erick said he would be out of town this week." Kate's attention focused back on Nathan's photo.

"Connor and I can go interview Nathan today, and I'll double-check to make sure Erick is actually out of town."

"I'd like to go." Kate was on her feet and feeling focused for the first time that afternoon.

"You're not going," Michael responded with a sharp voice. "Connor will stay here with you, instead. I'll go."

"Like hell." She folded her arms and stared at him, defiance burning through her. There was no way she was going to stay behind. "I need to be there. I need to see this man for myself."

"She might be able to help." Jake peered at Michael.

"No." Michael released the word so fast she almost missed it.

"I'm going, whether you like it or not." She exited the kitchen and made her way to the foyer. She grabbed her purse off the hall table and waited by the silver elevator doors.

"If I let you go, you don't leave my side," he warned upon approach.

Why did he insist on treating her like a child? Maybe she did need protection, and maybe she was scared, but he didn't have to make her feel so damned weak. "Fine," she bit out, hating herself for not fighting back at his use of the words "let you go."

"Come on, then," he said after an obvious sigh.

She slid into the back seat of the SUV a few minutes later and clamped her hands together on her lap as they drove. Her body tensed as Michael talked with ease to Jake and Connor as they drove to Nathan's law firm. She hated the fact that he was different with them. More laid-back.

His face didn't strain with anger at the slightest provocation when he was talking with them.

The SUV rolled to a stop in front of a three-story brick building on the outskirts of town after a short drive. "This is it?" Kate shifted in her seat to gain a better view out the window, peering past Connor, who sat to her right. "I was expecting some shiny glass tower."

Jake, who was riding shotgun, turned and looked back at her. "It might not look like much, but he's a well-known attorney."

She nodded and stepped out of Michael's SUV. An uneasy anticipation grew inside her as she stared at the building. Her purse vibrated against her side, and she took a moment to glance at her phone, but she tucked it away when she saw who was calling. It was her father, for the twentieth time that day.

"You ready?" Jake asked, looking to Michael and Connor. They nodded back at him and followed him inside.

When they entered the lobby, they were greeted by a cute brunette, who was clearly doing her best not to stare in awe at the three gorgeous men standing before her. "Do you have an appointment?"

Jake held up his FBI badge. "We need to see Mr. Nathan Williams. It's urgent."

The woman hurriedly reached for her phone. She mumbled a few words and motioned for them to follow her. She stopped outside a conference room. "Please wait inside. Mr. Williams will be with you in a moment."

Once the receptionist left, Kate sat down at the large, oval, glass-top table and stared at the dim shadow of her reflection. She wasn't sure how she should react toward the man who might not only be her stalker but her mother's killer.

"I won't let anything happen to you." Michael rested his hand on her shoulder before moving toward the window and pressing his palm to the glass. He had changed out of his suit after they came treacherously close to having sex earlier.

What had she been thinking? One minute they were talking about the redhead and the next—he was going down on her. Her legs tightened at the memory.

When Kate looked up and saw Nathan Williams open the door, her body tensed for a very different reason.

Nathan's dark eyes locked onto Kate's as he stopped in the middle of the doorway. The man shifted his black blazer away from his hips as his hands slid into his pockets. The pull of his brow, the pinched skin on his forehead—he looked nervous.

She assumed it was her, or maybe it was the fact that there were three former Marines in the room.

Jake directed his attention to Nathan and reached for the man's hand. He introduced himself, Connor, Michael, and then Kate. "Thank you for meeting with us on such short notice." Jake sat down and waited for Nathan to sit, as well, but Nathan remained standing near the door.

"What can I do for you?" Nathan's accent was thick, and Kate guessed he was originally from Alabama or Mississippi. He folded his arms and leaned against the interior of the doorway.

Kate studied him. He was tall, well-built, and had a sort of Russian-meets-cowboy look to him. "I'm Kate Adams. I believe you knew my mother?" She was surprised by the sound of her voice. She hadn't planned on breathing a word during the meeting, but she found that her curiosity overwhelmed her common sense.

Nathan blew out a breath, a low whistle noise escaping his lips as he did so. "Um. Was your mother Elizabeth?"

"Yes," Kate softly replied.

"Yes. Yes, I knew her." His shoulders sank a little. "What—what is this about?"

"What can you tell me about your relationship with Elizabeth?" Jake swooped in to speak before Kate could.

"Listen, I'll answer any questions you have—but you need to tell me what this is all about." The lawyer in Nathan broke to the surface.

"Someone has been stalking Kate, and this person may be connected to Elizabeth's murder," Jake replied with blunt honesty.

Nathan's face paled a little, and then he approached the table and sat down. "Why are you coming to me?"

"Kate saw you a few times since she arrived in Charlotte—and, well, you're connected to her mother," Jake said.

Michael came up next to Kate and sat. It was comforting having her own personal superhero.

Nathan clasped his hands on the table and looked straight into Kate's eyes. "I'm recently divorced. I don't normally frequent nightclubs, but I was out one night, and I saw you dancing. And my heart stopped. I thought I saw a ghost. I thought I was looking at your mother. You're identical. I freaked out and took off." He paused for a moment while rubbing his hands together. It was clear he wasn't a poker player. "I saw you again in Uptown and then at the Maddox event. I had no idea you planned the ball. When I saw you there and heard your name . . . I realized you were Elizabeth's daughter."

Kate had to remind herself to breathe. She felt like she was swimming under water and wouldn't make it to the surface in time.

"I was your father's roommate in college. I hung out with your mother a lot because of that. But I had nothing to do with her death, and I am most certainly not stalking you."

"My father never mentioned you." But he'd never mentioned that her mother was murdered, either.

"We were best friends, but after what happened to your mom, he shut me out. I've bumped into him a few times in New York, but he had no interest in reconnecting. I guess I reminded him of his past, of your mother."

"Is there anything else you might be able to tell us that would help out?" Jake asked as he rose to his feet.

"Not that I can think of." Nathan stood and reached into his wallet for a business card.

"Do you know Erick Jensen?" Jake asked while taking the card from Nathan.

Nathan's lips pressed together, and his gaze shifted down. "I know all the big-name lawyers in town, but he also went to school with me. I didn't know him that well while we were in school, though."

"And now?" Jake pried.

"I'm a real estate lawyer. He's a defense attorney. Our paths rarely cross. I did see him at the ball, though." He folded his arms in front of him and directed his attention to Kate. "You really are your mother's daughter," he said with an affirming nod of the head.

She rose to her feet, and her knees almost buckled.

"We'll be in touch," Jake said.

Nathan held Kate's gaze until she looked away and exited the room. Something in her gut didn't feel right.

"I don't believe him," Michael said as soon as he slid behind the wheel.

Kate agreed, but she didn't say anything. She found herself in a daze as they drove back to Michael's place, only half-listening to the conversation. She wanted to be privy to the details of Jake's plan, but her mind reeled from meeting the man who may have killed her mother.

"Connor and I will follow up on Erick Jensen's story," Jake said as Michael pulled up in front of his building.

Jake's words shook Kate free of her stupor. She reached for the door handle to exit, but Michael had already come around and beat her to it. The gentle touch of his hand on her arm as he helped her out of the car made her spirit liven a fraction. "Thanks."

"I'll bring Kate upstairs," Michael said as he tossed his car keys to Connor. "See you guys later."

Kate and Michael rode the elevator in silence to his home. She watched as he turned on the security cameras and alarms. He investigated every inch of his loft before allowing Kate to wander freely, just to be on the safe side.

"You're being a bit overprotective," she announced when he returned to the front entrance, where she had been waiting.

"Better to be safe," he warned.

Perhaps seeing Nathan had put him on edge. *Great.* Just what she needed. Michael even further on edge.

"So, what should we do while we wait for the guys?" she asked, lacing her fingers together.

"Hungry?"

"Are we . . . should we talk about what happened earlier?" She moved toward him, and he took a cautious step back and into the kitchen.

Was he afraid of her? Afraid of losing control again? For a military man, he seemed to lack self-control when it came to Kate.

"What is there to say? We almost screwed up. We can't let that happen again. We need to concentrate on finding your stalker." He turned his back to her and grabbed a bottle of water from the fridge.

She watched his tan throat as he gulped down the cold water. She needed to cool off, herself. The circuits were misfiring in her brain. A crazy person was spying on her, and she could only think about how Michael's hands would feel on her body. But a distraction from her dark life might be what she needed. "*Did* we screw up?" She moved closer to him. The words that tumbled from her lips contradicted the cautious whispers inside her.

He withdrew the bottle from his lips and set it on the counter. "Yes," he said without hesitation. "Being with you again would be amazing, but you want more. I mean, you said you don't want a relationship because of your job, but you also don't just screw, right?" He scratched the back of his head and squinted a little as he observed her. "I guess I'm a little confused as to what you want, but I do know what I can and can't do."

She inhaled at his words and released a slow breath. "You help me forget the craziness that's going on in my life. I feel safe with you."

He moved closer to her and tilted her chin up to look into her eyes. "You shouldn't feel safe with me. I'm fucked up." His voice was low.

He almost looked—dangerous. But he was trying, too, wasn't he? To get her to be the one to back away?

Her eyes shut. "You don't scare me."

"I should. Do you know how many people I've killed? Do you know the things I've been ordered to do to get terrorists to talk? I'm a killer, Kate."

The grittiness to his voice and the reality of what he'd said caused her eyes to flash open.

She remembered the three scars on his chest, and she reached for him, but he recoiled.

Her hand remained outstretched in the air, cold and alone. She finally pulled it back to her side and narrowed her eyes on him. "You aren't a killer. You were saving lives."

He cupped the back of his neck and moved his head around a bit. He was uncomfortable—she could see it in his movements, and in the now-blank look in his eyes. He was shutting down on her. Again.

"I can't be with you. As much as I want you," he admitted and took a step away.

"But I need you." She'd never said those words to any man in her life. She'd never needed to.

"And you have me—to help you. But that's all I can give."

"Michael, you're not a bad guy. Please, believe me."

"You don't know me," he said with a hollow look in his eyes.

"Let me get to know you," she begged, taking a step closer. She was willing to sidestep her plans if it meant having a chance to be with this man.

"I'm sorry. I just can't." And then he turned and left.

She tried to fight the sick feeling that was enveloping her. She couldn't believe her life right now. Her mother had been murdered. She had a stalker.

And she was allowing herself to fall for a man with a field of ice around his heart.

* * *

KATE PACED BACK AND FORTH IN HER BEDROOM, TRYING TO WRAP her head around her situation, as well as her feelings for Michael.

She stopped moving when she thought she heard something.

Were Jake and Connor back?

She opened her door and started to walk down the hallway but halted at the sound of a voice—a woman's voice.

She edged down the hall as quietly as possible and peeked around the corner.

The redhead.

"You need to leave." Michael had his hand on the woman's forearm as he motioned with the other for the elevator.

"Please, I need to make things right." The woman's voice was muffled, as though she'd been crying.

"It's okay. Don't worry about it, but this isn't a good time to talk." Michael moved to the elevator and pressed a button. "Where are you staying?" he asked as the doors opened.

"Where I always stay," the woman responded as she stepped into the elevator.

"I'll be in touch. I promise."

Kate jumped back around the corner when the elevator doors closed, and Michael turned around. She rushed as fast as she could with light footsteps to her room and pulled the door shut behind her. She was thankful that his doors didn't creak upon closing.

Michael wasn't the problem, she realized while sitting on the bed. She was. She was letting this man affect not only her confidence but her ability to think rationally.

"You need to eat." Michael was knocking on her door a few minutes later. "I have a sandwich for you."

"I'm okay, but thank you," she said when he entered.

He ignored her words, placing a food tray beside her. "Eat." He folded his arms and stared down at her. Was he going to stand before her and watch while she ate? He had some nerve.

"Please." He softened his stance a little, but he didn't move. His eyes shifted to Kate's legs, and he took a step back from the bed. "I'll let you know when Jake and Connor are back," he said after clearing his throat.

Kate watched him leave and was glad that he pulled the door shut behind him. She stared down at the sandwich and fought the childish urge to throw the plate at the door. *Goddamn you, Michael Maddox.*

She felt something pulling inside her, swelling to the surface.

Tears warmed her cheeks, and she wet her lips. Her emotions pushed through her mind like a tsunami engulfing the shore. She tried not to give in to the pain, but she was at her breaking point.

CHAPTER SEVENTEEN

It was close to nine when Kate left her bedroom. She needed fresh air. She didn't see any sign of Michael as she entered the living room and exited to the balcony.

She wasn't sure how long she'd been standing there looking out at the city, but she could feel Michael's presence before he spoke.

"I have an update."

She tensed at the sound of his words and slowly turned to face him. "Yeah?"

He sat on one of the lounge chairs and gripped the arms. "Erick Jensen is out of town. And I spoke to your father. He corroborated Nathan's story. He also mentioned knowing Erick, as well. But I feel like something is off with your dad. I don't know."

"You think he's keeping something from you? Why would he do that?" She rubbed her arms, trying to push away a sudden chill.

"I'm not sure."

She forced herself to take a seat on the chair next to Michael. She didn't think her legs would support the weight of her body any longer.

"You cold? The temperature here drops a little at night."

"No, I'm okay. The breeze feels good." The coldness of her body and skin had nothing to do with the weather.

"You haven't heard from your stalker since you came here. Maybe he or she got scared off." He rubbed his temples and glanced at Kate.

"Regardless—"

"You still want to know who killed your mom." He stood and tucked his hands beneath his armpits.

She nodded, then tilted her head back, looking at the starlit sky. Did she believe in heaven? God? Was her mom up there somewhere, the woman that she'd never met?

She could feel the tears brimming to the edges of her eyes. Being in Charlotte was too painful—even if she hadn't found herself in such a crazy situation, she should have known how coming to this city would affect her.

"Kate!" Michael shouted her name, his face scrunching as he suddenly charged her way.

Before she could even respond, he grabbed her by the forearms and yanked her forward out of the chair. He pressed her to the ground, covering her body with his.

She looked up at him, breathless, as he cupped the back of her head to keep it from hitting the ground. He braced himself over her like some sort of human shield—but why?

"I want you to crawl into the house, okay?" he whispered.

"Wh—what?"

"Just do it. Now." He shifted back off her as she went to her hands and knees and crawled toward the parted doors. Fear clutched hold of her heart, wringing it tight—but she forced herself to keep moving.

Once inside, Michael stood and shut the doors, and then he commanded the blinds closed. "We're okay in here."

"What the hell was that all about?" She wrapped her arms around her chest, her body trembling as Michael grabbed his phone off the table.

He didn't answer her, instead, he made a call. "Jake, get over here now. It's urgent."

"Talk to me," she demanded once he ended the call.

He came in front of her and gripped her forearms, steadying his gaze on hers. "You had a sniper rifle trained on your chest." He inhaled a sharp breath and stepped back, releasing his hold. "The glass is bulletproof. Don't worry."

"I—what?"

"Your stalker had you in his sights. A red dot sight. I know one when I see it."

She could feel her body tighten, her skin crawl. She wanted to hide inside a shell, snap it closed, and bury herself at the bottom of the deep sea. The situation was hitting her in an all-too-real way. Her skin grew clammy, and her vision blurred.

The next thing she knew, Michael was rushing to her side and holding her upright. "You okay?"

"I think I should sit down." He lifted her into his arms and carried her to the couch. "You could've been killed. You used your body as a damn shield," she bit out, angry at him for risking his life for her—a woman he barely knew.

"Are you crazy? Of course, I'm going to protect you, but—"

"No, I never meant for you to put your life on the line for me. Jesus, Michael, I should leave—" Michael's fingers came over her mouth, cutting her off.

"Hell no." His fingers slipped free from her lips. "I'm in this with you until the end. Until whoever just tried to kill you is in jail or six feet under. Preferably the latter. Got it?"

Her eyes narrowed as she digested his words. "And after— what happens after?" she softly asked. But she knew, didn't she? Michael would disappear from her life once she was safe.

Michael bowed his head for a moment, his hand resting on her thigh. But before he could answer, the elevators buzzed.

"What's going on?" Jake blurted the second Michael let him in.

Kate swallowed back her emotion and looked up to see both Jake and Connor standing before her.

Michael pointed to the closed windows. "Someone had a red dot sight focused on Kate's chest."

"Shit. Are you okay?" Connor sat beside her.

She looked up into Connor's light green eyes and nodded. "Yeah, I think so."

"We might be able to peg the stalker's location. Can you show me where you think the sniper was located?" Jake asked while approaching the balcony doors.

"No, don't open them. What if the sniper shoots?" Kate threw her hand in the air.

"I won't go out there right now, don't worry." Jake turned toward Michael. "I can pull up the hotel blueprints. We should be able to triangulate the position of the shooter and go from there. He must be staying in my damn hotel."

Michael nodded and then left the room for a minute. He returned carrying his laptop and handed it off to Jake. "Connor, maybe we should get Kate's father over here," Michael suggested.

"No," she said. "I don't want him to know what happened. He'll freak."

"It's your decision," Michael responded. "Why don't you get some rest while we figure this out?"

"You think I'm capable of sleep?" Kate rose to her feet and watched as Jake sat in the armchair opposite of her and began working fast on the laptop.

"No, but maybe you should lie down," Michael answered while coming around behind Jake's chair so he could see the screen. "You're safe, remember. Bulletproof glass."

Thank God you're paranoid. Who else would install bulletproof glass, other than the president? Or maybe warlords? "Fine," she said.

"Everything's going to be okay." Michael cocked his head to the side as his eyes connected with hers.

For some reason, she was getting the vibe that there was some other message embedded in his words—but she figured she was reading into it.

* * *

"Your stalker's playing games. I don't think he intended to shoot you. He used a fake identity to pay for his hotel room. And he left a note on the bed," Jake said.

"He what?" She looked away from Jake and over at Michael.

Michael's mouth was closed and his lips sealed.

Kate reached for the small half-sheet of white paper that Michael offered her. Scribbled in black pen was a message: "They can't protect you from me, but I'll enjoy watching them try."

"We dusted the room for prints, but he left no evidence behind. Well, other than that note. He knew we would find the room. Clearly, he wanted us to."

She handed the paper back to Michael as a numbness overtook her limbs. Numb was good, though. Numb meant no pain.

"We've started looking at the hotel surveillance footage to see if we can put a face to the guy in the room," Jake said.

She watched from a few feet away, hands clenched at her sides, as Jake sat in front of the laptop with Connor at his side.

It was now after midnight. It had been three hours since someone pointed a sniper rifle at her. In what world was she living now? "How do you know who you're looking for?"

"Well, anyone who goes out of his way to avoid the cameras would be a good start," Jake said before shooting her an innocent, sideways grin. "Plus, we've narrowed the feeds down to the time when he pointed the gun at you."

She rubbed her arms and looked at the closed blinds. Her stalker had been at the hotel across the street. For how long? And he had been in her hotel room, watching her sleep, not so long ago.

"Wait. Stop right there," Connor said. He reached for Jake's computer and shifted it onto his lap.

Kate came up behind him and watched as Connor pressed a few buttons and zoomed in on the screen, focusing on the reflection of a man in the mirrored elevator doors. "I know him." There was an air of confidence in his voice as his face registered alarm. "It has to be him." He rubbed his beard and exhaled. "That's Dustin Scott."

"Shit, you're right. A former sniper for the Navy SEALs," Jake said.

"And he's a fucking psycho," Michael added. He was standing next to her now, and he pressed a hand to her back.

"What? You think he's my stalker?"

"Well, he's on the FBI's most wanted list. He's a hired hitman," Jake said.

Terror threatened to bring down her entire house of cards in about two-point-five seconds if someone didn't make her feel better soon.

"Dustin was in the Navy until he was discharged a few years ago. Word is that he flipped sides and sold secrets to the Taliban insurgents—he's the kind of guy who will sell his own mother to make a buck," Jake said.

Just great.

"But the government could never prove anything while he was in the military," Michael noted.

"Dustin's good. Really good." Was Connor trying to petrify her? "This isn't his normal gig, though. Whoever hired him must be paying a substantial fee."

"Let's take a break for a second," Michael said and reached for Kate's arm, guiding her to face him. "Are you okay?"

No! She was losing her mind. She began massaging her temples.

Was a murdering ex-Navy SEAL really stalking her? And

whom should she be more worried about—the sniper or the man or woman who was paying the sniper?

"Do you think that Nathan's our prime suspect?" she asked after taking a breath.

"I have no idea," Michael replied in a low voice.

"I assume you're canceling the auction dates on Friday?" Connor asked.

"Of course," Michael responded without hesitation.

"You would probably want to kill me if I asked you to keep them as planned." Jake was standing now, facing Michael.

Michael snorted. "This isn't the time to be making jokes."

"Hear me out for a second." Jake held his palms up, showing that he wasn't looking for a fight.

Kate stared at Michael, wondering how he would respond to Jake. He stood tense and focused, with a clamped jaw and fists at his sides. He was ready to box.

"Don't even suggest it." Michael glared at Jake with dark eyes —there was some unspoken conversation going on between them.

"That we use Kate as bait?" Jake raised a brow and Michael tensed. "Dustin won't expect Kate to be out in public after the stunt he pulled. It will piss him off that Kate isn't scared. If we show Dustin we aren't up for playing his games, then maybe he'll make an uncalculated and irrational move—and we can get him." Jake crossed his arms. "He obviously wants a challenge. He practically all but guaranteed zero access to Kate by focusing the sniper on her. I don't know what his deal is, but I do know that he'll never expect Kate to be on that date. He'll screw up, and we can get him."

"So, you think we can draw Dustin out?" Connor looked a little too casual as he remained seated. He leaned back and crossed his ankle over his knee.

"Not going to happen," Michael said in a low, but firm voice.

"Do I get a say in any of this?" Kate raised her hand in the air. "As scared as I am, hiding away in Michael's fortress will only prolong things. Jake is right about that. And I really want this over. I want to know who hired Dustin. I want my life back."

Michael took a step away from Kate and gripped the back of his neck. "Maybe his mission has only been to scare you. If he wanted to hurt you—or even kidnap you—then he wouldn't be playing such games."

"Understanding the mind of a lunatic is not so easy," Connor reminded them. "He enjoys the hunt. The challenge. Remember, he used to scour the globe for terrorists."

Connor was now on the receiving end of Michael's icy stare. "The discussion ends here," he said, and then left the room.

Kate heard a door slam. While the discussion was far from over, in her estimation, she realized Michael needed to cool off. With time, perhaps he would come around to his senses.

Or maybe he was right.

CHAPTER EIGHTEEN

"WHAT'S HE DOING HERE?" KATE FOLDED HER ARMS AND STARED at the man who had lied to her for twenty-seven years.

"Kate, please, I'm so sorry." David Adams entered the kitchen, moving with cautious steps toward his daughter.

She stood, her body slightly trembling as she held her coffee mug. "I don't want to see you. Not yet." She bit her lip as Michael entered from the living room, wearing faded denim jeans and a soft-blue T-shirt that matched his eyes. "Why is he here?" She finally set her cup down on the counter, then strode past her father to face her steely protector.

"Jake insisted he come." Michael shrugged at her. "David, maybe we should all sit down and talk."

Kate's face was hot. Fever hot. Her anger with her father ran deeper than even she had suspected. "David." She didn't have it in her to call him dad. With a feeling of satisfaction, she saw him flinch.

"Kate, I've been trying to reach you," her dad said once in the living room.

"How could you lie to me all these years? You made me think Charlotte was a place of pain for you because Mom died giving

189

birth to me. All these years, I believed that I killed my mother." She touched her chest, fighting to breathe, to keep speaking. "I've felt guilty for Mom's death my entire life." *Don't cry. Don't give in.* She sat down on the brown leather recliner and pressed her palms against her knees, bracing for support. She didn't want to break down in front of Michael, Jake, and Connor. She had to find her composure—she was unraveling and fast.

David came to her side and knelt before her. "I was trying to protect you. I didn't know if her murder was premeditated or not. Who kills a pregnant woman? I worried about your safety, which is why I didn't want you to come to Charlotte. I begged you not to come." His voice was hoarse and his eyes a little red.

"Maybe if you had told me the truth, I would have been more prepared! Now I have some lunatic stalking me." She gulped and steadied her gaze on Michael, who was standing a few feet away with arms crossed.

"Just come home with me. You'll be safe, I promise," her father pleaded as his fingers draped over the arm of the chair.

"I'm not going to be safe anywhere, now." She stood, unable to stomach the proximity to her dad. He was a stranger to her.

"You have to trust me. Come home," he said and stood.

Kate turned her back on everyone and approached the closed blinds. "I want you to go," she said, her voice breaking—pain slicing through her. Betrayed by her own father.

"I agree."

Kate faced Michael, glad he was on her side.

"I have one question for your father before he leaves." Jake reached for a piece of paper that was lying on the side table by the couch. "Why did Nathan Williams call you last night?"

Kate stood still for a moment and turned around, allowing Jake's words to wash over her. She noticed the muscles in Michael's face twitch enough to showcase his disbelief at what Jake had said.

Kate shifted her attention back to her father, who appeared to have aged since she last saw him in New York. His forehead was riddled with lines, and his cheeks were a sallow color. "How—how did you know he called me? Are you tapping my phone?" He looked uncomfortable. Guilty.

"Not yours, but Nathan's." Jake handed David the paper. "Nathan was on the phone with you for three minutes around eight last night."

David's gaze flickered up from the paper as he shoved it back at Jake. "Nathan called me because he was worried about Kate. He told me that you all showed up at his office."

"When was the last time you'd talked to him before that?" Jake inquired.

"I can't remember, but it's been years."

"You don't think Nathan had anything to do with Mom's death?" she asked.

"I told your pals here," David said, waving his hand in the air, "that your mom mentioned being followed, but I don't think whoever followed her—if she was even being followed, for that matter—killed her." He lowered his head. "If I had only gotten to the house a few minutes sooner, I could have prevented her death."

"Or been killed yourself." Connor made his voice known.

David lifted his head to meet Connor's eyes. "Her necklace was worth a fortune. I scared off the burglars with my arrival, and they must have grabbed the first thing of value that came to hand. The cops found the broken clasp on the floor."

"And if the murder was premeditated, couldn't the killer have taken the necklace as a souvenir?" Jake tipped his head.

Her father had no response.

"You keep changing your story. One minute you whisk Kate away from North Carolina out of fear of whoever murdered her mother, and the next minute, you insist that it was a robbery gone wrong." Jake took a step forward and folded his arms. The muscles of his biceps bulged. "Which is it?"

Kate released her breath. If she held it any longer, she might have passed out. She looked down at the hand that rested on her forearm. Was Michael trying to soothe her? "Dad?" She finally said the word—a word that felt different now . . . foreign, almost.

"Kate, trust me. I'm better suited to keep you safe. New York is where you belong," her dad said.

"I can't leave. Not yet." She took a small step closer to Michael —to the man that was willing to take a bullet for her last night.

Her dad studied them and then started for the elevator doors after a moment. "I'm not leaving Charlotte until you do. Call me when you come to your senses," he said, loudly enough for her to hear before he disappeared behind the silver doors.

"Should we have told him about Dustin?" she asked, peering up at Michael.

"No. He would've had a heart attack." Michael moved his hand to her shoulder.

"He's probably confused about everything, which is why he can't get his story straight." Well, she hoped that was the case, at least.

"Maybe," Jake replied.

Michael's hand lifted at the sound of his ringing cell phone. He reached into his pocket and studied it. "Shit. I have to go." He placed the unanswered phone back into his pocket. "Can you manage without me for an hour or two?"

"Do you have a work meeting?" Kate asked. She must be throwing his entire work schedule off-balance.

"Uh, yeah," Michael muttered.

"I'll be fine with these guys watching me," she said.

Michael looked over at his friends, then gave her a quick nod before leaving.

"Kate, there's something we need to talk about," Jake said a minute later, coming up in front of her.

Her eyes glistened with the tears that threatened to challenge her composure. "Yeah?"

* * *

KATE HADN'T SPOKEN TO MICHAEL ALL DAY.

By the time he returned to the loft, Kate had taken notice of his obvious exhaustion. His shoulders were slouched forward— unusual for him—and his eyes were a bit bloodshot.

She didn't dare approach him and found herself feeling a bit afraid that he might see through her, as well. He might realize she was keeping something from him.

She spent her afternoon eavesdropping on Jake, Connor, and Michael as they studied the movements of Erick Jensen and Nathan Williams and followed up on leads with the FBI in regard to Dustin Scott. But she didn't feel like involving herself in their conversation. Their talk of intelligence and software was a bit over her head. Still, every once in a while, she crept down the hall and stopped shy of view from the living area, to catch up on the details.

On her fourth time down the hall, her ears perked up.

"Michael, I understand you don't want Kate on her date, and she postponed her date earlier today, but I think you should still go on your date," Jake said.

She couldn't see Michael's reaction, but she could envision his body tensing and his facial muscles growing taut. His body gave away his emotions far more than his words, particularly when the emotion was anger or lust.

"Why the hell would I do that?"

Jake didn't respond right away. Kate pushed her hands against the wall and moved her body a little closer to the edge. Still, she kept enough distance to avoid being seen.

"Let Dustin believe you're going about business as usual. Since you won't let me parade Kate around, at least let him think that you aren't worried about him."

"Why do I care what Dustin thinks?"

"We have to play his game a little, or we won't win. We can't beat a psychopath if we sit back and twiddle our thumbs."

"You think I am sitting here twiddling my goddamn thumbs?"

"Come on, Michael. This is my job. This is what I'm trained for. We're talking about Dustin Scott. He's been on FBI and Homeland Security's radar for a while now. We need to catch the SOB." There was a pause. "If anyone understands this, it should be you. You spend your life helping the government catch scumbags like him."

"You think whoever hired him is a terrorist?" Disbelief echoed in his voice.

"No, but next week he might be working with ISIS or freaking Vladimir Putin for all we know. He needs to be stopped."

"Don't make me regret asking you for help. I will not let you use Kate. If you've turned this into some OP for your sake—"

"Sooner or later I need to report that Dustin is in Charlotte. I can't keep this a secret."

"Fuck. I'm not asking you to, but I want this to be about keeping Kate safe and not about Dustin."

"Don't the two kind of go hand in hand?" Jake shot back.

Kate placed her hand over her mouth as shock plowed its way through each of her organs before slamming into her heart.

Can I really help bring down a traitor?

"Michael, Jake has a point." It was Connor. He was usually the quiet one in the room. But every once in a while, he spoke up, his words slicing the tension in the air—or creating new waves of it.

"I need to think. It's been a long day. I'm gonna lie down for a couple of hours. Wake me if you have news."

She hurried back to her room and shut the door behind her. She needed to give Jake an answer, and she needed to do it while Michael was sleeping.

But what would she say?

* * *

"So?" Jake stood at the sight of Kate as she entered the

kitchen.

"You wear glasses?" she asked, avoiding the question.

He smiled and removed the black-rimmed frames. "Only when reading, or if I've been staring at a computer screen for hours." He gave her a small smile.

"Where's Connor?" she asked while taking a seat at the kitchen table, drumming her fingers as she considered her decision.

He sat across from her and leaned back in his chair. "Tailing Nathan."

"Oh. Well, I've thought about your proposal." She took in a nervous breath. "I'll do what you think is best, but Michael will flip."

"I'll take the heat. I can handle it." His voice was calm.

"I don't want him angry with you." She moved her hand to her mouth and examined him. He looked every bit as intimidating as Michael. Well, almost.

"Trust me, everything will work out. This is my job." He stretched his arm out and reached for her hand. With his touch, she felt calmer. Safe.

When in fact, he was putting her in danger.

"What was that?" he asked as his body straightened.

Kate tilted her head in the direction of the sound. Her shoulders slouched forward, feeling Michael's pain—the pain he wouldn't share with her. "He's having a nightmare." She started to stand.

"I'll handle it." Jake motioned for her to sit back down, and then he left the room.

A few minutes later, she heard a commotion coming from down the hall. And then something broke. A lamp, maybe.

"You okay?" she asked when Jake came back in the kitchen with a bloody lip.

"Yeah." He grabbed a paper towel, wet it, and brought it to his mouth.

"Is Michael okay?" she asked, her voice stitched with worry.

"He will be."

CHAPTER NINETEEN

When Michael entered the living room, dressed in gray suit pants that were tailored to his body with perfection, Kate had to hold her breath. The luxurious material fit him in just the right way. Her eyes traveled the length of his body, slipping below his hips and moving slowly back up to his face.

It was Friday. Date night. She tried to fight the odd feelings that swirled around in her stomach. Worrying about Michael going on a date with the gorgeous Dallas girl should have been the last thing on her mind.

She had gone out of her way to avoid speaking to Michael since she had agreed to Jake's plan. Even now, she worried he might develop telepathy and read her thoughts. "Why haven't we heard from Dustin?" She forced the words from her mouth.

"He's playing a sick game," Michael said as he fixed the sleeves of his pressed, black dress shirt. He steadied his hand atop the nearby recliner. "You okay?" He tilted his head to the side.

She jerked her attention away from his eyes and found herself staring at his parted lips. "Yeah," she whispered.

It had been days since she'd thought about sex, but now her

mind was slamming into dangerous territory at full force. "Have fun tonight."

He took a step closer to her. "You know I don't want to go." He touched her shoulder, and his eyes drew her in.

She was surprised Jake had convinced him to go. As much as she believed Jake was right about drawing out Dustin Scott—it also scared the hell out of her.

"It's for the veterans," she reminded him. The ball had been only last weekend, but it felt like a million years had lapsed in between.

"I would have postponed. You know I'm only doing this because Jake insists." He removed his hand from her body. "Thanks for not fighting me on this. Thank you for postponing your date."

A twinge of guilt coiled inside her abdomen. She wanted to blame it on the excruciating workout she had completed that morning in the hopes of ridding her body of tension, but she knew it was something more.

"Connor, you'd better keep your eyes on her while I'm gone," Michael barked. Connor was in the kitchen, but Michael was loud enough for him to hear.

Connor stepped into the living room and looked at Kate, shooting her a sympathetic glance. A moment later, Jake came into view.

"You ready?" Jake tucked his gun in the back of his pants and slipped on a blazer to hide the weapon.

She'd never seen a gun up close before unless you counted passing by a police officer with one in the holster.

"You think Dustin will show up? Is Michael in danger?" she asked.

"No, I don't think Dustin will show his face tonight, but I won't let Michael out of my sight. Just in case," Jake answered.

"I don't need a bodyguard," Michael grumbled.

And he probably didn't. She was sure he could kill someone with his bare hands if he needed to.

"Michael, please be careful." Her brows drew together as she studied him.

"Everything will be fine." He gave her one last, long look and headed for the elevator.

She wanted to pinch herself, to wake up. Perhaps she was stuck in some sort of never-ending carousel of a nightmare.

But the pain and fear that streamed through her body were reminders enough that she was very much awake.

* * *

KATE TOOK A SIP OF HER MERLOT AND SET IT BACK ON THE TABLE with an unsteady hand. "What did you say? I'm sorry." She looked down at the sushi on her plate, feeling no sense of appetite.

Her date, Ethan, shifted in his seat and stared at Kate. "You okay? You seem a little preoccupied."

Normally a sexy Southern accent and incredible gray eyes would impact her, but right now all she could think about was her safety. And, of course, Michael. She couldn't stop the horrible images that spewed forth in her mind. Each scenario played out in her head, each ending with either her or Michael dead—or both. "I've had a lot going on lately. I'm sorry." She smiled at him and ran a hand through her blonde hair, which was flowing in soft waves down her back. "Thanks for doing the interviews and pictures with the newspapers before dinner. It'll help further the cause for the veterans."

She almost forgot about needing to have her photo snapped for the two papers. She had to bare her teeth and grin for the photographers. Would the images get her in even more trouble with whoever hired Dustin?

"Well, tell me about your business. I heard you were thinking of opening a third location in Charlotte. Is it true?" Ethan asked.

"I think I'm going to stick with New York and Boston, for now. I have my hands full with those locations, and I would probably be biting off more than I could chew by bringing my business to Charlotte." Her eyes scanned the room, searching for Connor. When she saw him at the bar, she felt a little better.

"Do you like what you do?"

She was in no mood for this conversation, but she forced herself to play the role. Pretend everything was normal, and that she wasn't scared of Dustin Scott. "Yeah, I think so. I didn't have much of a choice, though. My stepmother needed me to help out. But, it's probably the perfect job for me since I'm obsessed with planning things." *I didn't plan to fall for Michael, though.*

"Will you stick with it?"

"I think so." *If I survive.*

"You could always come and join the finance world. It's very riveting."

You have a great smile, she decided. And he was good-looking. He definitely had the angular features and soft eyes that she adored . . . even though he, and every man, seemed to pale in comparison to Michael Maddox. Still, she hoped he could distract her from the fear that was burning her insides. "For some reason, investments and acquisitions don't exactly sound sexy to me." She returned his smile. It was her first real smile of the evening.

When Ethan finished his sushi, he looked up at the approaching waiter. "You ready to order?"

"I'll have the egg noodles and chicken." She wondered if she'd be able to force herself to eat.

"Same for me." Ethan handed their menus to the waiter and focused his attention on Kate. "I guess we have similar tastes."

She could practically read his mind and almost felt sorry for him. He had no idea how little of a chance he had. It wasn't fair.

"Thank you again for bidding on me. It's for a good cause."

"I would have asked you out, regardless." He brought his glass to his lips, but his eyes never left hers.

She downed the rest of her wine and rolled her tongue over her front teeth. *Where are you, Connor?* Her nerves pushed to the forefront of her mind when she noticed Connor was MIA from the bar. Was everything okay?

"You're beautiful. I can't believe Michael didn't snatch you up for himself."

Ethan's comment snapped her attention back front and center. *If only you knew.* "His loss," she joked.

"Lucky for me." She relaxed when she spotted Connor near the entrance of the restaurant. He didn't look alarmed, so she shifted in her seat, hoping to seem casual.

After the meal ended and she carried her weight through the polite conversation portion of the evening, Kate proceeded with the rest of Jake's instructions.

Ask Ethan to a club. Get out wide in the open.

She couldn't believe she was purposefully becoming a target for a psychopath. But Ethan kept the drinks coming, and the alcohol soothed her, alleviating her nerves.

For a moment, she almost forgot that a murderous hitman for hire was stalking her—was possibly watching her at that very moment.

Tipsy became somewhat of an understatement, and she noticed Connor growing edgy at the bar. He had been against Jake's plan from the beginning, but he'd agreed to it when Jake explained that, once they had Kate's willing cooperation, they were under direct government orders to proceed. Jake had reported to the FBI that Dustin Scott was in Charlotte—and now her case was a federal one. No pressure . . .

"Come here," Ethan said, grabbing her hand and pulling her to the dance floor. They were at the nightclub where Kate had spilled her drink on Michael. That was the night her life had changed. No —her life changed the moment she received the phone call from Julia Maddox.

As much as she wanted to regret coming to Charlotte, she

would never have discovered the truth about her mother, and she wouldn't have met Michael. Of course, she wasn't sure if meeting Michael was a good thing or not. The jury was still deliberating.

Kate attempted to focus as she danced with Ethan, but the alcohol was going to her head. His hands brushed over her bare shoulders before skimming down the sides of her pale yellow, sleeveless dress. He pulled her closer and wrapped his arms snug around her waist when an Ellie Goulding song blared through the room. She shut her eyes as they moved around the floor, but she kept thinking of Michael.

When Ethan's lips touched hers, she blinked her eyes open in surprise. She took a step back, breaking their kiss.

She wasn't ready for the touch of another man's lips—alcohol or not. "Sorry, I just . . ." She didn't know what to say, and the music was so loud that it was probably pointless to speak, anyway.

"That's okay. Sorry."

She took a nervous breath and began to search for the beat once more.

Then terror struck her heart.

It wasn't Dustin watching her.

She gulped at the sight of him. "Michael," she whispered.

Michael stood a few feet away from the dance floor. His shirt sleeves were rolled to the elbows, and his hands were fisted at his sides.

Ethan followed her gaze and looked over his shoulder.

"Kate, it's time to go," Michael demanded after he'd stalked toward them with purposeful strides.

Kate looked back at Ethan, unsure what to do or say. He was reaching for her hips, but his touch felt foreign and wrong. Especially in front of Michael.

"Kate," Michael said with a strained voice. "Now."

"I should go," Kate said, pulling free from Ethan's grasp. "Thank you for the date."

Ethan looked to Michael. It didn't take a genius to figure out why she had pulled away from his kiss now.

"Goodnight," Ethan said. He leaned in and kissed her on the cheek.

She gave him an apologetic glance and then allowed Michael to pull her away. He moved so fast that she almost lost her balance in her four-inch heels. Holding her by the wrist, Michael guided her toward the door of the club.

"I'm so sorry," she cried as they stepped outside.

"Michael," Connor shouted, jogging to catch up.

Michael spun around to face Connor. "What in the hell were you thinking? And what the fuck is going on?"

Connor held up his hands. "I'm sorry. I'm following orders."

"Orders?" he bit out. "Whose orders?" he asked, leaning in toward Connor.

"Mine," Kate shouted. "I insisted I keep my date with Ethan. I couldn't stay cooped up any longer," she lied.

Michael released his grip on her and edged back a few feet.

Tell him the truth. She rubbed her wrist as if he'd burned her. "I'm sorry. I wanted to find Dustin. To draw him out. I'm tired of hiding."

Connor grimaced and shook his head at Kate, warning her with narrowed eyes. "Jake thinks you should take her somewhere else."

"Where? Somewhere else that's out in the open so Dustin can get to her . . ." Before Kate or Connor could respond, Michael reached for Kate's hand. "Come on, I know where to take you." He glared at Connor. "Tell Jake I'll call him. Don't have him waste his time calling me."

Michael's Audi was waiting near a valet by the curb, its engine still on, ready to go. "Kate," he ordered, opening the door for her.

Not wanting to upset him any further, she slipped inside the car without protest.

After tipping the valet, Michael got in the car, shifted gears, and pulled out onto the road. He gripped the wheel, his knuckles whitening. "What were you thinking? Might I remind you that a killer is following your every goddamn move?" He looked over at her. "You lied to me."

"How did you find me? You weren't supposed to know . . ." She hoped she could distract him for a moment.

"I installed a tracking device on your phone."

"What?" This time, she was the one seething with irritation. He hadn't even blinked as he admitted the gross invasion of her privacy. She reached into her clutch and touched her phone self-consciously. "When? Why?"

"After the ball."

He was out of line. She was too upset to talk, so she remained silent as they drove, and she was thankful he copied her.

"Where are we going?" she asked a little later when she realized they were leaving the city, heading north.

"To my place on Lake Norman," he replied. His foot pressed a little harder on the pedal, accelerating the car to an almost dangerous speed.

"You have a place there?" That was the last place she wanted to go. Lake Norman was where her mother was murdered.

"Yes." He continued to increase his speed.

"Be careful," she warned, noticing the roads were slick from an earlier rain shower.

He sped up a little more, probably just to spite her.

After twenty-five minutes of driving (which should have taken thirty-five minutes), they pulled up in front of a wrought iron gate. He punched a few buttons on the electronic keypad by the gate, and it opened. They drove almost half a mile. Huge trees lined the property and the long driveway.

Kate drew in a deep breath when they reached the house. "You have a log cabin?" She tried not to betray the shock in her voice. She expected a mansion, not a one-bedroom cabin on the water. And that made her like him that much more. "It's very . . . *you*."

He parked in front of the house and got out of the car. Without waiting for her, he walked to the front door and unlocked it.

There was no way she would be able to walk to his house in her stiletto heels. She stared down at the rocky ground and contemplated her options. When she looked back up, Michael was in front of her. He must have realized her dilemma. He reached for her and scooped her into his arms.

She looked up at him as he held her and walked. "Did you like kissing him?"

His anger toward her was for more than one reason, she realized. "You've got to be kidding! Why the hell do you care?" she asked as her feet found the ground once inside.

He ran his hands through his thick hair, mussing it up. "Do you want him?" His voice was like hard steel.

He had no right to be acting like this—no right. Being angry for keeping her date a secret was one thing, but being jealous about it? "Why'd you bring me here?" She crossed her arms, but before she could react, he was moving toward her, backing her up against a wall. He propped a hand on each side of her head, and she was imprisoned by his frame.

She looked at his tanned, muscular forearms, and her gaze traveled up to his shoulders, neck, and mouth. "Why am I here?" she repeated, her voice lower this time.

"You're safer with me. Away from everyone. I don't care what you think." He cocked his head to the side. His face hovered a few inches from hers.

His lips were too close.

"I don't feel particularly safe right now."

"I'm going to ask you one more time. Did you like it when Ethan kissed you?"

Who the hell do you think you are? She pressed her hands against his solid chest and tried to push him away from her. "Get away."

But he wouldn't budge—instead, his mouth covered hers. He

kissed her for only a few seconds before she pulled away. She was too damn frustrated with him to have his lips anywhere near hers. "Why are you doing this to me? You're hurting me more than any damned stalker could . . ."

"Shit. I'm sorry." He dragged his hands down his face.

She tried to swallow her emotions, but they were running skin deep. "Do you want me or not? I'm so confused." And what did she even want? Her mind was muddled, her feelings screwed up with everything that had happened to her in the last week.

He took a step back. "I can't get you out of my head. Even with everything going on, I just can't . . ."

She watched him for a moment, trying to anticipate his next move, and then she started to walk away from him. Through a long window on the other side of the room, she could see the lake, glinting in the moonlight.

He caught up with her. "I want you, Kate," he said gruffly. He turned her to face him.

The pain in her eyes must have been obvious because he softened his grip and dropped his head.

"Sex isn't enough for me. It never will be." She looked away and down at the oak floors.

He touched her face and tilted her chin up. "What if I want more?"

Could she believe him? "You don't. You just don't want to 'share' me with anyone else."

"Of course, I don't want you to be with anyone else. Seeing you with Ethan . . . slayed me. But I want you for more than that."

She lowered her eyes, hating her body for trembling, betraying her emotion. She wanted to believe that he wasn't speaking from some primal need to possess her.

Her breath hitched when he touched her mouth, rubbing his thumb over her lips.

Her fragile barrier was slipping. She tried to cling to it, but it was pointless.

She wanted him, too. To hell with her plans. She knew the moment they'd first kissed she'd rather live an uncertain and unplanned life—if it meant having a heart full of love. She'd just been too afraid to admit it then.

She released a ragged breath, and then pressed up on her feet and found his lips.

He cupped her face with his hands and brought her closer to him, giving him better access to her mouth. He growled as her tongue slipped between his lips, searching for an even more profound connection.

She stumbled, but he held onto her. "Michael . . ."

He took a step back, lifted her into his arms, and carried her to the bedroom. He flipped on the light as they entered. He set her on the bed and stared down at her.

She looked up at him in awe. He was the most incredible man she had ever encountered. She watched as he began to unbutton his black collared shirt. His hard body and gunshot wounds were exposed when he pulled his shirt off. His eyes never left hers as he maneuvered out of the rest of his clothing.

Naked, he moved toward her and took off her heels. He trailed kisses up her legs, and pushed her dress up, exposing her sheer white panties. She sat up so he could remove her dress. He slipped it off over her shoulders, revealing her strapless, white demi-bra.

He was taking his time—drinking her in and making her equally drunk with need. He brushed his mouth along her neck as he unhooked her bra and tossed it to the floor.

She murmured as he held his weight over her, pushing her back down, taking her breasts in his hands, massaging them—twisting and tugging on her nipples.

She gripped his back and arched her body when his mouth began to devour her breasts, teasing her with his tongue. His hand moved over her panties and dipped beneath the fabric, touching her sex with slow and deliberate movements. She was becoming almost painfully aroused. She reached for his cock and moved her hand over his long, hard length.

He groaned at her touch and released her nipple from his mouth. He captured her lips again as he pushed his fingers inside her. Her body tensed and shook with desire, needing more. He moved his mouth down her body and to her center. Her hips bucked as his tongue darted between her thighs.

Her nipples hardened, and she moved her hand over her own chest. She didn't want to orgasm yet, but she couldn't hold back. Her body exploded with the ecstasy his touch had built inside her after only a few minutes.

She motioned for him to flip to his back. She kissed his throat, and her mouth wandered over his pectoral muscles. Her lips moved down to find his happy trail and his hard erection. She kissed around the base and placed wet, sucking kisses on his inner thighs. She captured his hard-on with her mouth, and he groaned.

She took almost all of him in one languorous swallow. He looked down at her as she tightened her mouth around him.

"I want you," he said in a low, guttural voice a few minutes later.

And with one quick movement, she was on her back again, and he was braced over her. She hadn't even seen him reach for the condom, he was so quick.

His eyes tore through her, making her feel so many emotions that she couldn't think straight.

And then she felt him. He moved inside of her—slow at first, and then deeper and faster. He leaned down to kiss her as their bodies collided. His kiss rocked something free inside of her. She'd had her own walls up for so long that she hadn't even realized they were there. She'd protected herself with lists and plans—never letting anyone in, but Michael had broken through, even if he hadn't meant to.

And when their lips parted, he focused on her eyes, and she knew something was different about this time. The way he looked at her as they had sex—no, made love—it made her feel special, somehow.

Her body began to quiver and build again as he rubbed his hand over her wet center in rhythmic time with his thrusts. And then his head bowed as he found release.

She watched as the gorgeous man fell to pieces inside her.

"You're amazing," he whispered in her ear as their bodies parted.

She brushed the back of her hand over his cheek and shifted to her side to get a better look at him, her Man of Steel. "How did we end up here—again?"

He perched his head on his hand and ran his fingers through her long hair, pushing it off her face. "I guess I can't stay away from you."

CHAPTER TWENTY

"HOW'D YOUR DATE GO?" KATE LEANED AGAINST MICHAEL ON the porch swing with her legs crossed up over the edge as she eyed the lake. She brought the coffee mug to her lips and glanced over her shoulder, waiting for him to respond.

"Horrible. The whole time I was eating dinner, all I could think about was you. And when I went home, and you were gone . . ." He pushed against the ground, giving the swing a little more momentum.

"I thought about you, too," she admitted.

He wrapped his arm around her shoulder and pulled her closer to him. "I wish you didn't go out. Why would you use yourself as bait like that? Why lie to me? Was it really your idea?"

She watched a sailboat pass on the tender morning breeze. Could Dustin be on that boat? Watching them? Until they captured him, she would never be able to breathe easy. She had allowed herself to get caught up in the moment with Michael the night before, but now she had to put her game face back on and focus on the danger at hand.

"Kate?"

She pulled her legs off the railing and set her feet on the

ground, resting her cup next to the swing. "Why'd you decide to bring me here?" She was desperate to avoid the truth.

"Because the second I saw you with Ethan, I knew I had to have you all for myself. I want to keep you here for the weekend—keep you safe. Tucked away from all the Ethans and Dustins of the world."

His honesty was surprising. And refreshing.

"I won't let anything happen to you, I promise. But, if I'm going to keep you safe, I need the truth."

She stood and faced him. He remained sitting on the swing but brought the rocking motion to a halt. His bare feet pressed against the planks beneath his soles—veins slightly evident there. The man was always so tense—every part of his body.

"If I tell you the truth, will you promise not to flip out?"

"I can't make that promise." He cocked his head, his brows furrowing as he studied her.

Her shoulders sank forward. "Jake suggested I go on the date and not tell you."

He shut his eyes as his lips pulled together. "Go on."

Sure—and have you kill your best friend. But she knew there was no way Michael would let this go. "He explained to me the danger of letting Dustin remain on the loose for any longer. He told me the big picture. It's not about me. Dustin is a threat to national security. He's a danger, and if I can help bring down a traitor—"

"Let me handle Dustin," he interrupted as his eyes opened. "Your safety should never be sacrificed. That's non-negotiable for me." He set his mug down and rose to his feet. His hands swept up to both her cheeks. "If anything happened to you . . ." He shook his head, released her, and took a step back. "I'm going to kill Jake. And Connor," he grumbled and turned away from her.

"Please. Jake's doing what's right. And Connor was trying to protect me."

He crossed the deck and leaned his forearms over the side railing, looking out onto the greenish water.

"Jake's a Fed now. He may have to follow the rules, but I don't give a damn about anything right now but keeping you alive."

"That's not true." She lowered her forehead against his back and wrapped her arms around his body. "If Dustin gets away and hurts other people, and we could have stopped him . . . you wouldn't be able to live with yourself. That's not who you are, and you know it."

His hand covered hers against his core, and he released a deep breath. "Maybe we can just stay here forever," he said after a minute.

"Not a bad idea." Of course, she knew they were pipe dreaming. But she'd give herself one more minute to live in the fantasy world before they had to delve into something much uglier. "Is this another one of your getaways?"

He started to turn, so she dropped her hold and stepped back. He leaned against the railing and folded his arms. "After being in the Marines, sometimes I need to be alone. I need a place to silence the . . ." He looked down, but she reached out and rested her palm on his cheek, and he closed his eyes at the gesture.

"Not a day goes by that I don't think about Afghanistan. Or Iraq. That's what I dream about when I get those nightmares."

The buzzing noise of a distant boat and the soft sounds of the water lapping against the land became white noise as she stared at him.

"My men and I were on a routine mission. We were sent to gather intelligence in the Helmand province in Afghanistan. My platoon usually travels, does some recon, and makes sure that everything is safe before more troops come." He opened his eyes, and there was so much pain evident there that she could barely stand to look at him. He was hurting so damn bad, and he needed someone so much more than she realized. "It was supposed to be deserted, but our information was inaccurate. I can still smell the smoke. I can still see the debris of the IED explosions all around me. We were sitting ducks. Surrounded. Almost everyone died."

His tan throat moved as he swallowed. "An explosion blasted near me, knocking me off my feet, and then I felt the first bullet splice through my shoulder. I was on the ground, dust in my face as the boots approached me. The insurgent was dragging someone. A friend. The guy had a knife to him, and I was the last person he would see before his throat was slit."

Her heart slammed against her rib cage, hating the words he would have to utter next, and hating herself for making him relive the memory.

Two empty blue eyes were staring back at her, almost in a daze. "And then the guy took out his gun and shot me twice. Somehow, Jake got to me and kept me alive long enough until secondary forces swooped in to fight off the Taliban insurgents. Not a day goes by that I don't regret that I lived. I just keep seeing his eyes— looking up at me with such horror. It should have been me."

She couldn't fight back the tears any longer. They rushed free over her face. He moved his thumb across her lips.

"Don't cry," he said and cradled her head against his chest. "Please, don't cry for me."

* * *

"Answer." Michael slammed his cell phone down on the couch and rubbed his temples. He had called Jake five times in the last five minutes, with no answer.

He glanced over at the bedroom. The door was shut, and he assumed Kate was still resting. He'd burdened her with his past, and she'd broken down as a result. He should never have opened his mouth given what she was going through right now.

Stupid.

She'd need to eat at some point, though. His cabin had coffee and granola bars, and that was it. He couldn't risk going to the store, and he hated the idea of having a delivery man come to the house, but he had no choice.

He grabbed his phone and ordered a pizza online. After, he dialed Connor.

"Hey, man."

"Shit, Connor. What's going on? I can't get hold of Jake. Is everything okay?" He ruffled his hair and walked into the small kitchen.

"Yeah. Jake's working on some leads. He knows that if he talks to you, you'll just flip out, which you have every right to do."

"Where are you guys? My place?" He tried to keep his anger in check, at least for the moment.

"We're close to you, actually. We're staying at a hotel in Cornelius. Jake thought we should be nearby."

Michael was quiet for a moment. "Is Jake still using Kate as bait?" He pressed his hand on the counter, trying to steady himself.

"No," Connor said after what felt like too long. "He wants to keep a close eye on you and Kate. Give you some backup."

For some reason, Michael didn't believe him. "Tell Jake to call me."

He turned around when he heard the bedroom door open and ended the call, shoving the phone into his pocket.

"Something wrong?" she asked with a soft voice.

"Jake's ducking my calls. Afraid of me, I guess."

She gave him a weak smile and rubbed her arms as if a chill had snuck up on her. She was wearing some of his sister's clothes—skintight white jeans and a white T-shirt with no bra. Julia used the cabin every so often and had a few things stored there.

"I ordered pizza," he said while scratching the back of his neck, trying to look away from her nipples, which were poking against the thin material of the shirt. This wasn't the time or place to be getting a damn erection. *Jesus.*

She nodded and took a seat on the couch, clasping her hands on her lap. "I'm not hungry."

"You need to eat. It's getting late, and all you've had is coffee."

"That's not true. We split the granola bar you found in your cabinet earlier."

"Yeah, well, that's not enough." He came up next to her and sat down and reached out for her hand. Her fingers were freezing, and her hand was shaking a little. "Let me grab you a blanket."

"I'm fine. You can keep me warm," she said while looking up at him beneath long lashes, her eyes puffy a little from crying earlier. He was pretty sure she'd had a tear-jerker session as a result of a lot more than the heavy shit he'd laid on her—the woman was dealing with a whole mess of a situation, and he couldn't begin to imagine how she must be feeling.

Michael tugged her against him and held her tight. She rested her head on his shoulder, and her hand slipped up to his chest. His heart was racing, and he knew she'd be able to tell beneath her palm.

It was part nerves about what was going to happen with Dustin, but also because of fear—he'd opened up to this woman. He'd never opened up to anyone. And he had no clue if he'd be able to continue to be this man—the man she needed . . . or if he'd wind up hurting her.

The thought of causing her any more pain was unbearable, but he didn't know if he could trust himself. This was unchartered territory.

They sat in silence, holding each other until the delivery man sounded the buzzer at the gate.

Michael grabbed the 9mm he kept in his safe and tucked it at the back of his pants and then went to meet the delivery guy.

Fortunately, the guy appeared normal, and so he handed the kid a hundred. "Keep the change."

The delivery man's face cracked into a deep smile. "Thanks, man."

Michael watched the kid enter his car and waited until he was out of view before heading back into the house.

"I guess you didn't need your gun."

He set the pizza down in the kitchen next to the bottle of soda and put the gun back in his bedroom. When he came into the kitchen, he found Kate peeking inside the pizza box. "Looks like someone is hungry, after all." He grinned at her as she reached for a slice of pepperoni.

She rolled her eyes at him and slipped the pizza into her mouth.

He grabbed a slice, too, before reaching for his phone, hoping for a text, at the very least, from Jake. The sun was beginning to set. The gold light spilled onto the lake, and his concerns grew with each passing minute.

After finishing two more pieces of pizza, Kate spoke up again. "What's the plan?"

He moved away from the back door and faced Kate. Before he had a chance to answer, his phone began to ring. "Must be Jake." He grabbed his phone off the table by the couch. "I've been trying to get ahold of you," he answered with pained irritation.

"I'm sorry. We're trying to get some stuff worked out. Can you head over to our hotel?"

"I don't know if we should leave right now," Michael answered, contemplating the risks involved in traveling, especially at the late hour.

"You shouldn't stay there." There was a pause on the line. "Michael, did you know David had a paternity test run at the hospital the day Kate was born? Something has been bothering me about him, and I looked into a few things last night."

Michael looked over at Kate, wondering how she might react if she knew. And then there was a beep on his phone. "I'm getting a call, hang on." He transferred to the other line. "Hello?"

"Hello, Mike. Or is it Michael now?" The voice was low but smooth around the edges. It echoed loudly from the receiver—he must have bumped the speakerphone button by accident. "Did I catch you at a bad time?"

"Oh my God," she whispered.

His eyes locked on hers just as the power went out. The last bit of sun hanging above the water filled the room with blue shadows.

He moved toward her, gripped with sudden alarm, needing to protect her. "What the hell do you want?" Michael growled.

"Judging by the swarm of officers at the nearby hotel, I assume you all have figured out who I am." There was a deep and eerie snicker on the end of the line. "I guess the real game is about to begin."

Before Michael could respond, the call ended.

"We need to leave." She pulled herself tight against him.

"That's what he wants. I need to call Jake." But when he tried to call him back, he realized he didn't have a signal. "Shit." He blew out a heated breath. "Lost service. He's probably using a jammer, which means he's close."

"We should go, right?"

They couldn't stay there, but if they left . . .

With quick steps, Michael kept Kate at his side as he moved from the semi-dark living room to the bedroom where he retrieved his gun. "I don't want to take you out of here, but I guess we don't have a choice." Kate would be in danger no matter what he did—and it was all his fault. He should never have brought her to the cabin. He should never have fooled around with her last night when Dustin was out there, discovering his weaknesses.

They rushed outside, and he held his gun in one hand and the flashlight in the other. Kate pressed her hand against his shoulder, following his lead to the car.

He studied his Audi with the light, checking for any signs of tampering. "Stand back," he cautioned as he unlocked the vehicle and turned it on. He pulled up the LCD screen and tapped a few buttons, performing a quick, systems check for interference. He couldn't risk the car blowing up with Kate inside.

"All clear," an electronic voice from the car announced.

"We're good. Get in."

She secured her belt and shifted to better face him. "I'm scared."

"I know, but it'll be okay." He couldn't look her in the eyes as he spoke, because he wasn't sure if he was being honest. His gut was telling him they were already screwed.

He kept his eyes trained on the thick wood surrounding them as he drove down the long driveway. They needed to get out of the dark, and fast.

He tightened his grip on the wheel with one hand and repositioned the other to grasp hold of the gun in his lap, even though he wanted to be holding onto her, instead.

Where are you, you son-of-a-bitch? His eyes flitted each direction as they drove down the back road. There were still a few miles to go before they reached safe—or safer—ground.

When he caught sight of two bright headlights flashing on from an upcoming side road, he immediately braked.

But he was too late.

The sound of the two metal objects crashing into each other was deafening. The airbags were like a harsh punch in the face as they exploded inside the car.

His Audi slid off the road, only to be stopped by a tree, which caused a secondary jolt of his head forward and back.

Kate's screams shot through him. He tried to move, to free himself from the seatbelt, but the airbag was in his way. He searched blindly for his gun with a blood-streaked hand.

His hands slipped against the seatbelt buckle.

Get the fuck out. Get to her. His brain shouted desperate orders to his battered body.

When the buckle finally unlatched, he reached for the door handle and tried to fight his way free from the airbag. He tumbled out of the car and hit the ground with a large smack, the pain in his shoulder slicing through him.

He could no longer hear Kate, which made him more nervous. He started to get up when he saw boots closing in on him.

The same military-grade boots appeared in his mind. A memory of Afghanistan . . . of the Taliban insurgent who'd slit his friend's throat.

He shook the image free. He had to stop Dustin before he got to Kate. Where was his gun?

"You can't save her. Not today, anyway."

Michael started to push off the ground, ready to lunge toward Dustin. But the last thing he saw was a gun in his face. And the last thing he felt was an all-too-familiar pain.

CHAPTER TWENTY-ONE

"I GAVE YOU QUITE THE DOSE OF MORPHINE. YOU MIGHT FEEL A little nauseous."

Kate had surgery once. She'd had her wisdom teeth removed, and she had been nervous to be put under anesthesia, so the doctors had given her something to calm her down. It had felt something like this.

She struggled to control her thoughts and fight through the blur of memories in her brain. Where was she?

As if emerging from a dark tunnel, she started to see the light.

A car crash. Screaming—her own shrieks. Michael? Oh, God, what about Michael?

"Where is he?" She hadn't known that she spoke aloud until a voice answered from the darkness.

"In a hospital, I assume."

"Where am I?" She shut her eyes, hoping to quell the sick feeling that was building in her stomach.

She tried to touch her face, but she couldn't lift her hands. Kate forced her eyes open, fighting the grogginess that weighed her down. Cool metal chafed against her wrists as she twisted to find her hands.

They were shackled to a headboard.

She tried to move her feet, but they seemed likewise occupied.

"If you squirm, you'll just hurt yourself," the man warned as he stepped to the bedside and was dimly illuminated. He stared down at her and touched her face with the back of his hand.

It was Dustin. She couldn't make out his features, but she knew it had to be him.

She wanted to jerk her face free of his touch, but her head drifted to the side. "Where am I?" she repeated, mumbling.

He sat on the edge of the bed and clapped his hands. Dust choked the air as his hands smacked together. "The place has been vacant for some time now."

She tried to sit, to get a better view, but it was pointless—her head was too heavy, and she was cuffed. "Why am I alive? Why not kill me?"

"It's up to Michael if you live or die."

His words echoed in her ears for a moment, bouncing around as she tried to make sense of them. She moved her head toward the source of light beside her. Sitting on top of a bedside table was a battery-operated lantern. Either there was no electricity, or Dustin didn't want the lights on. Her body flexed against the restraints as anger stirred inside her. "What do you want from me?"

"What every man wants," he rasped.

Her stomach flipped and burned as waves of acid and nausea tumbled inside of her. *This can't be happening.* "No." She shook her head and strained against the handcuffs again.

"Money. Relax."

She stopped struggling. "My family has money if that's what you want." Kate allowed herself a thin glimmer of hope.

"You don't have the kind of money I'm looking for, but thanks for the offer." He stood and crossed his arms.

She could almost picture what he must have looked like in Afghanistan, with a sniper rifle strapped to his body and a shit-eating grin on his face. "I don't understand." The drugs were becoming less potent, and she was beginning to feel the effects of the accident. She bit back the desire to cry as a sharp, stabbing pain shot through her shoulder and right arm.

"Need more meds?" he asked while tilting his head.

"No." The last thing she wanted was to be drugged by a psychopath.

"Well, if you change your mind . . . You're no good to me unconscious."

She flinched as he approached her. "Please, don't touch me." She squeezed her eyes shut and sucked in her bottom lip, fear enveloping her. Her eyes opened when something wet touched her forehead. The sensation trailed to her shoulder.

He dabbed at the blood with a moist cloth and taped gauze over the small gash in her shoulder.

She stared at him in surprise, worried about his true intentions. "Please, just leave me alone."

"You should be okay now. Does it hurt anywhere else?" he asked, wiping his hands clean of her blood.

What in the hell is going on? "Are you crazy?" *Yes, of course, he is.*

"Michael won't help me if he sees you battered and broken— looking dead."

"What are you talking about?" She stared at him, her body vibrating with fear. *Please.* She glanced over at the nightstand and saw a gun. She hadn't noticed it before.

Dustin sat back down on the bed, close enough for Kate to really see his face. She could feel his eyes on her chest, and she remembered she wasn't wearing a bra.

"You're going to do something for me. Well, you already have, without realizing it." He made some sort of odd sound, like a snort. "You're going to get Michael to give me . . . everything."

Confusion swirled inside her. "This doesn't have anything to do with my mom?"

"Sweetie, you're a pawn in a much bigger game. Your life,

your past, is meaningless to me. But I do need to give some credit to your father. If it weren't for him, I'd never have stumbled onto such a golden opportunity." He leaned in toward her, the whites of his eyes bright as the light of the lantern played off his face. His lips curled on the ends into a grin. "If you haven't figured it out by now—your father hired me."

* * *

THERE WAS TOO MUCH DAMN BEEPING. HIS HEAD WAS GOING TO explode.

After a few attempts, Michael opened his eyes, and he was greeted by a piercing white light.

"Kate." He grumbled her name.

"She was taken, Michael."

Connor's words trickled through his mind, eating at him like a piranha on the attack. He couldn't believe it. Refused to accept it. "No." He struggled to sit, but felt Connor's hand on his shoulder, guiding him back down.

"We're on it, don't worry." Connor left the room for a brief moment and returned with Jake at his side.

"You okay, man?" Jake asked as Michael fought to sit again. "You were in an accident, and you've been shot. Relax."

Michael shook his head. "I have to find her. I need to get to her." He ignored the pain blitzing his system and removed the wires that were fixed to his chest. The monitors in the room began shrieking at obnoxious levels. "Get me out of this hospital," he demanded.

"Buddy, you were shot in the shoulder—not too far from your other bullet wound. You need to stay here."

"The fuck I do." Every nerve in Michael's body powered to toxic levels. Adrenaline was taking over with the need to get to Kate—to hell with pain.

But two nurses rushed in the room. "Please, sir, if you don't stop struggling we will need to inject you with something," the nurse to his left insisted.

The thought of being drugged halted his struggle for the moment. "Fine," he said, waving his hand at the nurse. He sat back and allowed the nurse to hook him up to the machines.

"I should be dead. Why am I alive?" he asked, feeling a little breathless.

Jake exchanged a knowing look with Connor.

"What is it?" Michael all but shouted.

"A lot has happened in the five hours you've been asleep," Jake said with a steady voice. He took a few steps closer to Michael's bed.

"Five hours?" Michael started to sit up again.

"I won't tell you anything unless you calm down," Jake warned.

Anger seethed through his bones. "Fine."

"When I discovered Dustin Scott was the one tracking Kate, I had to call my superiors, as well as Homeland Security. I'm sorry I couldn't tell you, but catching Dustin is a matter of national security. I have a team of agents nearby, working together to locate his whereabouts. I received direct orders to use Kate to draw out Dustin."

Michael clenched his hands at his sides but remained quiet.

"I asked Kate to take her date to the nightclub. I knew you would track Kate down and become furious with me, with Connor . . . I knew you would do something irrational—like take her to your cabin. I expected that, and I needed you to do that. Dustin needed to be able to access you and Kate to make his move." He held his hands in the air and furrowed his brow. "I'm so sorry. I was under orders."

Damn Jake—always following the rules. What the hell!

"I didn't want to betray your trust, and I hated putting you and Kate in danger, but I had no choice. We're talking about a man with connections to notorious terrorist cells throughout the world."

Jake was trying to convince his case, but the man had no idea what it was like to have a woman he cared for in harm's way. If it had been his mother or sister, how would Jake have felt . . .?

"Yesterday we did a search of any recent hotel and home rentals nearby. Someone matching Dustin's description rented a rather isolated property on the lake a mile from your cabin," Jake said.

"Which is why you wanted me at my cabin." Michael released a breath. "Is Kate there?"

"No. Surveillance shows no thermal body imaging. But we did discover something interesting—the place is being monitored and is rigged with explosives."

"He set a trap for us," Connor said from across the room.

"What about her phone? Can you track it?" Michael asked.

"Unfortunately, she doesn't have it on her. We found it at the scene of the car accident," Jake said.

This couldn't be happening. "What does Dustin want with Kate? If he wants us to get blown to hell, why didn't he just kill me?"

"I'm pretty sure he wants you alive, but the rest of my team—I doubt he cares about them."

"Because?" Michael tried to roll his neck a bit, to free some of the stiffness, but the pain in his chest and shoulder shocked him to stillness.

"He sent you a video message an hour ago."

"Show it to me." His voice was cold and thick with resentment.

Jake pulled his cell phone from his pocket and queued up the video.

An image of Kate appeared on the screen. She was wearing torn and blood-stained clothing, with her hands and feet shackled to a bed. The pain in Michael's body slipped away as rage enveloped him.

He was going to throw up. "If he fucking touched her—"

"Just listen," Jake urged.

With a strained voice, Kate said, "Michael, I'm so sorry. Dustin says he'll kill me if you don't do what he wants. But, don't—" The video ended, her words hanging in the air.

Jake didn't even give Michael a chance to process what he witnessed. "Following the video was a text message, which explained that you would be receiving an email soon. And he requested that you don't show anyone the message." Jake moved the phone away from Michael's view.

"But you haven't received any emails. At least, not to your phone," Jake said.

"And if I do, I'm sure as hell not sharing them with you." He couldn't trust his best friend right now, and it burned him. "I'll handle this on my own. Dustin wants me, and if I have a chance to save Kate . . . I need to do this myself."

"You know I can't drop this. I have the upper echelon of the U.S. government on my ass. They're demanding a win."

Before Michael had a chance to respond, he looked over to see David Adams entering the room. "Connor called me. Are you okay? Where's my daughter?" His words tumbled out in an almost incoherent jumble. He rushed to the side of Michael's bed.

"What the hell are you keeping from us?" Michael asked, gritting his teeth. "Kate was taken. We have no idea where she is."

David took a step back and pressed his hands to his face, his fingers trembling. "Oh God, I am so sorry. I never meant for this to happen. I didn't know who he was. I tried to stop it. But he wouldn't return my calls." He sank into a nearby chair.

"What are you talking about?" Michael shot out.

David attempted to catch his breath. "Ever since Elizabeth died, I've been worried Kate would discover the truth. I tried to keep her away from this place, to keep her safe." His breath hitched. "I lied to you all. Two weeks before her mother was murdered, Elizabeth told me that she could no longer live with the secret that she had been carrying around with her. She told me she'd cheated on me around the time she became pregnant. She didn't know if the baby was mine."

The paternity test. That part made sense now.

Michael tipped his head back a little, trying to keep calm.

"I was angry, and we fought. I didn't want to know who she slept with—I didn't trust myself. I didn't even talk to her for those two weeks. I refused to take her calls. Even when I got a message on my answering machine from her the week before her death, I ignored it. She said in her message that she was scared, that the person she'd slept with was obsessed with her—following her around. I thought she was just trying to get me to speak to her." He pressed his hands against the chair handles. "The day she was killed, she left me another message, asking me to meet her at her parents' house. She begged for me to come, to at least talk." He released a breath. "I decided to go, to talk to her—but I didn't get there in time. I told the police about Elizabeth's concerns about being stalked . . ."

"Apparently a little too late," Michael said while shaking his head.

David nodded and rose to his feet. He began to pace alongside Michael's bed. "I didn't want Kate to know her mom cheated on me and that we fought before her death. I wished I didn't even know that. And how do you explain it to a child? Then, when Kate told me she was considering opening a third location for her business in Charlotte, I panicked. I was worried she'd discover the truth somehow, that she would hate me. That she would find out that I might not be her father."

"Are you?" Jake asked.

"I don't know. I never looked at the results of the paternity test. I have them in my safe, but I loved her the second the doctor put her in my arms. I didn't care what the paper said—she was mine."

"How does Dustin fit into all of this?" Michael eyed David as he clung to his last grain of self-control.

"I'm a defense lawyer. I asked one of my clients if he knew of anyone who could tail someone for me and frighten them without doing harm. I wanted to scare Kate away from Charlotte. She's so headstrong. I knew it would take a lot, but I never meant for any of this to happen. I didn't even know the name of the guy I hired. I was given a phone number and a location to drop the money. I provided the person with her name and picture."

"Jesus. You hired an assassin—an associate of terrorists—to follow your daughter," Michael said in a low, disbelieving voice.

"I didn't know, I swear. When Kate called me about her mother, I realized everything had gotten out of hand. I tried to call the job off, but I couldn't reach him. I flew down to Charlotte right away, but I didn't know what to do."

"You should have told us the second you arrived," Jake said while reaching for his phone. "I need to make a call. Before I leave, is there anything else you'd care to share with us?" Flippant sarcasm laced through his words. "Like who gave you the man's contact information in the first place?"

"I can't divulge client information."

Michael glared at David. "Tell him."

"Alexander Konstantin," he grumbled, his cheeks reddening a bit.

"The Russian mob boss at Brighten Beach?" Michael's forehead wrinkled in shock. "You don't deserve to be called her father. Get the hell out of my room." He looked to Connor, and then to Jake. "Everyone. Leave."

"I DON'T UNDERSTAND." KATE RUBBED HER WRISTS AND STARED AT Dustin. He was sitting on the bed she had previously occupied, having moved her to a chair an hour ago. Only her ankles were tied to the legs of the dusty seat.

"If your original job was to scare me back to New York, why all the stuff about my mom? What kind of badass hitman sends flowers?" *What in God's name is wrong with me? I'm taunting a lunatic!* She swallowed back her nerves, trying to keep her head high and poker face on.

Dustin averted his eyes from the computer screen on his lap and fixed them on Kate. "Listen, my love, I don't have a clue about any fucking flowers, but I am a genius."

She squeezed her eyes shut for a brief moment, then returned her gaze back to the dark eyes of the madman. "Well, you failed at your job. I didn't leave Charlotte."

"And thank God for that. Running to Michael for protection triggered my idea."

God, she was dying to strangle the bastard.

"I mean, when I discovered the intense dynamic between the two of you . . . I simply couldn't resist. I guess you could call it fate. I was given a precious gift. An opportunity to cash in on much more than a worried father . . ." He chuckled, and the shrill sound of his laughter was disturbing. He belonged in a mental institution. "Of course, your father had no clue that I was much more dangerous to you than Charlotte could ever be." He lifted his long fingers from the laptop for a brief second to crack his neck. "What does he have against this place, anyway? I noticed that you visited your mother's grave—she died here, huh?"

What is wrong with you, you sick prick? A sour taste filled her mouth. She couldn't wrap her head around the truth. Her father had hired a deranged psycho, and now he was using her to get to Michael. She chose to ignore his mention of her mother and responded, "Michael will never give in to you."

"He has a nasty hero complex, sweetie." He wet his lips and arched his shoulders back before moving the laptop onto the bed. "Sure, Michael has a reputation for tossing women to the curb, but I knew that Michael would fasten his superhero cape and soldier around like the savior he thinks he is." He stood and moved toward Kate before kneeling in front of her.

She tried to hide her trepidation as he placed his hand on her knee. She could feel the bile rise into her throat.

"I never anticipated it would be so easy, though. I wanted to be sure he truly cared about you—the look on his face when I aimed my sniper at you was priceless."

He ran his cool fingers up her cheek, and she jerked her hand up, ready to hit him, but he caught it in the air. When she responded by swinging her other hand at him, he gripped her wrists so hard she had to bite her lip to fight the pain.

He released her and rose to his feet, taking a step back. "Feisty thing, aren't you? I see why he likes you. And why he'll do whatever I want."

She angled her face up and narrowed her eyes. "He's a patriot, first and foremost. He won't sacrifice the safety of the nation for me. I won't let him." She gripped the arms of the chair. "Money is one thing, but giving you access to national intelligence . . . you're certifiable."

"I have men already bidding top dollar for the information— the bid is nearing eight hundred million dollars. Come on, even you can appreciate a good auction." He winked. "He'll give me what I want. And if not, I'll empty the few hundred million from his bank account into mine and kill you all. Mother always told me to have a backup plan."

She could never let Michael endanger the nation's secrets for her. But who was she kidding—she knew she didn't need to worry about that. He wouldn't betray his country.

"How many times are we going to recycle this dialogue? Michael won't sell out his country. He doesn't care for you. Blah. Blah. Blah." Dustin cocked his head. "Do I need to tape your mouth?"

"Asshole," she muttered.

"Hey, you really should blame yourself for all of this. What kind of moron goes on a date when there's a gun-toting stalker following her around? You should have stayed penned up in

Michael's cozy loft." He guffawed. "You could be asleep in his arms right now. Instead, you followed the orders of Michael's FBI buddy—which I counted on. I knew that I could rely on Homeland Security to draw you out for me." He exhaled a breath and his eyes shifted to her mouth. "I'm always two steps ahead, baby."

"Just kill me now. Get it over with." Gone was the pain and sadness that had infiltrated her earlier in the night. In its place was the reality of her situation.

"Where would the fun be in that?"

She hated how he towered over her. Solid muscle pressed against his black T-shirt. She felt weak. Powerless.

"If Michael does give me what I want, I plan on sparing his life. Imprisonment as a traitor of the U.S. government is a fate worse than any death I might deliver."

"You son of a bitch." Without hesitation, Kate jumped up from her chair with her hands out in front of her, ready to claw at his face. Instead, she fell to her knees and pulled the chair down with her.

She looked up at him, hands pressed against the dusty, hardwood floor. Her ankles sang with pain from rubbing and twisting against the rope as she fell. "He's going to kill you," was all she had managed before he knocked her unconscious.

CHAPTER TWENTY-TWO

IT WASN'T EASY TO ESCAPE THE HOSPITAL WITHOUT SETTING OFF all the bells and whistles. But Michael was never one to hide from a challenge.

He called a taxi from his bedside phone before sneaking out of his room. The taxi brought him to a hotel a few blocks away, but he was careful to avoid the one where the Feds were camped out.

He entered the lobby of the hotel wearing his worn and bloody clothes. It was three in the morning. Seven hours had passed since he'd last seen Kate. The pain in his shoulder throbbed as he made his way to the conference room in the lobby. He ignored it as he settled behind a computer.

He accessed his private account—his untraceable, unhackable email account. How had Dustin known about it? He held his breath as he clicked open the only new email.

He lowered his face into his palm after he read the message.

There was no way in hell he could turn over sensitive government information to that psycho. Or give him carte blanche access to the encrypted intelligence software currently being used overseas. He couldn't even consider the option. He had to try and negotiate with him—offer him money, something . . . anything else. He would trade his own life to bring Kate back alive.

His fingers stabbed at the keyboard.

When he pressed the send button, Michael sat back in the chair, fingers in a steeple at his chin, waiting. When the sound of new mail binged a minute later, his eyes burned as he read the note.

Bring what I want in exactly two hours. Meet me at the place where her mother died. And send your buddies to my rental home. Come alone, or she dies.

Michael closed out of his email and erased any evidence from the system. He rushed out of the hotel lobby and back to the taxi that he'd paid to wait on standby. He needed to get to his office in the city, and fast.

* * *

"He has five minutes." Dustin looked over at Kate as she sat in the chair next to him with cuffed hands and roped ankles.

The headache she had from being knocked out by Dustin was nothing compared to the pain pooling in her gut in nervous anticipation for what was to come.

This can't be happening. She glared at Dustin before glancing at the laptop. The computer displayed a home on the lake, one that was rigged with explosives, or at least, so Dustin told her.

"Your friend Jake should be credited for allowing my plan to work so flawlessly." He shook his head and brought his hand to his chin as he focused on the screen.

She swallowed her fear as she watched men cloaked in black uniforms, guided by headlamps and long-range weapons, move in on the house.

Don't go. Don't do it.

An explosion blasted from the home moments later. Smoke billowed from the scene. The camera went out.

She struggled against the cuffs as tears filled her eyes. Had

Jake or Connor been there? God, how many people died because of her? How could Michael follow Dustin's commands? Didn't he know it was a setup? And what further hell did Dustin have in store?

"So many Feds. So many dead Feds." He raised an eyebrow, and his eyes lit with obvious excitement. "Next." He tapped a few buttons, and the screen switched to her grandparents' home.

She held her breath and watched with trepidation, her face mimicking the panic that swelled inside her. "Please . . ."

It was dark outside. The sun had yet to slip into the sky, but she could see a dark figure approach the back of the house. He moved toward the door with a large briefcase in his hand. There was no gun in sight. *God, Michael, no!*

"Good boy," Dustin said, staring with intense focus on the screen.

Kate's eyes widened, and she tried not to betray her sudden shock.

"I guess you win," she said, trying to mask her excitement. The body of the man in the video was leaner than Michael. And his hair was a little too short. "I can't believe Michael would really betray his country." Dustin diverted his attention to Kate, a smile of victory planted on his face. "You win," she said again, trying to hide the fact that she'd caught sight of a shadow on the deck off the kitchen.

"I guess that means he loves you. Too bad he'll never get to be with you." He reached for the gun that hung from his sidearm holster strap.

She shivered as she heard Michael's voice. "You're always one goddamned step ahead, but not this time."

Dustin pivoted in his stance, finding Michael a few feet away.

Before Kate understood what was happening, she heard a shot ring through the air. She flinched as flecks of blood splattered her shoulder and arm.

Blood spurted from Dustin's hand as his gun clattered to the floor. He pulled his hand to his body, cursing.

"Michael," she cried.

Michael shifted his gaze to Kate for a second before focusing his weapon back on Dustin. "You thought you could outsmart me? That you could trick me into that house? Do you think that what you saw at the rental home was real, too?" He shot Dustin again without hesitation.

The bullet pierced his shoulder and Dustin took a step back, moving farther away from Kate.

"You believed what I wanted you to," Michael said.

She was so close to him. If her hands weren't cuffed, she'd reach out and touch him, just to make sure he was real.

"The Feds want me to keep you alive." He tilted his head and studied Dustin, watching the blood ooze from the open wound. "I don't know if I can do that." He trained his weapon back on Dustin, aiming for his head.

"Put the gun down," shouted a loud voice.

"No," Michael responded, his eyes laser-focused on the bloody figure before him.

Jake entered the room with a few other officers close behind him, dressed in full SWAT combat gear. "Michael, please, we need to interrogate him for information. We need to know his sources. Please." Jake moved up behind Michael and placed a hand on his shoulder.

"Kill me," Dustin taunted. "You know you want to."

"Michael, no—it's what he wants. Death is too easy for someone like him." Jake was desperate.

Dustin kneeled on the ground in the living room a few feet away, still holding his bleeding hand, the hole in his shoulder gaping and bloody.

"Michael, don't do it." Her own words surprised her. She wanted Dustin dead as much as Michael, if not more.

At the sound of Kate's voice, Michael directed his attention to her. And after a few long moments of staring into her eyes, he lowered his weapon. "Kate," he muttered as federal agents swarmed the room.

"Michael, I—"

"Are you okay?" He swooped to his knees in front of her and began untying the ropes at her ankles. A nearby officer tossed him a cuff key, and he freed her wrists.

She flung her arms around his neck, holding him as she sobbed. She felt him flinch, and she pulled away. He was hurt—of course, he was hurt. They'd been in a crash. "Are you okay?" She swiped at her tears, trying to focus.

"You're okay, so yeah—I'm great." He helped her out of the seat and pulled her close to his body. "I'm sorry it took me so long to get you."

"How'd you know I was here?"

They held onto each other as they exited the cabin through the front door.

They were greeted by a swarm of flashing red and blue.

"I realized he would take you to the last place I would ever think of." He walked her toward the waiting ambulance.

"Your own cabin," she concluded and shook her head in disbelief. "I was at my grandparents' place. That was where he first took me—I didn't even realize it until he rushed me out of there." She sat on the bed in the ambulance and reached for Michael's hand once he was next to her.

"I don't know what I would have done if something happened to you." He tipped her face in his direction. "Dustin didn't . . . um . . . he didn't hurt you, did he?"

Understanding flashed in her eyes. "No." *Thank God.*

"This is all my fault. He used you to get to me. I'm so sorry," he said, his voice thick with guilt.

"I'm pretty sure it's my dad's fault."

CHAPTER TWENTY-THREE

Michael walked the few blocks to Kate's hotel, his nerves twisting like melted steel with each step. It had been a few days since the showdown with Dustin. He still couldn't believe everything that had happened.

When he reached Kate's room, he stood in front of her door, trying to figure out the right words.

His arm felt heavy as he lifted it to knock. The pain from the gunshot wound and the bruises from the accident were still fresh and very much active. But some other weight was dragging him down.

"Hi," she said in a small voice once opening it.

He studied her as he entered the room. She looked better than yesterday. Her face had its natural glow back, and her eyes looked a little brighter. "How are you?"

She rubbed her hands against her thighs and gave him a slight nod. "As good as can be expected." She took a seat on the leather sofa. "How's Julia? You saw her today, right?" She teased her tongue between her teeth before biting her lower lip.

She was nervous. Was she nervous because of him?

"Yeah, I saw her." He took a seat in the chair across from the sofa.

"Does she know everything?" Her voice quivered a little with each word.

He nodded and looked down at the ground, lacing his fingers together, resting his elbows on his knees. "When are you planning to go back home?" There. He'd said it.

She scooted back on the sofa and looked out the glass balcony door. "I'm not going back home. I'm going to rent a place in Boston. I can't live in the same city as my father right now."

"What about here?" He wasn't sure what his own question implied, but he had to ask.

"Michael, I—I don't know if we should—" She stopped herself. "Dustin forced us to be together for his own game, and now . . ."

"Dustin is not why we were together. He didn't manufacture my feelings for you."

"And what feelings might those be?" She lifted her brows and focused her blue-green eyes on him.

Shit. She wanted him to say it, didn't she? She didn't believe he was really capable of handling her heart without breaking it. But what could he say? "I care about you, Kate. I told you at the cabin that I wanted to give you more."

"And what does more mean? I'm sorry to do this right now, but after everything we've been through, I need to know where we stand. I need to know if I'm making the right decision."

"You mean the decision to leave Charlotte? To move to Boston?" He straightened in his chair.

"I don't know. I guess. I just found out I've been living a lie. Nothing seems real . . . So much for making plans, right?" She faked a laugh and smoothed a hand over her cheek. "I'm trying to understand this thing between us. You're the man who doesn't do commitment, who was seeing someone else while sleeping with me . . . I just don't know."

What the hell was she talking about? What woman? "I've only slept with you."

"The redhead." Her cheeks deepened to a rosy hue as if she were embarrassed by her jealousy.

"Trisha?" Michael stood, needing to be grounded to say what he was about to. "I told you—we're friends. Nothing happened between us. Nothing would ever happen between us." He could tell she needed more by the way she averted her eyes. "The day I was shot in Afghanistan, I lost a lot of friends," he explained slowly. "One of them was Eddie, and he left behind a wife. He was the only one of us who was married, and I promised myself I would look after her, always, for him."

He watched as Kate's gaze shifted toward his. She stared at him, blinking a few times. "September is a rough month for her, and for me. It's the anniversary of the day he died. I guess her feelings for me got a little muddled, and she kissed me. I explained to her that I could never feel that way for her. She agreed—she was embarrassed, even. She wanted to see me again to apologize." He moved toward the couch and sat beside her. "I should have told you, but this stuff is hard for me to talk about. You know that."

She reached for his hand and held it. The gesture sent a jolt through his system. God, he cared about this woman—more than she could possibly understand. But he fought the urge to take her in his arms and hold her—to promise her that everything would be okay.

He didn't know the future. He didn't know if he could promise her forever. He released her hand and was back on his feet, moving toward the window.

She rose from the couch and approached him, standing by his side.

"What we have is real, but I don't know how much of me there is left to give."

His words must have alarmed her because she took a step away.

"Kate." He faced her and extended his arm, but she slipped out of reach. "I'm not too different from Dustin if you think about it. I've killed countless people. I've taken lives without hesitation when ordered. I would have killed Dustin if you hadn't stopped me."

"You're nothing like him." Standing across the room from him now, she turned her back.

He lowered his head and focused on the carpet beneath his shoes. He heard the distant sound of the radio playing from the nearby bedroom. It was Sam Smith's song, "Stay With Me." How perfect . . .

The lyrics sounded in his ears, making the hairs on his arms stand on end. "I don't know if I'm going back into the military, Kate. And as much as I care about you—I can't let you be like Trisha." He paused and tried to fight the pain that was slowly seeping inside him. "I can't be Eddie. I can't be off in the Middle East worrying about you. I can't leave behind a woman I—"

She faced him, her eyes watery. "I've fallen for you, Michael. I've never truly felt this way before. I didn't want to. Not yet. I had plans." Her hands trembled.

Her and her damn plans.

"But I can't try and turn you into something you're not. I can't ask you to give me more if you're not ready. I'm going to leave tomorrow as planned."

He watched as she tried to slip a mask over her face, to shield her emotions, but he knew better. He felt as shredded, just as broken. "Kate—"

"No, don't. Don't say anything." She turned back away from him. "Please go."

He stared at her long blonde hair, dying to run his hands through it. He wanted to kiss her. To lose himself. To feel human.

But it was pointless. He'd never be able to shake the pain of his memories away. He'd never be the man Kate deserved.

And so, he forced his feet to the door.

CHAPTER TWENTY-FOUR

KATE EXITED HER BROWNSTONE APARTMENT IN BOSTON AND TOOK in a breath of the fresh air. It was a beautiful Monday morning in October. The temperature was hovering in the low fifties, but the blue sky made it feel warmer. The sun beat down on her shoulders as she walked down the tree-lined street, loving the golden-orange and red leaves that danced in the breeze.

It had been a month since the day Michael had walked out of the hotel room. A month since she'd heard the sexy baritone of his voice.

She had told him to leave. It was her own fault. She just never imagined his absence would hurt so much.

Julia had called her like clockwork twice a week, although she never uttered Michael's name. And neither did Kate. Instead, they spoke about daily details, made jokes, discussed business. Julia had told her she'd decided to put the next Maddox Gala on hold for a little while. Although she didn't say as much, Julia was probably hoping Kate would change her mind and host the New York event as they'd originally planned. But Kate didn't think she could do it. She had offered Julia the services of the New York office, which was certainly up to the task, but still, Julia had hemmed and hawed.

As she rounded the corner and the cafe came into view, she saw his tall, muscular frame. It was unmistakable.

"You shaved your beard," she teased.

Connor rushed toward her and scooped her into his arms, hugging her. "So good to see you." He set her down and pinched her cheek like she was his kid sister. "Glad we could meet up. When I heard from Julia you were living in Boston I thought I'd give you a call. I just finished a job."

"Hopefully it wasn't another kidnapping case," she joked.

"No, a basic bodyguard assignment." He motioned for her to have a seat at the nearby table. "I went ahead and ordered you a drink," he said, sliding a latte across the table.

"Thanks. So, how have you been?"

"Pretty good. How about you?"

She thought about how to answer his question. She wanted to ask him about Michael. She was desperate to know how he was doing, but she was too afraid to ask. Plus, she knew she would set herself up for pain. "I'm adjusting to my new life." She rubbed her cheek. "I opened the paternity test a week ago. I was relieved to discover David is my father." She exhaled after her admission. It was the first time she'd said those words aloud.

"Are you talking to him yet?"

"No. I don't think I'm ready for that. It's a bit of a challenge to forgive him after what happened. I've seen my stepmom a few times, and she keeps trying to convince me to see him. But I need more time." She cleared her throat and forced a smile to her face. "Anyway, I think I'll be staying in Boston for a while. I'm running my company in Boston only. I gave up my position in New York and put my New York loft up for sale."

He smoothed a hand over his clean-shaven face. "And you're happy here?"

"I've been focused on putting together the Mayor's Ball. Kind of crazy that I'm working with Erick Jensen on this whole thing, but it has helped keep me busy."

"You didn't answer my question," he responded with a firm voice. "I'm worried about you."

So am I. "I just don't know if being an event planner is all that fulfilling anymore." She shrugged. "Maybe I'll quit altogether, someday. I sort of feel . . . adrift."

He studied her for a moment before responding. "I know the feeling. When my time was up in the military, I had no idea what I wanted to do with the rest of my life. My father wanted me to run his business, but that's definitely not what I wanted. Thankfully my younger brother is up for the challenge once he's out of the Marines. But me—I should've stayed in the military."

"Why do you say that?"

"It's honestly hard to explain what it's like to be in the military, to be on a tour of duty and never know when or if your day is up. And to watch people die—to kill people. It's hard for civilians to understand." He clasped his large hands on the table. "But in the service, everyone gets it. We've all been through it together." He laughed as if shaking off his heavy comments. "If being in war doesn't screw with your head, then you must have been pretty screwed up, to begin with."

"Is it hard for you to be in a relationship? You know, because of your time in the Marines?" She leaned forward, wondering if Michael was the only one with the issue.

He took a moment to drink his latte. "I think it is, for a lot of people," he responded, without answering the question for himself.

Connor had a wall up almost as high as Michael, she realized. She watched as his eyes narrowed in on a blonde in a short skirt.

He averted his attention back to Kate. "Uh, hmm. Sorry." His lips curved into a smile. "I'm not ready to settle down."

"Well, when you think you are, consider moving to Boston. It would be nice to have you here."

"Do you mind if I tell Michael that I saw you?"

She didn't know how to answer.

"Kate?" He waved his hand in front of her face. "I take that as a no?"

* * *

MICHAEL SAT BEHIND HIS DESK AND STARED AT THE COMPUTER screen. The numbers were becoming blurry. He couldn't focus. He glanced over at the time and realized that if he didn't leave soon, he'd be late.

He hurried out of the office. It was almost four o'clock, but he only needed to walk a few blocks.

He arrived a few minutes after four and apologized to the receptionist. He was always a prompt person, and he hated being late to anything.

"He's ready for you. You can go on in," the receptionist said.

He headed down the long hall and to the office. He knocked on the door and waited for a response before entering.

The doctor rose from behind his desk and walked toward Michael to greet him. "Good to see you. Have a seat." He walked back to his desk and grabbed a notepad before seating himself in front of Michael.

Michael rubbed his palms against his gray slacks and waited for the doctor to speak.

"So, this is your third week in therapy. Do you feel like you're making any progress?"

"No," he said flatly. "I still feel shitty."

"Because?"

"Because I'm here—instead of with her."

"Kate?"

Michael nodded and looked down at the floor.

"Have you made your decision about rejoining the military yet?"

He asked him this question every time he visited. And Michael's response was always the same. "No."

"But you want to be with Kate?"

"Yes."

"But you don't know if you can be?"

"Yes." Michael knew the game. He knew the series of questions he would ask. He knew his answers before he was even asked.

"Are you having the nightmares?"

"Yes." He pinched the bridge of his nose and shut his eyes. The dreams had been coming every night, but the nightmares were no longer about the day he almost died in Afghanistan.

"Tell me about it."

He nodded, his eyes still shut. "I watch Dustin slit Kate's throat. Powerless to stop it."

"Why do you think she dies in your dream?"

He had answered this question before, too. "I don't know."

The doctor usually moved on to another question, but this time he pushed. "I want you to really think about it. You used to dream of watching a fellow Marine die in Afghanistan. His throat was slit, and you couldn't save him. Everything you dreamt about was true. Why do you think your mind is altering the reality of what actually happened now?"

"I don't know," he responded, almost angry.

"You saved her life when you couldn't save the Marine. But for some reason, I think that you're afraid that if you love her, you'll somehow kill her. You see yourself as the enemy."

Michael let the words sink in.

"You should talk to her," the doctor suggested.

"I can't. It's been too long. She must hate me." He leaned back in the chair and crossed his ankle over his knee.

"Do you think the nightmares will stop once you see her?"

"I don't know."

"Do you want Kate or do you want to be a Marine?" He was always direct, which is what Michael needed.

"They need me. People are dying."

"You're only one man."

"The military is made up of men and women. If everyone thought like that, there'd be no military." He rose to his feet, stuffed his hands in his pockets, and walked to the window.

"Don't you deserve happiness?"

"No," he was quick to answer.

"What about Kate? Does she deserve it?"

"Of course." He kept his eyes trained on the view outside. The room felt like it was closing in on him. He was struggling to breathe.

"What if you are her happy ending? What if you rob her of that?"

"She'll find someone else. Someone better. She deserves better than a murderer."

"So we're back to that, huh?" The doctor set his notepad and pen on the coffee table in front of him and stood. "Why do you call yourself a murderer?"

"Because by definition, that's what I am." He turned to face the doctor, his lips twitching with irritation.

"So the military is made up of a bunch of murderers?" The doctor stood a few feet in front of him and crossed his arms.

He was taller and more muscular than Michael would have expected, and he had gray hair that was cut close to his head. Michael noticed for the first time that he had callouses on his hands.

"Am I a murderer?"

"You were in the military?" He could see it now—the edge to the man. He wasn't sure how he'd missed it before.

"Navy. Ten years. Served in Vietnam. Killed more people than I can remember. I tried to keep count like it would somehow make it okay, but eventually, there were just so many." He shook his head. "But I'm not a murderer. I followed orders. I was in a war."

Michael bit his bottom lip, which triggered an image of Kate to flash into his mind. Beautiful and stunning Kate, biting her lip . . .

"How many men have you saved? How many Marines are alive because of you?"

Michael shrugged and looked away.

"That may be a better number to count." The doctor joined him at the window and looked down at the street.

Michael let the words sink in, but his attention shifted to a woman exiting a limo on the street.

A stunning blonde woman. Similar age. Same height. A dead ringer for Elizabeth, for Kate's mother—for Kate.

CHAPTER TWENTY-FIVE

Don't be nervous. Everything will go as planned. Kate walked around the ballroom, apprehension building inside of her.

The last three weeks had been a whirlwind as she prepared for the Boston Mayor's Winter Ball. It had served as a well-needed distraction from Michael, though. She still couldn't believe Michael never even gave her the courtesy of a call.

Over two months of silence. But she knew in her heart that hearing his voice would only make things harder for her. It was probably for the best.

For the last few weeks, she'd been spinning a story in her head, telling herself she had only fallen for Michael because of the circumstances. She had simply been a character in a movie, falling for the rich playboy, going against everything she believed in because she had been in close quarters with him and was scared.

That wasn't love. Just context. True love and fairy-tale endings were exactly that—fairy tales.

Every day she told herself that story. And every day, she felt she was getting a little closer to believing it.

Kate smoothed a hand over her sleek, white chiffon dress. The one-shoulder gown reached her ankles but also gave her some breathing room with a long slit up the side leg.

Take a deep breath. I'll be fine. She shut her eyes for a moment, allowing the music to fade into the background. *Just breathe.*

She gave a nervous swallow as she opened her eyes and moved toward one of her employees, gliding in strappy heels across the ballroom floor. "How are things going?" she asked, trying to sound as upbeat as possible.

The young brunette looked up at Kate and smiled. "Everything is perfect. The guests look happy. The mayor looks ecstatic. The music is divine." She nodded and looked toward the orchestra.

"Excellent. I think you guys have everything covered. I'm going to go outside for a bit and get some fresh air."

"It's pretty cold out. The forecast shows snow, which is way too early for November."

"I'll be fine." Kate smiled, grabbed her jacket from the coat check, and reached the large set of glass doors, noticing a slight tremble in her hand.

She ignored the alarm bells that sounded in her head as she stepped out onto the empty patio area. She rubbed her shoulders a bit, but the cool air was a welcome change to her heated and flushed skin.

She looked up to see the sun beginning to set, offering a blur of orange and pink that settled midway in the sky.

She tried not to feel a little empty as she glanced inside the ballroom through the glass doors, watching the happy couples move around the dance floor. She tried not to remember that she'd met Michael because she had been hired to plan his gala.

But the memory of their first kiss on the night of the ball slipped into her head and filled her with a mixture of pleasure and sadness. She missed his lips. The way they tightened when he stared at her as if he was struggling to control his desire.

Breathe. How many times would she need to remind herself to gather oxygen into her lungs? Tonight was such an important night. Thoughts of Michael bopping around in her head would only get her in trouble.

She forced her feet to move, to walk farther out into the maze that was the ghost of a garden. She found a bench and sat, careful not to rip her dress as she pulled the soft coat snug to her body. She clasped her hands on her lap and shut her eyes.

"I thought that was you. What are you doing out in this frigid weather?"

When she opened her eyes, she found herself looking at Erick Jensen. Throughout the coordination of the event, she had spent a lot of time working with him—at his insistence.

"Taking a break," she said, offering him a small smile. "How's your wife? Feeling any better?"

"She has a touch of the stomach bug." He took a seat next to her and rubbed his hands together. His black blazer was most likely not keeping him warm enough. "You did an amazing job tonight. Your mother would be proud." He moved a little closer to her, his leg brushing up against hers.

She gave a polite nod and forced herself to respond, "Thank you."

The touch of his cool hand against her cheek stunned her. She pulled her brows together and studied him with caution, her shoulders arching back.

"God, you're spectacular."

She ignored her nerves and moistened her lips. "Do you miss her? Elizabeth?"

The pad of his thumb had brushed across her lips before he placed his hand on her thigh. "Having you here has made me miss her a lot more."

She could see him swallow. "The flowers you had delivered to my office two weeks ago—the white tulips . . . you said they were my mother's favorite, right?"

He nodded, his eyes darkening as he focused on her mouth.

"When you had tulips delivered to my hotel back in Charlotte in September—how'd you even know I was in the city?"

"I—" He tilted his head to the side and eyed her. "Eh, what are you—"

"Do you ever visit my mom's grave?"

"Kate, what's going on?"

"You loved her, didn't you?" His hand on her forearm sparked a warning inside of her, but she disregarded it. "Erick, please, just tell me—did you love her?"

He looked up to the heavens and back at her again, his eyes ablaze with . . . something. "Yes."

"Do you want me? Do you want me because I look like her?" Erick's mouth dropped open, and he gaped at her in silence. "Erick?" She stood.

"I cared very much for her, and you look so much alike. It can be confusing." He rose to his feet and braced his hands on her shoulders, urging her toward him. "Yes—yes, I want you."

"Then tell me the truth. Tell me what actually happened to her. I won't blame you. I promise. I need to know what happened."

Without responding, he reached for her, his mouth covering hers.

She struggled against him and pulled free. "You killed her," she rasped, unable to stop herself. "You killed my mother. Admit it." Her voice was raw now. And her body warm from adrenaline.

Erick had changed at that moment. He no longer studied her with a lovestruck gaze. His face grew taut with emotion—with rage. "I want you, Kate. I need you. Let's forget the past and move forward."

"I love someone else."

He shook his head, his face twisting with anger. "No. You've been flirting with me these last few weeks. Wearing slutty clothes and brushing up against me. You've been teasing me." He shoved his hands through his hair before balling them into fists at his sides. "You're a whore like your mother." He grabbed her by the arm and tugged her against him, his hot breath on her face. "Your mother fucked me, made me fall in love with her, and then wouldn't leave that asshole, David. She was everything to me. Fucking everything." His voice, a low growl, echoed through the air.

She could feel his spit on her face as he yelled. "And you're just like her—a manipulative bitch."

"Why'd you kill her if you loved her?"

He ignored her as he began to yank her arm, trying to force her down the path, farther away from the ball.

"No." She twisted and turned in his arms. She slammed her heel into the top of his shoe.

"Bitch!" He released his grip for a moment before seizing her arm again. "Your mother wouldn't be with me, but—goddamn it —you are."

"Let her go." A familiar voice roared through the air.

Kate shut her eyes at the sound. *No, not yet. I didn't get it yet!*

Michael was on Erick in a split second. He reeled his hand back and socked him in the jaw, knocking him off his feet and to the ground. He kneeled down and reached for the lapels of his blazer before twisting Erick's arms behind his back, effectively disabling him.

"Get the police," Michael yelled while flipping him over, shoving his knee into Erick's back, pushing his face against the concrete.

She chucked her heels and rushed with bare feet down the cold path to the ballroom, screaming for help as she neared the doors.

The security guards were at their stations, and there was a crowd of police, as well. The Boston Police Department was being honored at the ball this year. "Help!" she hollered as loud as her lungs would allow.

Everyone in the room stopped dancing, and the orchestra members dropped their bows. The party came to a screeching halt.

She was shaking.

The armed security guards and unarmed, uniformed police officers followed her down the trail. They rushed to action when they saw Michael standing over Erick's body.

The guards aimed their weapons at Michael. "Back away!"

Michael looked up from Erick, his exhaled breath evident in the cool night. He held his hands up as he locked eyes with Kate.

"No. No, he's the one who saved me," she cried out, but no one seemed to hear. She watched in horror as they cuffed Michael and his eyes never left hers.

* * *

"Explain what happened tonight," the detective said while sitting across his desk from Kate.

Kate glanced around the room, wondering where they were holding Michael. Why wouldn't they let him go already? But why was Michael even at the ball?

Kate looked down at her hands in her lap and back up at the green eyes of the middle-aged detective staring back at her. "I have something I'd like you to hear." She took an uneasy breath and reached into the pocket of her jacket.

The detective cocked his head and leaned back in his chair as Kate set her phone on his desk.

"Listen." She hit the play button.

When the recording ended, the detective squinted and leaned forward across his desk. "I didn't hear him say he murdered your mother. Angry at her, yes . . . and he certainly hit on you. We can charge him with assault."

Kate pressed her palms against the desk, knowing she needed to speak fast. "Twenty-seven years ago, my mother was shot while she was eight months pregnant with me." She continued to explain the story, as well as the events that had led up to Dustin Scott's arrest two months ago. "You can verify the story with the FBI." She sat back in her chair, a little breathless.

"What finally tipped you off that Erick, a friend of the mayor's, allegedly murdered your mother?" He scratched his chin and reached for a pen.

"The flowers." She blinked a few times, still a bit shocked by how everything had come together. "When I was in Charlotte, white tulips were left on my mother's grave and delivered to me anonymously at my hotel. I thought it was my stalker, but it wasn't. Erick gave me the same flowers a few weeks ago, telling me they were my mother's favorite. Something in my gut told me he was the guy." She took a moment to replay the last few weeks in her mind. "I wasn't sure, so I put my theory to the test. Flirted with him. Made him feel at ease with me. And then, tonight, I had hoped he would make his move—and he did."

"A little risky, don't you think?" he said, looking up from whatever note he was jotting down.

"I knew there were dozens of police officers at the ball. I wasn't too worried." *Maybe it was a little stupid.* "But I needed to draw him away from the ball. Make him feel comfortable."

"And then you secretly recorded him?"

She nodded.

"And your friend, Michael Maddox . . . was he part of the plan?"

No. "You'd have to ask him what he was doing there." She bit her thumb, nervousness settling in now that the adrenaline rush had dissipated from her system.

"I guess I'll go talk to him myself." He stood. "Don't go anywhere," he warned before walking through the maze of desks and toward a closed room.

CHAPTER TWENTY-SIX

KATE PARKED HER CAR AND WALKED A BLOCK OR SO DOWN THE street to her brownstone apartment, feeling safe in the dark hour, even though she'd been attacked by Erick not too long ago. He was in custody, after all. They'd made the official arrest, which meant Michael should've been on his way back to Charlotte.

The detective never told her what Michael had said to him, but it must have helped since Erick was now in jail. She wished she could have seen him, though. She would like to have thanked Michael, at the very least—and had the chance to ask him what he was doing at the ball.

She felt like she was losing him all over again.

As she neared her home, she stopped a few feet away from the steps. Her heart plummeted into her stomach with no parachute—there was no saving her.

"Hi," Michael said, looking up at her from the front stair.

She couldn't move. She couldn't think. She stared at Michael. His hair stuck straight up like he'd been running his hands through it for hours. His jaw was tight, and his blue eyes looked pained. He was in a tuxedo. Only his tux was in pretty bad shape.

He rose to his feet and approached Kate, who was still standing before him, a statue. "You okay?"

"You're here," she muttered, toying with the straps of her purse.

He stopped inches from her. He pushed his hands into his pockets and swallowed. "Of course I'm here."

"How'd you know where I live?" Stupid question. This was Michael.

He dipped his head down a fraction and looked up at her from beneath black lashes. "I'm sorry about tonight."

"For which part? Saving me? Or spying on me?"

"I saw Erick's wife a week ago." He took a deep breath and continued. "She was stepping out of a limo alone, and I approached her. I asked her who she was, and then I saw her necklace." He reached into his back pocket and retrieved his wallet. "Here," he said while handing her a photo.

Kate stared at the photo of her mom.

"His wife looked like you, and she had a necklace that resembled the one that was stolen from your mother." He placed his hands in his pockets. "I did a little research, and I discovered that Erick had two other wives before this one. All of the women in his life had plastic surgery, becoming clones of your mother."

Her mouth parted in shock. *No wonder I never met his wife.*

"I told the police that if they obtained the necklace, the serial number of the diamond would most likely match the one from the police report in regard to your mother's murder." He cleared his throat and took a step back.

"I don't even know what to say."

"But it looks as though you already figured out who Erick really was . . ." He removed his hands from his pockets and rubbed the nape of his neck. "I can't believe you approached him like that—alone."

She angled her chin up and studied him. "I guess I wasn't alone after all."

"I went to the police as soon as I had my suspicions about Erick, but they wouldn't listen to me. So, I began following him. I didn't want to tip him off. I was hoping to somehow catch him— but you beat me to it."

"Well, thank you for rescuing me." She bit her lip for a moment. "Again."

"Am I too late?" His brows snapped together.

In what direction had their conversation just turned? The pain his absence had inflicted upon her tugged at her heart. "Too late for what?" Before he could answer, she added, "I appreciate you saving me." A hot thread of anger coursed through her all of a sudden. "You kept your promise to find my mother's killer, and for that, I'm grateful. But I'm not naïve enough to believe that means that you wa—" He silenced her with a finger to her lips, closing the gap between them.

I can't handle any more heartbreak.

"Kate, I've wanted you ever since you spilled your drink on me." He removed his finger from her lips.

Startled, she moved backward a little, needing space from his overwhelming presence. "That's not what I meant."

"For more than just your body." He wrinkled his brow. "Kate, can we talk inside? Please." He moved forward, but she held up her hand, warning him back. "It's cold. You're shaking."

She averted her attention to the soft, powdery coating of snow that must have fallen while she was being held at the police station. But she wasn't shaking from the cold. "Michael, I gave up on the idea of you." She wanted to cry as her gaze drifted upward over his creased tux.

He rubbed his palm against his own cheek. "I didn't want to do this out here, but okay. I'm not giving up without a fight." He released a deep breath.

She crossed her arms, feeling the chill despite her thick coat— or maybe she just felt cold from the loss of his touch. The simple graze of his finger to her lips had warmed her body.

"I told the military I'm not coming back."

She remained silent, her thoughts a frenzied mess.

"I want to buy a home in Boston—if this is where you plan to live."

She dropped her purse to the ground, feeling too weak to hold its weight. Her knees trembled, despite the renewed spike in her body temperature.

"I've been seeing a therapist."

Her lips twitched.

"I wanted to try and get better before I saw you again. For the first time in my life, I realized I needed help. I want to work through my shit. And I want the nightmares gone."

She looked down at her purse, which was lying on the thin cushion of snow. "Two months isn't a lot of time to work through what you dealt with in the Middle East. To get over your anti-relationship feelings." She had to be realistic. She needed to think rationally.

"I don't think of myself as a murderer—even though I wanted to kill Erick."

And she'd almost wanted him to.

"I know I'll need to keep seeing someone for a while—I know I'm not a hundred percent out of the woods, but I can't wait any longer to be with you. I know it's unfair of me to ask you this, when I'm still so broken, but I promise I will get better for you —for us."

Oh, God. His mouth was dangerously close to hers, and she could still smell his cologne, despite the fact that he'd been at the police station.

"I need you, Kate. I want you."

She wasn't sure if she was still breathing.

"I've never said those words before. Ever. But I mean them—*I need you.*" His voice was deep and strained by emotion.

She wanted to believe him, but she was scared. "What about the military, though?" Her voice broke as she spoke. "Are you serious about not going back? I don't want you to think you have to choose."

"I thought that was the only place I belonged until I met you." He touched the side of her face. "I'm in love with you, Kathryn Elizabeth Adams."

His words hit her hard. A tornado of feelings spiraled through her; she felt weak. "How do you know?" she asked, still not sure if she could trust him. "How do you know you love me?"

Michael shut his eyes and tilted his head back. "Because being away from you has caused me more pain than all of the bullets that pierced my chest. Losing you has eaten away at me, making me feel weak and alone." His eyes flashed open and found hers. "And because your smile tugs at something deep inside of me. Your humor and your sensitivity, your sweetness and personality . . . you make me feel different." He exhaled a slow breath. "You make me feel human again. I feel like life is possible if you're in it."

She stared in disbelief at the man in front of her. Was this really happening? "Can we go inside?" she asked, and her bottom lip trembled.

"You okay?" He touched her arm.

She nodded. "Yes. But if we don't get inside soon, we'll have to make love out in the snow."

He released a laugh and pulled her into his arms. "You love to drive me crazy, huh?"

Her eyes sparkled. The dead weight she'd been feeling for months was gone. She no longer needed to silence the memories of her past—she wanted to create new ones. "We've been apart longer than we were ever together . . ."

"Thankfully, I've made extensive plans about how to make up for lost time."

She smiled. "*You* made plans?"

"Yup. Want me to show you the list?"

"Oh, don't make me call your bluff." She wet her lips. "What exactly is on your list?"

"Mm." He pressed his lips to hers briefly. "Kissing."

She perked a brow. "Yeah? And what else?"

Michael looked over his shoulder at her home. "Let me show you the rest inside."

"Mm. Now that does sound like a good plan."

Michael took a slight step back, his eyes settling on hers. "Kate —I hope you know that I'll do everything in my power to earn your love."

She shook her head. "You already have it." She touched his lips with her index finger. "I love you, too."

"Thank God," he said, shoving his hands into her hair. "And I never want you to stop."

EPILOGUE

"PLEASE TALK TO HIM." KATE REACHED FOR MICHAEL'S FOREARM. "You're like brothers."

Michael lowered the bottle of beer from his lips and eyed Jake from across the room. "He could've gotten you killed back in Charlotte, Kate."

She turned into him, pressing her body against his as she reached for his beer and set it on the table next to them. "This is our engagement party. He came all the way here. Please. For me." She looked up at him and purposefully bit her lip.

"You're not playing fair." His hand swooped down her back and cupped her ass, squeezing it a little.

"Well, I learned how to play dirty from the best." She chuckled.

"Hey, I've been nothing but a good boy since I met you." He lifted a brow and leaned forward, softly nipping at her lip. Even that small gesture had her legs tightening. He'd been out of town for work all week, and then they had to come straight to the party. They hadn't had time to make love since he'd been home.

Seven days without feeling Michael inside of her? Unbearable.

But he was *trying* to distract her with sex right now, so she had to resist.

"Don't make me threaten you," she said softly, narrowing her eyes. "I bought this tiny little red number I was going to wear for you tonight. But maybe—"

"What happened to my fiancée? I go out of town for one week, and when I come back, there's a—"

"Watch yourself," she teased, "or you'll be going another week without getting any."

She could feel his erection harden against her body, and she tried to hold back the soft mewl that threatened to escape her lips. She wanted him so damn badly . . . but she wanted him and his best friend to make up, even more.

"Fine," he grumbled, "I'll talk to him. But I want you naked in my bed in less than an hour."

"What about the red—"

He leaned forward and pressed his mouth to her ear, the sensation sending chills through her body. "Screw the lingerie—I just want you."

Something inside her body squeezed as her eyes flashed, and she had to check a wild impulse to drag him right out of the pub and take him home.

"Hey, two can play at that game," he said, giving her a quick pinch on the ass.

She folded her arms and blew out an exaggerated breath as he walked toward Jake, who was standing on the other side of the bar alongside a few of Michael's other buddies: Connor and another guy she'd met earlier tonight—Ben Logan was his name. Ben was also a former Marine, and he now ran a private security company out in Vegas. Michael was already making plans to visit him . . . and to get in a lot of trouble in Sin City, she was sure. Of course, he'd told her that they'd be spending most of their time in bed, but who was she to complain?

"You got them to talk? It's a bloody miracle."

Kate glanced over her shoulder at the man to her right, and then she looked back at Michael as he scratched the back of his head and began talking to Jake. "It's been months, so I thought our engagement party was the perfect time. Thank you again, Aiden, for throwing the party. I'm used to being the event planner, but you and Julia really surprised us. Your pub is great. Love the Irish charm."

In fact, Kate and Michael had been two buttons away from skipping the red lingerie when his sister had come barging in their front door, demanding they come with her to the pub. When they had arrived, they found fifty of their friends and family there.

Kate glanced over at her dad and stepmom as they chatted with some of Kate's old college friends. She still couldn't quite wrap her head around what her dad had done, and maybe she never would. But she had forgiven him, even if she worried that she might never quite trust him again.

"When's the wedding going to be? Might I recommend Ireland for a setting?"

She'd gotten to know Aiden in the last few months they'd lived in Boston, and she was beginning to feel a little sad that Michael's best friends were all unattached. They were fun and always kind to her, but it would be nice to have a few girlfriends around. When they had fiancées and wives, then they could all go on couples' trips together.

There was the planner in her. She hadn't quite managed to kill that compulsion, but maybe she shouldn't. Being a planner could be useful . . . just as long as she allowed herself to be flexible when the situation called for it.

"I've never been to Ireland, but I've heard great things about it." She released a deep breath when she saw Michael patting Jake on the back. Then the two of them began to head toward Kate and Aiden.

"I think they're mates again," Aiden said.

"Thank God."

"Congrats again, Kate," Jake said, and Michael narrowed his eyes a little at her before angling his head toward the door. The man had his priorities. Fortunately, she shared them.

But she had friends and family here, and they couldn't ditch their own party, could they?

"How was London last month? As boring as I remember?" Aiden brought his beer to his lips and took a swig.

"Actually, it wasn't anything like I planned," Jake answered, his brows pulling together. Kate felt a surge of curiosity, but she didn't want to pry.

"You met someone, eh?" Aiden asked.

Michael was standing next to Kate now, and he slid his hand up the back of her silk blouse. At the feeling of his warm fingers on her skin, her breasts tightened with need.

"It's complicated," Jake grumbled.

"Complicated women can surprise you," Michael said, and Kate wasn't sure if she wanted to elbow him in the ribs or kiss him.

"Yeah, well, we'll see . . ." Jake smiled and raised his drink. "In any case, cheers to you guys. May you have years of wedded bliss and lots of babies and yada yada yada."

Kate chuckled. "Maybe you shouldn't give a speech at the wedding," she joked.

Before anyone could respond, Kate noticed Connor, Julia, and Ben coming up behind Jake.

"I'm thinking this party needs a little livening up," Connor said, giving a mischievous shrug. "No—don't have him play that techno shit of yours," Jake called as Connor turned toward the DJ's table.

"It's better than that twangy country shit," Connor shot back.

Julia folded her arms and shook her head. "Boys."

When the music blasted, Michael tilted his head back and laughed. He shook his head back and forth, spreading his fingers over his belly.

"What? What am I missing?"

Then she recognized the tune—"Thunderstruck," by AC/DC. As Jake, Connor, Aiden, and Ben came up alongside Michael, their heads began to rock forward and back like guitar players at a metal concert.

Michael was still smiling.

"We used to listen to this in the desert," Michael said into Kate's ear. "Got us pumped up before missions."

Kate grinned. She loved to hear about his good memories. She hoped they would one day help him shed some of the pain. And seeing him here with his friends, happy, was the best engagement gift she could imagine.

"Come on, man. Belt those lyrics," Ben said to Aiden, a smile spreading across his face.

"You sing?" Kate laughed as she began to groove to the music.

Aiden threw his hands in front of him and began playing an air guitar, and Kate clapped her hands with glee as these five badass Marines joked and played around together like boys. She grabbed her phone from her purse and snapped a photo of them, capturing the moment, loving every moment of her life as they formed new memories together.

BONUS SCENES

*Get 3 free bonus scenes in mini-book format starring Michael &
Kate.*

Get the **exclusive bonus scenes** written only for subscribers when
you join my newsletter! Learn more at BrittneySahin.com.

Also, join my new Facebook group – Brittney's Book Babes

ALSO BY BRITTNEY SAHIN

Hidden Truths

Beyond the Chase - Fall for the sexy Irishman, Aiden O'Connor, in this romantic suspense.

The Hard Truth – Read Connor Matthews' story in this second-chance romantic suspense novel.

Surviving the Fall – Jake Summers loses the last 12 years of his life in this action-packed romantic thriller.

The Final Goodbye - Ben Logan's book (June 2018)

*Connor Matthews guest stars in the new romantic suspense, *My Every Breath*. Learn more.

Stealth Ops SEAL Series

Finding His Mark (Sept 20, 2018)

Stand-Alones

Someone Like You - A former Navy SEAL. A father. And off-limits.

The Story of Us - Fall in love in Rome with the sexy Italian soccer ("football") player.

On the Edge - Travel to Dublin and get swept up in this romantic suspense starring an Irish businessman by day…and fighter by night.

My Every Breath - a sizzling romantic suspense. Businessman Cade King has fallen for the wrong woman. She's the daughter of a hitman - and he's the target.

ABOUT THE AUTHOR

Thank you for reading Michael and Kate's story. If you don't mind taking a minute to leave a short review, I would greatly appreciate it. Reviews are incredibly helpful to us authors! Thank you!

Sign up to receive **exclusive excerpts** and **bonus material**, as well as take part in great **giveaways**, which include gift cards, swag, and signed paperbacks.

For more information:
www.brittneysahin.com
brittneysahin@emkomedia.net

Made in the USA
Columbia, SC
17 April 2020